Contents

I.	Setting Out	3
II.	Across The Void	11
III.	A New World	17
IV.	S'zana	36
V.	Murz Ten	42
VI.	Dolish	67
VII.	Dureen	86
VIII.	Hreek	112
IX.	Across The Solid Sea	123
X.	Edge Of The World	141
XI.	The Tower	152
XII.	The Last Guardian	169
XIII.	Lucky Bastard	183

Thanks for backing this!

In Gratitude

This book is only possible because a number of backers on Kickstarter were willing to pay cash up front for me to write it, commission the art, and print it. I recognize what a tremendous act of faith that is, and I've tried to write a book that matches what I promised them: A classic sword-and-planet adventure written not as parody or deconstruction, but as a new entry into an old genre. Flying ships, swordfights, lightning guns, romance, strange alien landscapes, deadly monsters... I've managed to get them all in. Also, personality-shifting half-plant gorilla people, ornithopters, government conspiracies, military bureaucracy (both human and otherwise), and monomolecular blades.

When I set up the Kickstarter that funded this book, I did not think about creating appropriate titles for backers at different tiers of support. Thus, I'm sort of improvising the divisions here. One more thing on the "Now I know, and knowing is half the battle." list.

Supporters Of The Genre

- Adam Muszkiewicz
- Alex Dingle
- Andy Fix
- Brian Newman
- Brook West
- Christian Brock
- Christian Wanamaker
- Christopher M. Plambeck
- Glenn Porzig
- Henry Lopez
- Hogan Brimacombe
- James Groesbeck
- Jeff Rients
- Jeffery Sergent
- John Fiala
- Joshua Kellerman
- Paul Allan Ballard
- Raeve
- Sean L.
- Tom Ryan
- Aaron Bosanko
- Charles Fitt
- Dain Lybarger
- Jeffrey Gomez
- jgnow
- Michael Bentley
- Patricia Pennow Healton
- Sean Patrick Fannon
- Silverback Press & Legendsmiths

Fans Of The Author

- blackwelll
- Catherine Faber
- Craig Hackl
- David Chambers

Doug Bailey
Eric Coleman
James Jandebeur
john hayholt
John Heine
Lee DeBoer
Leibowitz
Owlglass
Yaron Davidson

Admirers Of The Printed Word

"Filkertom" Tom Smith
BlackWyrm Publishing
Cliff Winnig
Hector Escobedo
James Collier
john ackerman
Jon Ryers
Laura Chapman
Lisa Cortes
TacoWaffle
Thomas Ladegard

Worldbuilders: Namers Of Names

eric Sowder
Michael Dancy
Sarah Hulcy

Connoisseurs Of Fine Literature

Asher Green
Chris
Christian Lindke
Doug Lanford
Edward M. Van Court
Jerome Comeau
Laura Antoniou
Miles Matton
Philip Reed
Steven Mentzel

Worldbuilders: Crafters Of Concepts

Celia Triplett
Rob Jackson
W. Banks Miller IV

Commissioners Of The Arts

David Johnson

Special Thanks And Gratitude To

David Mattingly, for talking me through all of the zillion things I didn't know about getting a book ready for print. If you're reading this on dead trees, it was due to his help.

Gareth M. Skarka, who volunteered his graphic design talents towards creating the title and author credits on the cover, as I have the artistic ability and grasp of composition of a sea cucumber.

Elizabeth Harac, for scribbling all over badly-faded hardcopy printouts with an orange marker and insisting I decide how many "m"s there should be in "hmm" and mandating I stick with it.

Rocket and **Toaster,** for testing the tensile strength of my keyboard, protecting me from dangerous monitor rays, and keeping the printer from hurling deadly pieces of paper at me by sleeping in the output tray.

Deirdre Saoirse Moen, for coming to my rescue when I realized I could not, in fact, teach myself GIMP in about 15 minutes and do the cover layout.

If you're reading this via a downloaded, but not necessarily purchased, copy... if you like it, then please consider purchasing it. There's no huge publishing house or corporation here, there's just one author who would much rather write books than financial software for a living. I can write a lot more books if I can write full time, so if you enjoyed this one, it's in your own self-interest to make it possible for me to produce more.

Prologue

One of the very few benefits of wasting far too much of your life online since the days of CI$ and 1200 baud modems is that, if you post megabytes of rants, thoughts, and comments on everything from Usenet to Facebook, sometimes, against all odds, you get silent admirers in interesting places. Every so often, one of these lurkers decides to contact you. That's how I got my hands on the transcripts.

It's well known that an awful lot of data collected by NASA has been rendered useless by the loss of formatting information and/or media destruction. A few people, working on shoestring budgets, are trying to recover this. Often, it's done on their own time, with their own gear, out of a love for knowledge... and that's where this starts. Someone, I will call him Scientist X, had found hundreds of boxes of fan-fold printer paper covered with seeming gibberish. It turned out to be text dumps of image data, gathered by a satellite which didn't, according to official records, exist, and misfiled in the wrong basement of the wrong building. Barely legible scrawl on the boxes marked it as scheduled for incineration... around 1975. Scientist X spent a few months deciphering the format, and then recreating the images, and then enhancing, cleaning, and filtering them. And then he saw the patterns, pulses and flashes from a place where nothing should be. A few more months of very quietly working to eliminate every other explanation, including a ridiculously elaborate practical joke, and he confirmed his first suspicion -- the patterns were a simply trinary code, two lengths of 'on' and a single length of 'off'. It was also one of the most familiar codes known, in use on Earth since the early 1800s. Morse.

Even more careful digging, confirmation, examination. It was clearly an error, or a hoax -- perhaps the Soviets had been trying to fool one of our spy satellites. Nothing, however, could match the signal source, and the more analysis he did, the more he found it impossible that anything near Earth, or in our solar system, could be appearing at that point, at that distance -- more than a light year away, and moving quickly, nearly 1% the speed of light.

The first guess, then, was that some other species had picked up our early Morse transmissions, and were using them to contact us, perhaps assuming we'd have evolved from radio to laser by the time we got them. Then, he began fully translating and ordering the data, a difficult task. Distortion, Doppler effects, missing fragments... it took a few years, he said, to put it all in order. Then, realizing what he had, he also realized that it couldn't be revealed as truth.

That's where I come in. Scientist X contacted me, decided he could trust me, and we agreed I'd take the raw material he decoded and present it as a novel. No one was going to believe it anyway -- and anyone seriously trying to research it might end up vanishing -- so why not? Now, any kind of word analysis of the text to follow will show it's very clearly written by me, and not by the putative writer. This is to your benefit, because Maj. Falconi, for all this other virtues, wasn't much of an author. It wasn't his job to be. He was making a report. I had to fill in a lot of gaps, infer some things, totally make up others, and provide a lot more dramatic flair. I'm sure Darth Vader's official statement about the destruction of the Death Star would have been pretty dull reading, too. Besides, given the circumstances of the transmission, it was obviously going to be pretty terse, as well as being poorly organized. There were a lot of bits of "Addition: Prior to events as described in 1.3.1 to 1.4.2, the following..." in the data stream. I've really only worked with the first batch of files; it's possible some of the assumptions I made to fill in the gaps were dead wrong.

If you're smart, you won't believe a word of the foregoing. It's self-evidently a flimsy framing sequence in the classic tradition. So, please remember: This is all fiction, even the part that claims it's not. Really. I'm a writer. Would I lie?

Chapter 1
Setting Out

Anything about my life prior to October 1973 ought to be a matter of public or military record, if they haven't scrubbed it by now. Some file clerk can dig it up for you: Ryan Patrick Falconi, Major, USAF, Serial Number FR 1787421. I'm starting with the parts that *won't* be on the record. This transmission is being made in accordance with the general orders I was issued on October 20, 1973: "Report all findings as soon as it is possible to do so." If I've done everything correctly, I've set this message to repeat indefinitely. I also want to state: No rescue or recovery is possible. Do not attempt it under any circumstances. Do not allow anything I will describe to convince anyone that the rewards of coming here outweigh the risks -- there is no *risk* of failure, there is an absolute *certainty* of failure. No one returns from this place. Any person suggesting otherwise should be court-martialed, stripped of their command, and executed -- not necessarily in that order.

Now that that's out of the way...

On October 14, 1973, I was flown to the testing range near Groom Lake, Nevada. I understand that even mentioning the existence of this base breaches security -- but it's impossible to produce this report without revealing far more. I can only hope the only people who would know where to look for this have the kind of clearance necessary to read it. No one told me anything about why I was being brought there. They probably didn't know and couldn't tell me if they did. My hope was that I was being assigned as a test pilot; I'd made no secret that was where I wanted my career to go.

Thirty minutes after landing, I was sitting in a bland, featureless office. Grey filing cabinets. A black phone. A meticulously empty inbox. A framed photograph of President Nixon on the wall was the only decoration. The man on the other side of the desk from me matched the room. I could spend a week with him, and then be unable to pick him from a small crowd the next day. A small nameplate stated he was Colonel R. Jeffries.

He studied some papers carefully, looked up at me, looked down at the papers. I recognized my photograph among them. He spoke, hesitating a moment before each sentence, reading a line from a script scrolling behind his eyes. "Firstly, Major Falcon, I..."

I winced. "Excuse me, Sir. It's 'Falconi'." He started slightly, the script interrupted by this improvisation. When he didn't say anything for a few seconds, I continued. "'Falcon' is, uhm, a nickname I was stuck with from flight school. Falconi... Falcon... Air Force..." I shrugged. This wasn't the first time I'd dealt with this bit of silliness.

He frowned slightly, then looked back down at the papers, paging across them. "Mmm. Says 'Falcon' here." He frowned more deeply, then looked up at me, scanning my face for signs of some sort of deception. The *papers* said one thing, I said another -- surely, it must be the person, not the paperwork, that was in error. Finally, he sighed and gave in. "Ah. Hm. Firstly, Major *Falconi,* I want to offer my condolences on your father's passing. If it's any consolation, that's what got you short-listed for this, which is..."

I'd let him go on as far as he did because I was trying to really grasp what he'd just said. "Sir? My father's what?"

Annoyance replaced the forced, and false, look of empathy he'd been trying to wear. One interruption might be tolerable, but two was surely a court-martial offense. He breathed deeply, recalled some handbook somewhere that described appropriate responses, and continued. "Your father passed away approx 1400 hours, on 10-01-73, from a..." he looked at the papers again..."'coronary event'." Another pause. "They didn't tell you the cause of his death?"

I struggled to maintain composure. I'd learned to respect the uniform, if not the man. "Sir, I was not informed of the *fact* of his death."

He tapped his fingers for a second, then concluded that since this wasn't part of the script, he'd just ignore it and move on. "Hmm. Usual mail SNAFU. You should be getting the notice soon. Give it a week or so. These things happen. Point is, as I was saying, with tragedy comes opportunity. Your came up earlier, but we didn't want anyone with close family ties. Pony Express kind of thing, you understand. Once news came in, you got moved to the front."

There's an old military joke everyone knows, and I was suddenly the punchline. As his words passed around me, I tried to think. Why didn't anyone else tell me? My current posting wasn't secret. I was stationed stateside, easily reached by phone or Western Union. I hardly lacked for relatives. Even a small family gathering of either the Falconis or the Patricks usually got Brooklyn's Finest out to keep things calm... those who weren't already part of the celebration. I flipped through my mental rolodex of aunts, uncles, cousins, and more. I could think of only one reason everyone had been silent, and it was both painful and plausible. Shock and grief congealed into anger.

The Colonel looked at me expectantly. "So, do you accept?"

I was sure, even in my state, he hadn't ever said what mission, or posting, I was being considered for. I didn't particularly care. "Sir, yes, sir."

Fortress At The Top Of The World

With that bit of illusory closure, I got my mind back to the present. "Uhm... Sir... what did I just accept? I don't think you actually told me."

"No. I couldn't, until you accepted. Very dangerous, and very, very, classified."

Almost certainly, I thought, testing something. Something so new, so experimental, they can't even reveal it exists to *be* tested. This would keep me too busy to think about anything else, which was a good thing. "Sir, since I *have* accepted..."

He nodded, but ignored my implied question. "Yeah, we thought you would. Congratulations." He picked up the phone and pushed a clear plastic button. "Falcon is go. Tell Catering and Supply Services."

"Sir, I'm flattered, but given what you just told me, any kind of party would be..." He waved dismissively as he stood up. "That's just what we file the expenses under. No one looks too closely at how much it costs to entertain the VIPs. Come along, Major. I'll show you what you've signed up for." He walked out of the office; I followed. He kept talking. "Your gear and possessions will be packed and shipped here. Until the end of this assignment, you will not have any contact, on or off this base, except as specifically ordered."

I'd expected us to go outside, to a hanger, but we instead went down one blank corridor after another, ending in an elevator door with no call button, guarded by a 2nd Lieutenant who snapped to instant attention. "12-B" was the only thing Colonel Jeffries said. The guard turned a key in the lock and stepped inside, followed by the two of us. The Colonel withdrew a key of his own and inserted into one of many locks lining the left side; the guard did the same on the right. Two clicks, and the door shut, and we descended. After what seemed an unusual period of time, we stopped, and the doors opened onto a corridor identical to the other. Jeffries gestured for me to exit, and I did. There was only one direction to go, so I turned, and found myself staring into a vastness. If you've ever been to the Houston Astrodome, it was about that big, but perfectly circular.

It was also bright, illuminated by dozens of powerful beams glaring from the ceiling. We were standing on an encircling catwalk. Guards stood sentry at a dozen points. There were a few other places on the walkway that looked like they led to other elevators, but I was focused on what was at the center of the room.

Two items dominated the area. The first looked like something from any one of the dozens of magazine articles that had come out since the moon landing, showing visions of "America's Next Steps Into Space". A large, cylindrical body, maybe the size of a boxcar, atop a sweeping, triangular, pair of wings. A rear fin for stabilization. Dozens of people scrabbled over it, attaching, welding, and hammering.

The second was harder to describe. Probably, it had been teardrop shaped once, with pod-like projections that looked like they may have been jets. It was badly burned and scarred. The skin of it was torn and twisted in places, but it looked more like molten plastic than torn metal. It was around half the size of the first craft. People were working on it, too, but they were disassembling it, not repairing it. Watching for a while, I saw a steady stream of technicians and engineers carting pieces, not easily identified, from it to the larger vessel. The bits being moved varied a lot: Glowing coils of cable, things that looked like the blobs in a lava lamp reformed in silver metal, complex parts like engine blocks: Half metal, half diamond and sapphire.

Col. Jeffries let me gape for a couple of minutes before he started in. He gestured to the more recognizable vehicle. "That's part of our reusable orbital fleet. Two or three years from now, NASA will announce they're starting work on them." He pointed to the other ship. "That one's... well, NASA won't be announcing anything like it."

There has been rumors and claims of a cover-up going back almost thirty years. "Roswell, sir?" I asked.

He didn't quite laugh, but his lips twitched in what might have been an attempt at a smile. "No. That was just aerial surveillance. We planted the whole alien crap to keep people off the real story. You ever hear of Aurora, Texas?"

"I can't say I have, sir."

"Good. It means me and the folk before me have done their job. There's some public records... back then, it was harder to keep things out of the papers, but we've kept it from blowing up big. Eighteen-nineties, there were a whole bunch of what people today'd call flying saucer sightings, though they called them 'airships'. Most of them were hoaxes. Once the first ones started everyone wanted to get in on it. One of them, real one, went down in Aurora. The government, even back then, protected the fine citizens of this great land from anything they were too dumb or skittish to know about. Called in the Pinkertons to deal with it, and any extraneous other things. They dutifully gave it to the War Department, and after there was an Air Force, it made sense they'd pass it on to us. And we've had it for about fifty years now, figured out a little of it, not sure what to do with it."

"Does it... work? Fly?" I was still watching the constant activity below, teams of ants streaming back and forth between two corpses.

"It did. We tested it a few times. You'll be getting all the reports, you can read them. We only had the one, and while we could figure out how to work it, we couldn't really figure out how it worked. We couldn't make more. Bit of a white elephant, really. Then, six months ago, we had Incident 41."

"Sir, I'm not sure I follow you."

He nodded. "Yeah, this place doesn't get a lot of visitors. Everyone here tends to know what's going on, so we get out of the habit of explaining things. One of our engineers, a Lieutenant, uhm, Cohen, was doing a routine check of some of the instruments, and noticed something new. The same old pattern we'd always seen on one particular gizmo, we'd decided it was probably a kind of radio, had changed. Started doing some non-routine checks, looking at parts that hadn't done anything interesting in eighty years, and they'd started doing interesting things. Every couple of days, more and more of the machinery began to work."

He pointed up to the ceiling. I could just barely see a dark, charred, scar.

"Shot out some kind of space ray, once. We had to tear out the bit that shot it, but it gave us an idea, that if it was picking up a signal, maybe it was trying to send a reply. So the slide rule boys did their thing, and we figured out where it was aiming. We told the people who don't exist where to aim the satellites we don't have, and we saw something." He looked at me with a hint of a smirk, challenging me to guess, so I could guess wrong and he could feel smart.

"Another ship, sir?"

The smirk widened. I'd made the right, wrong, guess.

"Another *planet*."

Standing in the same room with a flying saucer that had crashed eighty-odd years ago, I was not going to blurt out "But that's impossible!" I just nodded a little.

He continued. "Moving across the solar system at an angle. Came from somewhere far away, seems to keep going on, just passing through. Lucky for us, not near any planets. It was moving fast, fast enough the eggheads wet themselves. We don't know much about it. We do know it's got a moon, a tiny one. We also know someone's there. The people watching it saw some flashing lights, they said it was patterns, not natural. A code, they figure. That thing, there..." he pointed to the torn teardrop... "inside it, there's a gadget which started flashing the same kind of patterns. One of the reports you'll read goes into how they 'see' each other, I won't claim to understand it. My job, for thirty years, hasn't been knowing things. It's been keeping other people from knowing things." He was silent for a moment, looking down at the work area, tapping one finger on the railing. Then, whatever door might have opened in his mind slammed shut once more. "As you can see, that thing might fly a bit, but it's not going to space. We've disconnected everything we can figure out, what we call the engines and the 'light radio' and the rest, and we've jury-rigged them into the..." he pointed at the human-made craft below, rustled some papers to find the name, "some genius called it the *Bellerophon*. Schedule says, she launches in a week. That's as long as we've got, by our best guess, before the target is out of range forever."

He waited for my response. I tried not to ask any of the usual stupid questions. "Is it safe?" "Are you this thing will fly?" "Do we know if they're hostile?" "Will I come back alive?" The only honest answer to any of those would be a big shrug. I'd walked into that elevator thinking I'd have months to stew over my personal issues; now, it looked like I'd have a week of utterly ignoring them, and after that they'd be extremely moot. My life was getting simpler by the minute. "Sir, you said there was documentation? Something about how to fly this thing? I'd like to start in on it right away."

"Your assigned quarters are in section 14-J. One of the APs will escort you there. You'll get your documents, and full orders soon. I knew you were the right man for this."

I didn't need to ask what might have happened if, having been shown this, he'd decided I wasn't the right man after all. Were there wrong men before me? No, wrong question. If there's only a week left until launch, the question is, how *many* wrong men were there before me?

If anyone's allowed to read this, it's likely you'll have access to the documentation and research notes and pretty much pure speculation I was given, so I'm only going to go into the details as they become relevant to this report. I recognized some of the names on the notes, and I wonder if the one who served the Nazis and the one who fled the Nazis ever discussed this in person. Probably not. Sketches, photographs, film recordings, audio on wax and vinyl and tape, everything but the most basic details floating in a sea of "if", "we think", "it seems", and "probably". Nothing could be tested before go-time. No models could be built in wind tunnels. No glide flights, no unmanned launches.

I didn't feel like I was committing suicide, though, no matter the odds. I felt more like this was just the trajectory of my life, and I really had no more say over it than an arrow did once it was fired from the bow.

Normally, ships like the *Bellerophon* were carried aloft on huge fuel tanks, aided by booster rockets. For this mission, though, it was strapped to the back of a heavily modified commercial jet, one that could skim the thinnest edge of the atmosphere. Then, if everything was right, if all the assumptions were correct and the engineers, working with guesses and estimates and hopes, got everything right, the probably-propulsion and maybe-navigation systems would kick on, and I'd orient on the signal, and then do this, that, and the other thing, and I'd be moving faster than any human has ever travelled, heading to an unknown point.

The mission profile didn't include landing. The equipment added from the Aurora craft worked poorly in an atmosphere when it was removed from the original ship. With that out of the equation, the *Bellerophon* had the aerodynamics of a brick and needed a lot of runway. The hope was that I would, somehow, make contact in orbit, that they'd be friendly, that we could communicate. If no one was there, I was to orbit as long as possible, get as much information as I could, launch some satellites that would keep monitoring and transmitting back to Earth, and then, right at the edge of estimated endurance, break orbit and head home.

No one pretended I'd actually make it back. I appreciated the general honesty about the mission.

There was a week, more or less, of training. First on the general flight controls of the *Bellerophon,* to familiarize myself with them. They were designed like standard control systems, and it took me a handful of hours to be proficient. Then, I started using a mechanical simulator that modeled how the ship *might* fly when the alien machinery was implanted.

The alien machines played games with gravity, with space itself. I'd been told that they didn't so much move the ship, as move space *around* the ship, so that the ship was like a silver ball on a tilting wooden surface. The flight controls, in effect, tilted the universe, and the craft rolled merrily downhill, whichever way "downhill" happened to be. Tip too far, and you careened out of control across the "board" of the universe. Tip too slowly, and you rolled to a stop. The engineers said there was a kind of "friction" in space, as weird as that sounds. Learning to fly this way, hoping the simulator was accurate, took me most of the training time I had. I heard some of the others mumbling astonishment at the fact I'd learned anything at all.

What can I say? Flight was one of the things, maybe the only thing, that ever came perfectly naturally to me. It's hard to talk about it without sounding like a barroom braggart, but if I wasn't good -- "scary good", I heard an instructor say when he thought I wasn't listening -- I would have washed out early on. They kept me in, despite my problems, because they thought it was worth the effort of turning me into a decent soldier. As I restarted the simulator for another test, I concluded they were probably right. Col. Jeffries was still walking, after all. I'd learned what I had to.

Then, the day came.

No speeches, no press conferences. I was poked, prodded, measured, and almost skinned alive by people taking samples and readings. Someone said they wanted to be sure that if I came back, that I was me. I think they watched too many movies on the late show.

The interior of the *Bellerophon* was roomy, much larger than the cramped capsules of the Gemini and Apollo missions. There was room to walk around, and I'd been told that, hypothetically, I actually *would* be walking, as "gravity induction" was part of the package deal. There were a lot of supplies, and some reprocessing equipment to stretch those supplies in ways I didn't want to think too much about. TV cameras and microphones were everywhere. Everything I did or said was going to be transmitted back to Earth, to watching orbital eyes.

Time compressed. Hours passed after I entered the *Bellerophon's* cockpit and began familiarizing myself with the new controls and systems. Tests were done -- mostly on the type of things that might cause everything to explode before we even lifted off. It was an old, familiar, pattern: Request and respond. This is go. That is green. The ritual kept everyone calm.

At 0213, 10-20-1973, *Bellerophon*, strapped to the back of a 747, left Earth's surface.

Chapter 2
Across The Void

The stars sharpened minute by minute, as the air thinned. I watched the countdown dials carefully, as well as listening to status reports from the pilot of the plane below me, his voice crackling in my headphones in calm, professional tones, as this was the most routine mission ever. Minutes collapsed to seconds, and then, to nothing. There was a shudder as the connection between the jet and *Bellerophon* was severed. I began the routine I'd rehearsed during training.

Bellerophon's controls were mostly modified airplane controls, designed to be as straightforward to a skilled pilot as possible. However, they ran into and through wholly alien devices, with some of the connections and linkages being based on "high-probability conjecture," or more precisely, "wild-ass guessing".

Bellerophon had been released on a vector out of the atmosphere. I needed to cut in the "lifters", the devices that "create a field which is mostly impervious to gravity", and then fire the actual Earth-made rockets to provide the final kick. I did the first, and there was a wave of *something* that passed through me and everything else. My body and the ship had become just barely translucent. It was eerie seeing the black shadow of the control throttle through the back of the hand I had wrapped around it. Looking down, I saw through the floor the faintest hints of a blurred Earth and a grey blob that was the descending 747.

No time for pondering, though. I gunned the engines. The thrust slammed me back into the chair as the engines ignited, but not nearly as much as I'd expected... or maybe as much as I should have expected, if I'd been thinking about it more. The sky, sharp and clear through the windows but a discolored blur through the rest of the translucent hull, darkened rapidly.

So far, I wasn't dead. I suspected I'd already caused some people to lose their contributions to the betting pool.

I signaled base. "Catering, this is champagne delivery. Leaving the highway. Over."

Minutes, taking their own sweet time about it, ambled by. Some of them seemed to take an hour or more to get where they were going. Then the signal came back. "Delivery, you are at the intersection. Left turn. Over."

That meant I was far enough out of orbit that I could turn off the rockets and move on to the next part, the "autopilot". The world had been calling to the alien ship ever since it drew near, and everyone was pretty certain they'd figured out how to connect the pulses of light and sound produced by what seemed to be a kind of radio to the "propulsors". If they were right, *Bellerophon* would point itself at the signal and all I'd need to do was ride it home. If they were wrong... I think the pool had 5-1 "crash into the sun", 3-1 "crash into the Earth", and 2-1 "drift forever in the all-devouring void of space".

There was no control button for this bit of unknown science. I had to manually touch a length of "cable", one which looked like cold light formed into a thin, flexible, tube to the diesel-engine-mixed-with-diamonds device precariously bolted to the controls next to me. When I did, there was a small, cold flash, and it fused seamlessly and perfectly -- though I didn't test the connection by seeing if I could yank it out again.

A second or two passed with nothing happening. I was preparing to signal and ask for further instructions, when *Bellerophon* began to vibrate, going from barely noticeable to tooth-rattling in seconds. The "radio" was showing an in-air display of lights, squiggles, and lines, all flowing faster and faster, with geometric shapes appearing, growing, and fading with increasing speed and intensity.

I found the "propulsor" switch and activated it. Somewhere in the back, bits of scavenged machinery shifted and connected.

Bellerophon spun violently. If I hadn't been safely strapped in, I'd have been flung at concussion speeds against the hull. Even so, it still disoriented me. The vibration continued to build, but it felt smoother somehow, more aligned and controlled. I recovered my bearings and reached for the speaker, only then noticing how the Moon loomed in the cockpit window.

"Catering, I have checked the map. We may have a traffic jam. Over."

Surely, I thought, whatever autopilot these aliens built could avoid the Moon. Then I remembered two things: It was recovered from a *crash*, and the humans who installed it only had guesses at how it worked.

I think Collins had "Crash Into The Moon" in the pool, at really long odds. Lucky bastard.

There was a definite sensation of acceleration, far less than there should have been, since the Moon was growing visibly in the window. Base still hadn't replied. "Catering, this is champagne delivery. I want my last words to officially be f..."

Then the world turned into a speeding blur. The moon grew to screen-filling size in an instant, and then, it was gone. I checked the small TV screen that showed the rear camera view... there it, and Earth, were, dwindling in the distance. The radio crackled. "Champagne... ring. We ...." There were a few more bursts of static after that, and I kept making regular reports, hoping they'd be picked up by "ears" a thousand times more sensitive than the ones on *Bellerophon*, but those distorted words were the last things I would ever hear a human being say.

Then, there was waiting. I'd blindly accepted Jeffries' offer, at first, partially because I had hopes it would keep me too busy to think. Now, I had little to do but think, and occasionally check various controls and hope, each time I gave in to the need for sleep, that the ship wouldn't simply explode before I awoke.

The "radio" started making noise about three weeks into the journey.

Ever since we'd passed *through* the Moon (I may never know quite how that worked), the hovering lightshow had been a steady sequence of simple geometric shapes, colored squiggles like oscilloscope patterns, and occasional complex forms composed of many lines, akin to what someone might imagine Chinese writing looked like if they'd never seen it. Now, new patterns were appearing, such as six squares arranged in a circle and spinning slowly, or an octagon flashing from blue to purple to red in a slow pulse. And it kept making noises -- a whine, a beep, buzz.

I'd become used to the somewhat smeared and washed-out view through the windshield -- an impressionist planetarium. Now there was something new. When I first noticed it, it was perhaps half the size of the Moon as seen from Earth. A dark shadow blotting the stars, with jagged red lines occasionally visible. There was a glow around one edge.

I took a pouch of lunch, rehydrated with lukewarm water, from the small galley and sat down to watch the view and the "radio", occasionally sending back my reports. Supposedly, everything was being transmitted back behind me, so my opinions were probably redundant, my guesses as to what I was seeing laughable to the eggheads. I spoke anyway. Maybe it would be in history books someday. It wasn't stirring stuff, I know.

Over hours, the target loomed larger, and the glow grew stronger, and then, in a process so smooth that I really noticed it only as it was completed, the dark void ahead was illuminated, and a smaller shadow, maybe an eighth its size, was clearly outlined, a tiny moon eclipsing the world below it.

A sun, of sorts. An artificial sun, orbiting the world. If there were an alien Galileo here, he would have been very disappointed.

The world appeared twice the size of the Moon, now, and details clarified. The most obvious feature, a large ocean, stretched pole to pole, looking like a split seam. Clouds swirled across the surface. The surface was mottled in more colors than I'd seen in pictures of the Earth from orbit -- browns and tans were there, but purples and blues and yellows formed blotches and blobs beneath the clouds. As the 'sun' moved across it, and its apparent size increased, I saw that the rightmost edge of the world... the western side, if I decided that the 'sun' was moving east-to-west... was glittering. Ice? Something else?

I'd become used to the bleeps and boops and late-night-creature-feature electronic noises of the 'radio', so I admit I twitched a little when they were replaced with something else.

Words. I didn't understand them at the time. I'm not one of those savants you sometimes see written up in *Reader's Digest*, who can recite a speech after hearing it once, so I can't tell you exactly what they were saying. Based on everything that happened since, I can guess it was something like "Unidentified craft: Please provide authorization code." To me, it was just a garble of noise. I tried answering.

"This is the *Bellerophon*, of Earth. We wish peaceful contact." There were non-engineers working on this thing, too, sociologists and psychologists and all of the other types who tend to spout definitive-sounding statements about things that no one could be certain of. The guys who worked with the slipsticks, graph paper, calculations, and equations splattered everything they wrote with "probably" and "appears to be," but the ones who worked with thoughts and feelings wrote with certainty and conviction, even though none of them agreed with the others about anything. They'd concluded that any "advanced" culture would have a universal language, or some other way to understand what was being said. (As it turns out, they were almost right, but not for any of the reasons they guessed.) They also decreed (although no one else believed them, and they were right not to), that an "advanced" culture would be "beyond war and violence", pointing out that the crashed ship had no evident weapons. I mentioned to one of them that this could just mean we hadn't found what we could *identify* as weapons, or that just because someone crashed their family station wagon didn't mean there weren't also fighter planes. I heard him mumbling something about "typical military mindset..." as he ignored me and walked away. No one else I spoke to believed that bull either, but they did believe any weapons the aliens had would be so advanced that arming *Bellerophon*, or even giving me a sidearm, would be a waste of time and might trigger a hostile response. That I understood, though I really didn't like it. No matter how useless I knew a simple pistol might be, it would still make me *feel* better to have one.

The plan was that if I had a chance to talk, I should take it -- and pick my words carefully. I'd been given several pages of "things to say" that had been written over the years. I was heavily tempted to ignore them and follow my instincts, but I was being recorded, and I'd been given orders. It may seem stupid, since I knew there was effectively no chance of going home and I couldn't be punished, but I'd sworn oaths and I meant to follow them.

Time passed. The *Bellerophon* was near to the back of the artificial sun now, and I could see it was a virtual cityscape of strange structures and protuberances. Millions of lights, fixed and moving, were arranged in grids and triangles and circles, shedding just enough illumination that I could make out the shapes of structures. It felt like flying over Manhattan at night, but this 'sun' was several hundred miles across. I kept talking. Hopefully, the aliens might understand my words, but not how emotionlessly I was saying them.

"...seek only understanding and communication, that we may discover each other's ways and share them in the name of..." I sighed. I'd read this nonsense for an hour, and there'd been no change, except that the display was getting more and more frantic and the voice shifted from repeating one pattern of sounds to another, and another. Then, it really changed. It began to speak in a rhythmic, formal, pattern, a sequence of short, definitive, sounds... and I realized it was counting down.

I cursed, unstrapped myself, and hastily donned the spacesuit. If the ship was damaged, I thought, it might give me a few hours to repair it, or maybe if they saw me drifting in space, they'd think I was harmless. I sealed the helmet and then realized I'd been an idiot. I pawed at the autopilot controls, a task made difficult by the thick gloves. I found the attached cable, and pulled. It was welded firmly, but adrenaline and desperation combined. It pulled free, causing a blinding flash that left spots in my eyes despite the tinted visor. *Bellerophon* shuddered as her engines abandoned the orders they'd been given and waited for others.

I shifted the 'propulsors' to manual. I could still hear the countdown going.

I pulled back on the throttle, and the cityscape below me zoomed downwards. I tapped madly on the jury-rigged controls for the alien engines, hoping to steer around the 'sun', maybe to get a look at the 'dark side' of this world. Every scrap of information I could get sent home would make my imminent death that much less pointless.

Then the countdown stopped.

There was a brightness behind me -- I could see it as a painful orange glow at the edge of the cockpit window -- and *Bellerophon* tilted madly. On the screen that showed the rear camera view, I could see pieces of what had formerly been the right wing tumbling off behind me.

That should have been it for me, but I wasn't flying using wings. I was a silver ball, rolling on the tilting plane of the universe itself.

I angled downwards, as another beam carved across the left wing and the rocket exhausts. The fuel explosion brightened the sky before me and then faded to a scattering of bright blotches on my eyes. *Bellerophon* bucked and twisted -- silver balls don't roll very well when they've been hammered out of shape a few times. I remembered they said the alien engines wouldn't work right in the atmosphere, but I felt the thuds and jolts of increasing air density, and they were still warping gravity around themselves.

Ahead of me, I saw a line of darkness, creeping over the edge of the globe. If I could get out of the weapon's sights before it shot again...

I wasn't aiming for anything but the ground. I wasn't trying to do much more than get *Bellerophon* to an angle where I could at least pretend it was landing. I hardly noticed how the ship kept flickering in and out of translucency, showing me flashes of the world passing below me.

The darkness deepened. No more attacks were coming, not that it mattered. I was riding a dead hunk of metal. I fought desperately with the controls. Slow it down -- tilt the wooden board back, bit by bit, until the silver ball stopped rolling... ease it a little, just a little, in another direction... but I was trying to do all this while riding a roller coaster. Blindfolded.

Flashes of colors -- reds and oranges, yellows and tans, the colors of childhood Septembers. The colors were inside and outside, and I made a brief effort to remember what I was supposed to pray just before I died. I couldn't, and instead tried to run through every obscene word I knew. I didn't make it a quarter of the way when it all went black.

Chapter 3
A New World

Something bright began to penetrate my closed eyes, but the creeping pain along my limbs was what first pulled me into consciousness. It was mild enough that I was still in a vague haze. I opened my eyes. *That* woke me up better than a bucket of ice water dumped on my head. (Fifteen years ago. Summer camp. The guy paid for that, I want to you to know. He still walks funny.)

Something like a splayed starfish with too many mouths was glued to my helmet, its half-dozen segmented tendrils clawing at it frantically. Still acting on instinct, I shouted a few choice words and tried to scramble back and away, not really grasping that it was stuck *on* my helmet. The motion to pull back triggered another wave of pain down my arms, legs, and sides, and I looked down to realize that vines and other foliage had been partially fused with my skin, torn free by my sudden movement. Blood trailed from the plants, and along my shredded suit.

I fumbled at the thing on the faceplate, which seemed agitated by the excitement. It quivered. Gouts of yellow and black ooze spurted from it, dripping across my vision, with the helmet's visor becoming clouded and cracked as the goo spread. Thankful beyond all reason that I was wearing gloves, I gripped the nightmare and pulled. It came loose with a hideous noise, and its claw-tipped limbs whipped in desperation and rage. I hurled it across the ruined cockpit.

Ruined. Yes, that was the only word. It looked as if it had been abandoned in the jungle for decades, not what I assumed was minutes. The plant life grew through it and around it, passing into and out of consoles and chairs, floor and ceiling. The automatic intangibility may have been a safety feature, activated on collision, but deactivated improperly, so that the ship and the jungle were still interlocked with each other. Maybe that's how it could move as fast as it did, the engines made it exist half in the universe, half out of it. I don't know.

Colors. The colors were colors of fire. I'd thought, coming down, Autumn colors... but these were bright and vibrant and strong, the colors of something overflowing with life. Pretty literally. There were things everywhere. Scaled things, slick and slimy things, furred things. Things with no limbs, four limbs, six limbs, too many limbs. Things with flapping, leathery, wings; things that leapt; things that drifted through the air, tadpoles inflated like balloons.

Many tried to explore the suit to see if it was edible; and, if not, to see if anything *inside* it was edible. I batted, kicked, and slapped them as I stumbled through the steel-and-tree maze the *Bellerophon* had become. The light that filtered through the many gaps in the ceiling seemed like sunlight, and I realized that since I'd crashed on the planet's nightside, I must have been out for a few hours, at least.

I had to remove the helmet. The corrosive spit of the, uh, jungle starfish had made vision impossible. The consequences were as bad as you might think. I realized I'd been breathing stale air for the last few minutes when I got a good lungful of the local atmosphere... and it was a second *after* I took that first breath that I bothered thinking about how I had no idea if the air was breathable. Then again, if it wasn't, what could I have done?

I didn't die from the first inhalation. The smell was overwhelming -- rot and moistness and perfume, sulfur and decay and smoke. Smoke? My crash had started a few smoldering fires, but the moistness of the place kept them from spreading. My eyes stung a bit, and I wondered why kind of wood was burning and what it might do to me.

I scavenged. I found water, dehydrated food, first aid supplies, a basic toolkit, some clean jumpsuits, and some bags, leftovers after a month of opening supply containers. I hooked the Swiss army knife from the toolkit onto my belt. I coiled up twenty or so feet of cable -- you never know when you might need rope. I also spent some time turning shards of hard metal, support struts, and stripped wire into a makeshift hand axe. Given the thickness of the jungle around me, it would be necessary.

So... now what?

There would be no rescue from Earth. Were the aliens looking for me? The crash site was obvious enough; they couldn't easily miss me if they were looking. Or maybe they could, or maybe they assumed I was dead. I could stand around forever playing what-if games, or I could move. I moved.

If there's anyone living here, I thought, if they're anything like humans, they'll use rivers for transport and food, they'll build their cities near them. Thus, I had a plan: Find a river and try to follow it downstream. This plan was based on a thousand assumptions, but every other plan I could think was based on even more. The number of facts I had to work with before setting out wasn't going to increase until I *did* set out.

Downhill, more or less, seemed the best way to find a river. The ground was generally rolling, but there was a grade it seemed to follow.

The trees were dense and the undergrowth was tangled, thorny, and sticky. Crystal formations, from tiny fist-sized clumps to man-sized outcroppings, were commonplace. They grew randomly, in every color and shade and degree of transparency. They ranged from brittle to hard, from perfectly uniform to madly asymmetrical. Plants partially engulfed many of them. I couldn't be sure, but after a few hours, I became convinced some of the smaller nodes could scurry in front of me just so I could stumble over them.

It seemed most of the local life was built with an excess of fangs, stingers, and claws, or maybe the herbivores just stayed well hidden.

After a few hours, I came to a "wall" formed of what I took to be fungus. Nearly my height, it stretched across my path, and going around it would mean backtracking and finding a way though much denser forest. I gently prodded the wall, and found it to be soft and slightly flexible. It was mostly colored in the same bonfire hues as the woods around me. It reminded me of a landlocked coral reef. Vaguely ovoid protrusions, ranging from the size of my clenched fist to the size of a pumpkin, grew randomly along the sides and top. There was a swarm of buzzing creatures around it, but there were swarms of buzzing creatures around *everything*.

I started to tear through it, and then it burst. A cloud of tiny insects, so dense it looked like smoke, roiled out. I shut my eyes, staggered back, and then real explosion happened. The nearest pods ruptured, and from them came swarms of larger bugs, waspish things over an inch long. The noise was hideous; the sensation of the things surrounding me was even worse. My suit, torn though it was, provided some measure of protection or I'd probably have died right there. Instead, given a paralyzed moment to choose to run back or forward, I chose *forward*, smashing full-on into the hive-wall, feeling it resist for a moment, and then give way as I propelled myself forward -- covering my face as much as possible, feeling a billion points of contact as the things landed on me, crawled into holes, tried to find any point of flesh they could contact to sting and bite. Each sting felt like a needle of flame.

Two or three minutes of almost-blind running, opening my eyes in quick blinks and peering through to see just enough of the path ahead to plot a few more steps, then repeating... and the ground vanished under me. I plunged into a pit of brackish, vile, liquid, warm and foul smelling, so thick with red and orange ooze that it barely qualified as water... but the swarms retreated. Given that moment of respite, I heaved myself out of the muck, and collapsed on my back, trying not to think of how many scratches, cuts, and wounds I'd just exposed to whatever exciting diseases this world had to offer.

I began to hope the aliens did find me. Either they'd kill me cleanly with some sort of ray gun, or they'd take me back to their lab to dissect me, but in that case, they'd want to clean me up first! That would almost be worth it.

They didn't seem to be coming, though. I did what I could with the first aid kit and the peroxide. Maybe I could stop the worst of it. There were some antibiotics as well; I took one. I poured one of the bottles of clean water into a bag of grey pebbles and yellow flakes that claimed to be some kind of Swedish Meatballs -- it was more like mildly salted mushy cardboard and paint chips, but it was food. Sort of. I realized I had only a few days, at most, and then I'd have to start finding out what could be eaten on this world... besides, according to most of the local wildlife, *me*.

I put my flight suit on again, and the remains of the suit over it. The suit was hot and uncomfortable, but it continued to provide some protection. I set out.

Then I heard it. Rather, I heard the silence. The continual chorus of chitters, buzzes, squawks, and other things which couldn't be identified went dead. Station WJNGL was off the air.

So far, I hadn't seen any animals much bigger than my head. My own size and presumably alien shape and smell had not been enough to terrify the locals into silence. So, what had?

It was silent, as well. I had only the barest warning before I saw it, a pattern of colors moving where other patterns were still. Dappled in shades of black and yellow, it slid by just a few feet ahead of me, and then I heard a louder noise, a rustling of leaves, branches breaking, and a shrill, buzzsaw-on-granite sound that seemed designed to send rusty knives across my every bone and nerve. Its warcry done, it heaved fully into view.

Serpentine. Thirty, forty feet long. Its body was as thick as mine, and its head and jaws could easily engulf me. Two segmented, insectoid arms grew out from it, below the neck, and those were tipped with long, armored, pincers.

It reared up, and back, and peered down at me, a master predator which had no fear of a hairless ape. Slitted eyes narrowed. Tasting the air, a foot long tongue flickered in and out.

I watched it, waiting for the lunge to attack, hoping this thing might have some body language I could read. It was still staring though, weaving, trying to lock my eyes with its own... trying to make sure I was looking *at it*...

A noise, an instinct, a whisper from St. Joseph of Cupertino... something told me to spin, right then, right now. Spin, see it, curse loudly, lean left, turn the lean into a fall and the fall into a roll, spin, get my feet under me, push up, and bring my axe down on the tail of the beast -- an armored, segmented, whip terminating in a stinger the size of my arm, a stinger which a second earlier was heading straight for my back.

The axe hit hard. The impact with the shell jarred my arm, but the momentum kept going, and the hard chitin cracked, and there was a spray of black ichor and a noise from the thing -- different from the triumphant screee! of the hunter it had made a moment ago. This sound was louder, filled with fury and pain.

Well, so was I.

Eight years old. Staring up at a boy half again my age and twice my weight, one of the many predators who prowled the pavement savannah or lurked in wait by the dime store watering holes. His face red and contorted, his left hand clutching his right wrist, his right index finger twisted and cracked after he made the mistake of poking me one more time than I could stand... which was once. We circled, crouched, each ready to charge or flee, each watching the other, and the crowd watching us. The predator could retreat and lick his wounds, but he'd be torn apart by his fellow beasts if he did, and he knew it. I'd hurt him, and he feared me, but he feared his own kind more.

Twenty seven years old. Facing a snake-scorpion on an alien world. No intelligence glinted behind those serpent eyes, not that much ever shown in the neighborhood thugs. It cared about survival, not status... but if its instincts told it to run after every pain, it would never survive. It skreee-klikked and lunged, fangs agape, claws snapping and seeking.

The neighborhood lion pounced, roaring his pride in a stream of profanity and threats. If he hadn't been so desperate to show off his courage, he wouldn't have been so open. If he'd been a little more cautious, a little more controlled, I would have been lying broken in the street, bleeding and crying until some adult took pity on my and called my parents, as if that would have been any sort of mercy. But he wasn't cautious. I stepped into his charge, before he'd built up momentum, and grabbed at his already crippled hand, the one he couldn't form into a fist. I twisted at the broken bone, and when he screamed and tried to turn back and pull away, I put all the weight I had into a shove that sent him into a sidewalk display of soda bottles, his own bulk doing the rest, casting him down into a mound of shattered glass and fizzing liquids.

I was cut, scraped, hungry, and exhausted. If I had taken a moment to realize how bad off I was, I would have died. I didn't take that moment. Instead, I took the axe and flipped it horizontally, then, as the snake-scorpion snapped at me, I ducked under the massive head and shoved the axe, using both hands, directly into and through the soft skin of its throat. I felt my hands sink into its warm flesh and the gush of black blood cover my hands, arms, face, and hair.

That should have been enough, but it wasn't. I grabbed a brick, a bit fallen from some building, and ran towards him, fully intending to smash his skull to pulp. That was enough for one of the adults, looking on from their bench, to finally act. Watching children beat each other bloody was just good, clean, fun, but being a passive witness to one child killing another might be considered immoral. He grabbed me, disarmed me, and hauled me off, screaming and kicking, to my father's shoe store.

I collapsed to my hands and knees, letting the axe fall. Breathing in great, wheezing gasps, I could hear the jungle noises slowly return. The thing in front of me twitched and jerked for long minutes, even as scavengers approached to enjoy the kill.

The thing's blood stank, and attracted even more than the usual cloud of insects. I had no choice. I abandoned the EVA suit, and used one of my few containers of water to wipe as much of the ichor off my skin and jumpsuit as I could. I hacked off a few chunks of meat -- why not, I thought, I may need it soon -- and wrapped them as best I could in some of the cleaner bits of the suit, and kept on.

Shadows had blossomed throughout the forest when I found the top of the cliff. Any darker, and I might have found the *bottom* of the cliff a second or two later.

Even through the dimming light, I could see hints of a river, a mile or so from the cliff. Getting down would have to wait until morning.

It was odd, looking at the sunset, to realize this sun was a machine orbiting only a few hundred miles away from the surface. Stranger still, then, that this world seemed so... primitive. But how many signs of modern civilization would an alien who crash landed in the Amazon or the Gobi see? Would he realize there were cities with millions of people, that we'd split the atom? Except... he would have seen the lights of our cities on his way down. I had seen such lights on the back of the 'sun', but nothing in my rapid descent across the world. There was no sign any local forces had scrambled craft to scour the area, looking for a crashed vessel. I imagined an antennaed, green-skinned man frantically trying to convince his antennaed, green-skinned co-workers that he'd seen a UFO.

They're aliens, I had to tell myself. Who knows what they're like? Maybe they don't even care if I crashed. Why assume they think like us?

I couldn't convince myself of that. I was sure that while there were countless ways to build a body, there weren't nearly as many ways to build a mind. If the builders of the ship had the kind of mind needed to study the world, to make tools, to travel to other worlds, those minds would end up being a lot like ours. I was pretty certain I'd received a warning message, and was attacked because I didn't heed it, which further supported that conclusion. So... where *were* they?

Note, I wasn't just standing there staring over a cliff while pondering this. I was semi-sheltered in an alcove formed by a couple of jutting rocks, getting a fire started. I hoped the light and heat would keep away some of the inevitable night prowlers. It would also serve to cook my snake-scorpion... eh, snorpion... slices.

The light faded to the waning moments of twilight, before true night falls, and then it happened.

The fire was casting back the darkness around me, but I could see the deep purple of the sky just beyond my small shelter of rock grow darker and darker, and then... light bloomed and spread. Peering out from the alcove, gazing around, I saw a million shifting pools of light, each soft-edged and faint, but together providing a glow brighter than the fullest moon of Earth. It came from the crystals. In the darkness, the uncounted outcroppings and formations became illuminated, each casting its own particular light, each pulsing and shifting in slow, spectacular, cycles. I strode to the cliff-edge, enraptured almost to the point of carelessness. Below me, spreading out, were two great lakes of light bisected by the dark gap of the river. Whorls and swirls and washes of color, a psychedelic display worthy of any hippie's imagination, played across the landscape below. The river was dark only by comparison to the brilliance on either side; it had its own faint glow, small pools of muted color cast by the crystals at the bottom.

And more. Here and there along the river were pinholes of light -- tiny but brilliant specks, sharper than the pastel auras that washed throughout the woods. They moved in ways that were not the random dashing and darting of insects, and some moved in groups, each point remaining at a fixed and constant distance from its brothers.

They were ships. Craft, of some sort, traveling up and down the river. Far distant, downstream, I could just barely see a constellation of such lights, regular and unmoving. A city.

So there *were* beings here, something like humanity. Beings who traveled in boats on the water, needed lights at night, built port cities.

They might kill me on sight. They might capture me and dissect me. They might place me in some kind of alien zoo. They might even welcome me. My odds were probably better confronting them than trying to remain too long in this jungle of nightmares.

I returned to my semi-secluded alcove. I roasted the snorpion meat, cooking it until it seemed very well done, hopefully enough to kill any parasites. I ate the tiniest sliver of it, and waited half an hour. No nausea, sweating, shakes, numbness, or other symptoms. I took a slightly larger bite, and waited yet again. Still nothing besides hunger. Finally, I tore through the whole slice.

It didn't kill me. I can't really tell you what it tasted like. Definitely not chicken.

I had to sleep. Other than hoping the fire would ward off predators... and not attract alien hunters or hikers or little green boy scouts... I had little I could do to increase my safety. I looked up at the stars as I lay down on the best bedroll I could make from the fragments of my suit and other bits of clothing and gear. I knew all the basics of orienteering and navigation, how to find my way home after a crash (or at least know exactly how badly screwed I was), but the stars above me were unreadable. Many of the familiar constellations were there, but this world was at a different angle, blending southern and northern skies. There was one star, three or four times brighter than any other, and I figured that was mine. The Sun. Sol. Just one more star now, among the rest, and the sun of this world was a great machine.

Tomorrow, perhaps, I'd meet the builders.

Something was tugging at my foot.

I jerked my leg back, then kicked furiously. I felt a thud as I hit something. My eyes tried to focus down my body as my hands scrambled to find the hatchet. At my feet was a hairy, six-legged thing about the size of a sheepdog. Its fur was a blend of reds and mauves and grays, and jutting spikes poked haphazardly out across its body. It had a long, pointed, and hairless face, the skin drawn so tight that it seemed almost mummified, and six eyes, black featureless orbs, three on each side of the long muzzle. It made a stuttering yipping noise, and its maw unfolded bidirectionally, expanding outwards to reveal row after row of grinding teeth.

Seemingly satisfied that it had told me what it thought of my interrupting its meal, it made a final "sssbrak" sound and loped off. Then I noticed how numb my left arm felt, and looked at it.

A glistening amber leech, six inches long, had fastened itself on my exposed wrist. Through its translucent skin, I watched for a few seconds as its internal organs bloated and gorged on my blood, clearly flowing in slow pulses into the thing's abdomen. I scraped the hatchet edge along my skin and cut it free, then stamped it to pulp. I spent some time with the first aid kit, cutting out the barbed bits stuck in my fortunately-numb flesh, and slathering on as much disinfectant as I could.

Then, the descent. I was a decent climber, but the *Bellerophon's* load-out had not included a climbing kit. The assumption was that, if I made it alive, I'd either be incinerated on the spot or taken on-board some sort of advanced alien craft. Wilderness survival wasn't on the list of scenarios. The cable I'd taken wasn't long enough to use to rappel down from here. I'd have to find another route.

Hours of walking later, always careful to keep myself close to the river, I found a rough but navigable path downward. I made my way along it carefully. Midway through the descent, I noticed a fruit-bearing tree, with deep auburn bark, broad ochre leaves, and branches heavy with lumpy, apple-sized spheres covered with a swirling skin of teal-flecked metallic blue. I plucked one, but as soon as it was detached, it unrolled into a giant millipede thing, its underbelly covered with squiggling legs surrounding a toothy "jaw" that ran the length of its body. Its legs flailed and its maw gnashed furiously as the creature twisted in my hand, trying to turn itself over and attack the warm flesh holding it.

I shouted and flung it into a nearby thorn bush... which unwrapped a dozen needle-tipped creepers and impaled the squealing arthropod, dragging the twitching body deep into its heart.

Earth has piranha swarms, spider wasps, and worse, I told myself. A tiger or a shark would look just as alien and monstrous to this world's people as these things do to you, never mind what humans do to each other.

Some hours of walking later, the ground leveled out. It would be a simple enough thing to find the river, and then? I wasn't sure. My plan was to observe at least a little, get some sense of what I was dealing with, maybe spend a few days, if I could, out of sight, working out the best way to approach them. It wasn't much of a plan, but it was a plan.

"No plan survives contact with the enemy." As true on an alien world as in every war in human history.

I heard a scream, then other sounds -- voices, even if I couldn't understand them -- and the sounds of a fight. I heard distinctly *metallic* noises, and none of the horrors I'd seen so far on this world had been made of iron.

Stealthily, or so I hoped, I made my way towards the noise. There was enough cover that I could peer through while remaining hidden. I did check to make sure these particular specimens of the local flora didn't find me edible.

I saw three people. Two of them are best described as "lizard rat men". They had muzzle-like faces, a long, naked, tail, and dexterous hands ending in sharply clawed fingers. Fur grew on some parts of their bodies, grey-white on one, and patterned brown-and-black swirls on the other. Those parts not covered in fur or armor showed heavy scales. Their eyes were reptilian, and they had no visible ears.

Each wore armor, formed of hardened leather, and (I later found) treated with a varnish to add toughness. They carried swords, which were currently sheathed. On their belts were all manner of small things -- a sack, something that could have been a drinking horn, a small knife. One had a collection of brightly colored ribbons tied into an ornate knot and fastened to his neck. Most of the gear they carried was festooned with brilliant bits of metal or colored glass, sparkling and reflecting the light of the artificial sun. One of them, the grey-furred one, was wearing a copper-colored metal helmet, rather visibly dented.

The third person in the tableau was the likely source of both the dent and the metallic noise. She was of a different species, much closer in form to humanity[1]. She was wielding no weapon but a large stick, and she was waving it in front of her inexpertly as the two lizard-rats moved cautiously around her. She was clearly frightened, but stood her ground, turning her head towards one and then the other, trying to hold them back as they closed in.

---

[1] (Someone reading this might notice I made a lot of assumptions. I didn't consider that I could be seeing one species with two very divergent-looking genders. I was assigning pronouns based on casual observation. Well, the kind of people who stop to second- and triple- guess themselves when in the field don't come *back* from the field. In the future, someone can write a book detailing all the assumptions I made and how *they* wouldn't have made them. This isn't that book.)

She was closer to humanity, but not human. Her skin was a deep violet-grey. She had short, black hair, and was wearing a simple knee-length, short-sleeved, tunic of tan cloth tied with a belt of shimmering green-scaled leather, the same material used for her boots. On her right wrist was a wide copper band. A basket was nearby, and I could see that it had previously contained an assortment of the crystal shards that "grew" throughout the forest.

She swung the stick; the grey-furred one grabbed it, twisted his arm and pulled it away, as the other one moved in and grabbed her waist. She flailed at her assailant, who ignored her blows. The other retrieved a set of chains from the sack at his belt, and approached. Their intent seemed clear.

Now, at this point, I probably should have considered how little I knew of the situation. For all I knew at that moment, the mauve woman was the most vile murderer in history, and the two lizard-rats were the local police or FBI. There were a thousand different explanations for the scene I was witnessing, all equally plausible, and acting on impulse, without trying to gather more information or make a reasoned appraisal, would have been incredibly stupid.

I charged.

Grey-Fur heard me and turned. He shouted something, then stepped back a couple of feet, drawing his sword in the process. Brown-Fur hesitated, torn between holding on to Mauve and either attacking me or running away. As I closed with Grey-Fur, he decided, delivering a heavy blow to Mauve and knocking her to the ground, then drawing his own sword and looking rapidly back and forth at myself and Grey-Fur, even as the distance between us vanished.

Grey-Fur was in a defensive posture. He was babbling at me, and gesturing with his empty hand in a way that seemed to be almost conciliatory, his hand open, palm towards me. He watched me, clearly wary, but showed no signs of attack. If his tone and body language were close to that of humans, he was saying something like "Hey, buddy. We don't want no trouble. Let's just talk about this, OK?"

I hesitated, just for a second. I might have stopped, at that point, stepped back, and made some gesture of my own, and perhaps everything from that moment forward would have been different... except that his pal, Brown-Fur, decided to take my brief pause as a sign to join in.

He sprang forward, attacking in a leap a human couldn't make. His blade came down in a powerful arc, and I sidestepped it only barely. The edge of it slammed into a twisted stump, splitting it... and the sword stuck. He tugged at it; and, in the instant between his realization that it couldn't come free and his decision to let it go, I struck, swinging the hatchet into his side. It cut through the hardened leather and I felt warm blood spurt out. As I pulled my weapon free, trying to keep an eye on Grey-Fur without turning my back on Brown-Fur, he collapsed to the ground. I saw him begin to crawl away, trailing blood more or less the same color as mine.

If Grey-Fur had any interest in parley, it was gone now. Whether Brown-Fur had seen some gesture telling him to attack, or if he'd acted as impetuously as I did, I'll never know. But I'd just smashed an axe into Grey-Fur's partner or friend or lover or sibling or something, and Grey-Fur was not happy about it.

Mauve was slowly pulling herself up, still coughing from the hit she'd taken. "Run!" I shouted, knowing she couldn't understand me.

Grey-Fur was more cautious than his partner. He knew he had greater reach than I did, and used it. He kept stepping in, making quick jabs, then withdrawing to parry. He was armored; I wasn't. He was using a weapon he'd probably trained with for years; I was using a makeshift hatchet. The only reason I wasn't already dead was that he was being extremely cautious, sizing me up, testing me. Once he was certain he had my measure, he'd move in for the killing blow. I had to shift the battle away from his strengths.

We danced around each other for another few seconds as I tried to think of a way to actually *do* that. A lot of possibilities appeared and disappeared as I had to work harder and harder on defense, his attacks becoming more sure, more focused. I spotted something. It was a ridiculous gamble, but it was the only one I had.

I hurled the hatchet. Clumsy and unbalanced, it was never made for throwing, and I'd certainly never mastered any kind of axe-tossing skill; the closest I'd come was drunkenly hurling daggers at a dartboard, at a seedy bar in Saigon, four years ago. I wasn't seriously trying to hit him with it, though, just distract him for one or two seconds, just long enough...

He misjudged the path of the axe, didn't see that it couldn't possibly hit him. He flinched, and turned his head, just for a moment, and watched it pass. If I'd tried to charge in, weaponless, he would have easily killed me. Fortunately, that wasn't my plan.

I'd maneuvered next to what I'll call a bugfruit tree. Grabbing one of the "fruits", I pitched it at my attacker. Classic fastball, straight over the plate. It unfolded mid-flight, and splattered directly onto Grey-Fur's muzzle.

That was when I charged. I smashed into him, hooking my foot behind his, and forced him to the ground, even as he was still trying to detach the hungry millipede-thing from his face. I leapt on top of him, my knee on his chest, and grabbed at his sword-arm with both hands. His other arm was still focused on removing the eyeball-eating creature, so I had the opening I needed to slam his weapon-bearing hand down onto a rock. The shock and pain caused it to open, and I took possession of the sword, turned it point downwards, and forced it through the gap in his armor between his chest and throat.

I staggered upright again, panting, scanning for Brown-Fur or Mauve. Brown-Fur was still lying a short distance from where we fought, unmoving. I was surprised; the wound hadn't seemed lethal, but then, what did I know of these beings' anatomy? Mauve...

Mauve was walking towards me, her tan tunic well-stained with blood. Given her strong, upright stance, the blood wasn't hers. In her hand was the knife Brown-Fur had been wearing on his belt. She was looking quite intently at me, very focused, and the way the knife moved in her grasp as she walked signaled considerable skill. The woman I'd seen struggling ineffectually against the two lizard-rats was no longer there. This was someone completely different, who just happened to be living in the same body.

She stopped, about ten feet from me. She looked at the corpse of Grey-Fur next to me, the sword still pinning him, a teal-and-blue crawling thing placidly eating his head. I saw a quick dart of her vision to the hatchet, closer to her than to me. Turning to keep me still partially in her view, she also glanced at Brown-Fur, and then back to me.

I considered reaching for the sword, but if there was any chance of getting out of this without being in another fight, that would end it. Whatever decision she was trying to make, I decided, I'd let her make it. I felt confident that if she moved to attack me, I *could* get to the sword in time. She seemed aware of this as well.

After half a minute of silence, other than the sounds of the jungle, she spoke. Actually, she shouted, a long stream of angry syllables punctuated by hand gestures and pointing -- at me, at the corpses, at the face-eating bug, at everything. A full minute of what sounded like fairly high quality profanity followed. She stopped, and stared at me, her eyes daring me to deny whatever she may have said about my mother, my talents in the sack, or my relationship with farm animals.

I shrugged, not knowing if the gesture would mean anything to her. "Sorry. I really don't understand a word. I'm, uhm, not from around here... uh..." I fell back on the speech I'd been forced to memorize. "'We wish peaceful contact between our peoples, hoping to create a productive...'"

She started to speak again, and I shut up. This time, the words were different -- not just the tone, but the language. When I provided another round of "Sorry, no parley fransay," she tried a third language, this one a painfully guttural series of throat-tearing syllables, while I stood there feeling that with each go-round, Mauve was downgrading her opinion of me. Then again, how was someone from this sort of sword-and-sandal matinee culture supposed to guess I was from another world?

At this point, I wanted to slap myself on the back of my head. I hadn't even thought, consciously, about the fact the first people I met on this alien world, a world with an artificial sun, were running around with swords. Had I just happened to land in a backwater part of the world, someplace the local version of *National Geographic* would visit? Except... the sun. This wasn't anyone's home planet. Someone had *built* that sun, and would the people who could do that still have 'primitive' areas? Maybe. There were parts of Appalachia, I'd heard, still without electricity.

Mauve was walking closer to me, talking in a calm, soothing tone, back in the first language she'd used. She hadn't dropped the knife, but was holding it loosely, as non-threateningly as possible while still being able to switch to a fighting position in an instant. As she talked, she gestured towards Grey-Fur's body, pointing to it, and back to herself, taking a few careful steps forward at a time and watching me for any reaction. I said "Go ahead", and tried to signal agreement. She bent over, cautiously, never taking her eyes from me for more than a second, and pointed to the bug on his face, and then to her knife.

I nodded, and took a slow step back. I got the impression we'd both be happier with a little more distance.

Using the blade, she flicked the thing from his muzzle, then she rooted under his armor and pulled something out, tearing the cord it has been attached to. It was a plate of grey stone, octagonal, three inches long and half as wide, a half inch thick. I could see a dozen colored dots, no, they were small gems, each a quarter-inch in diameter, on its surface. She wiped the dagger on one of the few remaining clean bits of her tunic, then held it in her teeth as she tapped on some of the gems and then *slid* some of them, *through* the rock, as if it were some kind of soft clay. There were no grooves or slots. She could push the gems around, but the stone remained perfectly solid. After a few such adjustments, she held it out to me with her left hand, though not before returning the knife to her right.

I accepted it. She stood back up.

The tablet felt warm in my hand, and it buzzed slightly. Almost all of the gems sparkled a glistening orange hue now; they had been a mix of blue, black, and yellow when she'd first found it. Jewelry? A weapon? A credit card?

She tapped the knife in her hand, and she said "*vizish*". She looked at me expectantly. She repeated the word and the gesture.

"Knife?" I said. The tablet produce a short, louder, buzz.

She nodded. Then she tapped the knife again, and repeated the word, "*vizish*"... but this time I *heard* my word, 'knife', overlaid on her word, separated by just a moment. The stone wasn't speaking, though. I heard the word in her voice, coming from her position, but somehow, it was translated for me.

Thus began the language lesson.

It took a bit to really understand what was going on. The tablet knew what word Mauve was saying, and would signal me when the word I gave wasn't the "right" one... so if she was naming the *color* of a leaf, and I kept saying "leaf", the tablet would make a particular kind of noise, until eventually I said "red", and the it would make the "finally, you got it" sound, and we would move on. When I spoke, I could hear my voice and the echo of my words in her language. Over time, I stopped noticing it unless I had to. It was like listening to a translator speak, if the translation started talking well before you finished.

Hours passed as we worked through many hundreds of words. Some things just seemed to *happen* -- tenses, plurals, all the stuff you fall down on after you get past "Tiene las orejas de un burro". Every so often, she would ask for the tablet, possibly move one of the gems, and hand it back to me. The gems were changing color -- the orange they'd been when we started altered to reds, blues, and greens, a bit at a time. I decided it was measuring something, or perhaps grading me on my performance.

The sun was starting to reach the horizon when she finally seemed happy with the pattern and color of the gems. She handed the tablet back to me. "Keep this near you, always. We have enough to begin. Over time, the words will be natural. When you stop hearing the echo, it is done."

I took the tablet. She continued, "Do you understand what's been going on?"

I slipped the flat stone into a pocket. "Yeah. This teaches words. I hear your words in my language, you hear my words in yours."

She smiled. "Good. Now that we can talk...*do you have any idea what a mess you've made of things, you idiot? I don't know what land you're from, but were you exiled for being stupid, or did you just get lost and wander across the world to end up here?*"

This was *not* what I was expecting to hear, for many reasons. Perhaps the least important of them was that words like "idiot" and "exiled" weren't words she'd used while teaching me. I actually didn't think too much about that until much later. I was too busy trying to find the best answer, and to keep myself calm. I have never learned to take insults gracefully, but there were three things keeping me under control. First, I'd learned very early that almost *anything* might be forgiven, except attacking a woman. Second, I'd been forced to learn how to endure and had trained myself to not throw the first punch unless I absolutely had to. Third, she still had the grazarn's knife, and I hadn't picked up the sword.

She took my moment of silence as further proof of my idiocy. "I know you can talk. Do so!"

I did. "No, I *don't* know how much I've made a mess of things... or even what 'things' you're talking about... and as for what land I come from, well, that's going to be a very interesting conversation. I'll say this, in my 'land', people tend to be thankful when someone stops them from being attacked!" I tapped on the word-finder. "Let's see... is there a word in your language for 'gratitude'? Yes, it seems there is."

We stared at each other for a second. I had no idea, I realized, what passed for proper behavior here; maybe you *weren't* expected to be grateful in these circumstances. Maybe I'd just insulted her to the point where she'd be justified in attacking me.

She relaxed, and I could see it was with effort. I knew the feeling. She spoke very carefully, picking her words one by one. "If... things had been... what they must have seemed... I would be expressing thanks." Unexpectedly, she laughed, and then leaned back against a tree, chuckling. "Undone by my own skill. I'll tell D'Valya of this. I'm sure he could make it some lesson in pride or arrogance."

She pushed herself away from the tree, and walked towards me. She was studying me intently. Despite our hours of language exchange, this felt like the first time she'd really *noticed* me. Perhaps she'd been waiting too eagerly for the chance to make her speech.

She reached forward, then stopped. "May I examine your clothing?"

I nodded.

She ran her fingers along the edge of my left sleeve. Despite the heat and humidity of the jungle, her skin was cool, and if she was sweating, I didn't notice it. I considered the past two days of swamp, muck, and exertion, becoming quite aware of how I might look... or smell.

Her hair, I realized, wasn't quite the deep black I'd thought. Up close, it glistened slightly in the fading light, and had a translucency to it. Not noticeable where it was thickest, as it thinned out, I could see it was almost like fibers of obsidian.

"I haven't seen cloth of this texture." She then pointed to the Air Force patch on my shoulder. "Or symbols like that." She touched my hand, and seeing that I didn't object or resist, turned it over, considering something. She let it go. "Is this sort of skin normal?"

Italian/Irish mutts? Americans? Humans? Did she mean color or texture or something else entirely? I shrugged. "It's common in some areas, less so in others."

Her voice became more distant. She was speaking to me, but also to herself. "Odd. You must be from very far, if I've never seen, or even heard of, anyone like you. To travel that far... you're not a trader. You're not a spy. You fight well enough, but a mercenary would have to speak some common language to seek work."

What, I wondered, was it safe to tell her? I would be hard to pretend I'd wandered here from somewhere else on the world, as I couldn't describe any of the places I may have passed through. How welcoming would they be to strangers from space? It might be best to shift the subject.

"I said, it will be quite a conversation. Your turn, since we're talking. What did I do wrong when I thought I was helping you?"

She glanced towards the sinking sun, and ignored my direct question. "The grazarn will have a camp not too far from here. It would be better to talk there."

I took the grazarn's blade and wiped it down as much as I could, keeping an eye on Mauve to see if she'd react. I wasn't about to wander off with someone who didn't want me armed. She didn't say anything, just waited until I was done, then turned and walked in the direction of the river. She stopped suddenly, spun to face me, and performed a gesture that involved looking backwards over her shoulder for a moment, then around, and then directly at me, pointed at herself, and said, "S'zana."

Chapter 4
S'zana

I imitated her gestures as best I could, and said "Major Ryan Falconi, USAF."

She repeated it back to me, and she couldn't suppress a slight giggle. I heard what I'd said to her echoed in her language, but I was learning the trick of listening to the words as she spoke them, and then hearing the meaning of those words within my mind, as the word-finder did whatever it was doing to my brain. *"Kalveer R'yan Faleekon Youesssaf".* "Kalveer", I guessed, was a military rank. "Youessaf" was just noise. My actual name didn't turn into any kind of words, directly, but "Faleekon" was extremely close in sound to a type of carrion eating creature not known for its cleanliness.

"Let's leave it at R'yan for now."

"'Kalveer'. Impressive," she said, with a slightly disbelieving air. We began to make our way along. The jungle was thinner here; there were several clearings and it was relatively easy traveling. "Alone, though, and with no decent weapon. Hm. Deserter, then? Fled from your far land to ours?"

"No. Not by a long shot." There was no keeping the anger out of my voice at this accusation. She noticed it.

"I see. I apologize. But you are a mystery." She stepped briskly over a tangle of roots. "I'm not sure what your archery skills have to do with it, though."

I laughed. That took the edge off. The translation of words was literal; whatever phrase she might use to mean "poor odds" or "very off the mark", it wasn't the same one I used. I explained.

"Strange skin, strange words, strange clothes. Hm. Through the Scour?"

We spotted an aggressive tangle of seeking vines and made our way around it. S'zana pointed out the smaller plants, baseball-sized knots of thorns, that would awaken the larger one in the center. By avoiding them, we could move unnoticed past it.

"Let's find this camp. Then I'll give what answers I can."

The grazarn camp consisted of two small tents, and a flat-bottomed boat tied up to a large tree. A swarm of winged worms had descended on a spilled ceramic cask of something sticky and alcoholic. Smoke trailed from a firepit.

S'zana pulled a branch out of the charcoal and waved it at the wriggling mass, but they were mostly undeterred.

"Fire drives them off?"

Her first expression was one of "How could anyone ask such a stupid question?" but then changed. She smiled slightly, as if I'd somehow told her something. "Yes. Give me a few minutes to get this going." (The actual 'minute' was not precisely the same as an Earth minute; the word she used referred to the same sort of timespan. It's not especially useful, for purposes of this report, to worry over the distinctions, so I'm going to continue to use similar Earth measurements of time, distance, and size, unless it matters.)

A cigarette lighter was part of the basic survival gear I'd packed from the *Bellerophon*. I found a branch that wasn't too damp, and quickly ignited it. The brilliant yellow and scarlet leaves emitted thick smoke. I walked to the hungry mass and waved the blazing wood among them. A few, too slow or bloated, caught the flame and exploded in brilliant bursts of blue fire. The rest scattered. The cask was already on its side; I kicked it a bit, and it rolled down into the river. Hopefully, that would keep the swarm from reappearing.

Based on that Bing Crosby film I'd seen on TV, I was expecting either shock or astonishment. Instead, I got, "Even your relics are strange."

"Relics?"

She nodded. "The word-finder. The flaming thing you used. Stormfire bows. Flyers." I handed her the branch I'd set on fire; she used it to bring the rest of the pit to life, then rooted in the grazarn's supplies to find food. Thick brown bread, very dry. A sweet paste of mashed fruit. Some jerky, heavily spiced. I contemplated rehydrating the supplies from the *Bellerophon*, but quickly chose otherwise. The local food hadn't killed me yet. She also found some smaller, unbroken, clay jars of the same sticky, obviously alcoholic liquid the worms had been so eager to devour. She handed one to me.

"Now. You asked what you did wrong. When I'm done telling you, you'll tell me your tale?"

I nodded.

"Within the witness of the Guardians, then. It shall be enforced." She said this in a formal, structured way. The last sentence, in particular, had a religious quality to it.

She dipped a bit of the jerky into the fruit sauce, took a few bites, a swig of the brew (called *klur*), and began.

"Three years ago, the Appointed Overseer of Murz Ten, a grazarn named Shial the Grand, with whom we'd previously had tolerable relations, lost his power, and life, to a challenger, Dolish of Unknown Reach. The Overseers of the Klurish League change like a *frar* molts, so this wasn't something we considered important. That was stupid. We'd grown soft. We'd forgotten how hard-fought our 'tolerable' relations with the League, specifically with Murz Ten, had been."

(S'zana's own species, according to the word-finder, were 'humans' -- which was what every species' name, in their own language, translated to. The exact word S'zana used, though, was *delnar*. Her nation was Alsoria, more completely the Covenant Lands of Alsoria.)

"Dolish wasn't content with the large fees we paid to travel the Tendran, or the other tributes we'd offered, such as our willingness to give the grazarn those criminals of the Covenant Lands who deserved it. He ignored our borders, allowed pirates to attack our ships, randomly seized cargos or imposed new fees and taxes at whim. In time, his stupidity would have aroused the guilds and factions of Murz Ten against him, as their own fortunes were being undone by his madness, but we weren't going to wait for them to gain the courage to act against him. The grazarn have a saying, 'Everyone wants to slit the master's throat, but no one wants to hold the knife'."

"My life followed an odd path. My parents and siblings were and still are successful artisans. They make dyed glass, for art or function, and can refine and shape *joziv* stones. We weren't wealthy, but we were comfortable. They were happy. I was bored."

I tossed a little more wood onto the flames. As the fire rose, something lurking in the strange mix of shadows and crystalline auras slithered back. "My father owned a shoe store. I understand."

"I chose the city guard for my service, when the time came to do so, even though my parents could have arranged for something trivial and safe. Soon after, the Listeners chose me."

("Listeners" was more literally translated to "Those Who Listen To Whispers, Those Who Watch Shadows In Darkness".)

"We couldn't send an army against Murz Ten, no matter what Dolish did. Even if we took the city, which would be beyond chance, the rest of the League would respond. There are Listeners in Murz Ten, and from them we learned much about Dolish. He sends his own men on raids to capture slaves and other tribute for him, instead of simply purchasing them from the market, a habit that makes even the slavers dislike him. He believes having his loyal followers do the work somehow makes *him* seem brave and strong. He looks for the odd and the unusual, or those with skills he needs. He had taken a cache of stormfire bows, but had few *joziv* stones for them. Thus..."

I tore a chunk of the dried meat from the slab we passed between us. I decided I liked it better without the fruit paste. I also decided I liked the *klur*. It was like drinking ninety proof maple syrup. "Thus", I continued for her, "since you could pass as a, uh, carver, you'd wander around where his raiders were..."

She nodded. "Dolish doesn't trust other grazarn to do the job. It would be too easy for them to steal and then vanish into the city. He would also be wary of a too-convenient solution to a problem, fearing a rival might be behind it."

The *klur* was having an effect. I was feeling distinctly relaxed. I leaned back against a stack of boxes the unfortunate raiders had piled near the firepit. "And I showed up." I shrugged. "There'll be other raiders, though. It sounds like you've put up with this bastard for a while now, what's a few more days?"

She shook her head. "There are times and cycles for these things. Dolish has prodded us enough, and is convinced we're toothless. He plans more than raids and piracy. He's going to move, in force. If we meet him in the field, we may win, but at a high cost, and other nations on our borders -- the Devout of Frashar, the Zulsair Province -- will see our weakness."

"So, now what?"

"I'll report what happened. We'll make new plans." She didn't seem optimistic about the outcome. "Do you understand, now, what you stumbled into? Is your question answered?"

"Probably as well as it's going to be for now."

She looked back at me with a set determination, and her voice once again took on that ritualistic, intoned, quality. "Good. Within the witness of the Guardians, we have a bargain. My promise has been fulfilled." She upended her own jar of *klur*, shook it a bit, and peered into the emptiness with a sneer, as if some significant amount of the beverage might be cowering at the bottom, refusing to come out. She tossed the jar behind her, and then scraped at the last of the fruit paste with another slab of dried meat. "That means, it's time for you to talk. Where *are* you from?" The question sounded half-rhetorical, along the lines of "Were you raised by wolves?"

I looked skyward. Yes, the very bright star, the one I was sure was the Sun, was still there. "That star... has it always been in the sky?"

"Are you saying you're from beneath the ground? Why are you asking about stars?"

"It's... it's important. Tell me when you started seeing it."

"Forever. It is one of the long stars, one that has always been known. Some months ago, it grew increasingly brighter. For a time it could be seen in the day, swollen and immense. Most considered it a sign, as such things occur every ten or twelve generations. No one agreed on what the sign meant, naturally. For everything large or small that happened while it was bright, there was someone who would claim it was an omen. Good fortune, ill fortune, a war here, a treaty there, and I'm not going to be distracted. Where are you from, and why are you here?"

I told her. It took a while. There was no word for "planet" in their language. There was their world, there was the sun that orbited it, and there were stars. The Guardians, I learned, lived on the stars, or perhaps were the stars -- the mythology wasn't clear, and even with the word-finder, we kept running into ideas that there weren't matching words for. We improvised.

"Three days ago, you say. The sun attacked your ship, the *Winged Steed Rider*, and you fell during the night."

This was our fourth go-round on the details. "Yes," I sighed. I hardly blamed her disbelief, and this was basic interrogation -- keep checking the story, seeing if there's a slip or an inconsistency.

"I think I saw it. It looked like the skin of the sky had been cut, bleeding red flame along the wound."

Earlier, I'd taken out most of the items I'd salvaged from the *Bellerophon*. She'd quizzed me on them, examining them closely. Now she went through them all again, carefully, reconsidering.

"'Fealkane'... a better name for you than *faleekon*, I think. R'yan Fealkane.'"

I heard her words, in her language, and in mine: R'yan Fallingstar. Well, if it was Fallingstar or Vulture, I'd pick the former. I remembered what she'd asked me, a few hours before, and I repeated those words to her: "Is your question answered?"

She nodded slightly. "It is. The bargain, as witnessed, is done."

"Now what?"

"We should sleep in turns, to keep the fire going."

"And tomorrow?"

"I told you. I'm going back. For you? I don't know. The story you told, the craft your people found... it was a relic, something made by the Guardians. If your mission is to find its makers, your mission has failed, for they are long gone, but you have no one to report this failure to. My advice is this: Take the grazarn's boat, go to Murz Ten, find work as a guard or a mercenary. The League is known as a place where those willing to be second to the grazarn can be equals to each other. It welcomes outcasts and wanderers who do as they're told. Hmm. Still, you're more outcast than most, and from all you've said, you would not find enough pride in serving the grazarn to satisfy you."

I had an idea. For the record, I think it was inspired by the *klur*.

"Wait. Dolish, your target. He collects the weird and unusual, right? Well, is there anything around now more unusual than me?"

"No... and I follow your thought, but his raiders have gone, and even if they took you as a freak, you'd be caged. As a crafter, even a slave, I'd have some freedom to roam the palace in the course of my work. I'd have ample chances to kill Dolish. I'd even be allowed to carry the sharp tools and knives I need to do my job."

I smiled, as pieces of my drunken plan fell into place. "Not quite what I was thinking. Despite everything going on, for right now, you're not at war. You still have some trade, you can still go into the city. So, we go in. You're a merchant or whatever. I'm your prize. From what you've told me about Dolish, he wouldn't let anyone else grab me. He has to be the one with the best toys."

She considered this, and then smiled. "Perhaps. No matter what he permits outside the city, once inside, he's more constrained. No one trades if they think their goods will simply be taken from them. He'll want to bargain. I could get us inside the palace. Once there, I could come up with something."

"There. Done. We'll head out tomorrow."

In retrospect, there was an obvious question about her entire plan, both original and revised, that I hadn't thought to ask.

Chapter 5
Murz Ten

Standing watch as constant waves of color created an ever changing pattern of light and darkness was a skill I would need time to master.

The fire kept most of the locals away, and the one creature which ignored it, a five foot long, brilliant green slug that used feathery antennae to perceive the world, fled (slowly) after a few prods with my sword. Despite the tents, we took turns sleeping in the raft's cabin, as the door could be barred. We understood and agreed to this without much trouble. Neither of us had done anything to arouse distrust, but we were both strangers to each other, in a land where, I was learning, there was a constant dance of allies and enemies. I'd already demonstrated I didn't know S'zana's oaths, values, or rules of proper behavior. I didn't know how much of her sense of what was just or proper extended to strangers. In a weird way, a certain amount of mutual paranoia was a form of respect.

S'zana emerged from the cabin. She'd washed the tunic as much as possible, but it was still well stained. Underneath it, she'd added on a breastplate, and the leg and shoulder guards of the armor the grazarn wore. The original group had been three in number, with one meeting some unknown fate, his or her gear scavenged and brought back.

The armor had been designed for a being with a slightly different body structure than her own. It fit oddly, and she kept pulling at it and frowning.

"Is it that useful? It didn't really help the one I axed."

She tugged at the shoulder piece and snarled at it, trying to intimidate it into fitting better. It didn't work. "Yes, you claim in your land, the warriors fight naked, like Valishi show-fighters."

She'd mostly accepted that my "land" (the only words we could use were "star" or "land", as nothing meant anything close to "planet", and we settled on "land" for now) was not on this world, but she seemed to find my descriptions of it exaggerated at best. She knew a number of stories, cast as folk tales, legends, or cautions for the young, about those who fooled around with relic flying ships, and were thrown away from the world, never to be seen again. She felt the same thing happened to me. Mostly, it was my claims that we could manufacture "relics" at will, or had cities housing millions, that she found too insane to believe. Every traveler, she told me with a condescending but not unkind grin, makes up wild stories of the wonders of their home. Mine were a thousand times crazier than most. More than once, during our long night, had she mentioned that I might consider becoming a storyteller of some sort, and promised she could induce someone named D'valya to give me advice in that area.

"No, we aren't naked. We fight with..."

"I know, weapons that tear through leather and iron. If you could make such relics, you'd make stormfire bows instead. Anyway..." she had given up trying to glare the armor into submission and had begun helping me root through the camp, seeking anything worth taking with us,"...without the armor to soften your blow, he would have been dead shortly after. As it was, he was not mortally hurt, not unless he did nothing to close the wound or seek healing."

She opened one more box, and emitted a small cheer, holding aloft another jar of *klur*. "Further, the less we look like targets, the less likely someone is to try to make us targets."

I'd managed to adjust the belt and scabbard to fit my waist, and fastened it on. Both items were glistening with tiny gemstones. "Gaudy", I said.

"Grazarn", she replied. "There's very little they won't try to make sparkle."

It was true. The raft was fitted with things that glinted and reflected on every surface. There were several places where the same sigil, an oval frame containing a clawed hand formed from a mosaic of olive and turquoise stones, the background filled with fragments of glittering quartz, was repeated. The symbol of Dolish, I was told.

Sailing lessons came next. The rigging was simple; a single sail, controlled and angled by a few lines and pulleys. Two people could handle it, one adjusting the sail, one on the rudder. As we were heading downriver, the current did most of the work for us.

Most of the first day passed smoothly. We talked a lot, our conversations somewhat hindered by a need to constantly explain things we each took for granted. We passed occasional villages, as well as other vessels. The rudder could be worked from inside the raft's cabin, and S'zana urged me to stay inside as much as possible. We didn't want the curious deciding to swarm us.

Towards late afternoon, the cabin darkened unexpectedly. I peered out. The sky had blackened. The clouds grew thicker as we watched.

S'zana peered up and down the river bank. "There", she finally announced, pointing to a spot on the shore. "We can drag the raft up there, far enough from the water's edge, and we can try to set up the tents against the rocks."

We pulled the raft up as the storm truly hit. There was no time to set any kind of camp. All we could do was ride it out in the cabin, and hope we'd tied everything as well as needed. I opened the crate with the *klur*, handed one to S'zana, opened one for myself, watched, and waited.

I'd experienced tropical storms before. I'd even flown through them, terrified and exhilarated at the same time. This one may not have been the worst I'd experienced, but it was close. The winds easily drove water through every tiny crack in the cabin's wall. The sound felt like the equal to machine gun fire. And the lightning...

The darkness brought out the colored auras of the jungle, and then the lightning set them on fire. The lights flared with the storm, changing from the soft-edged glows I'd seen before into spiked and jagged waves of energy. The jungle's brilliance seemed to reach for the clouds, each thunderclap causing the flares to shoot higher into the air. One crystal outcropping was near us, barely twenty feet away.

A bolt struck it, and I saw it shoot fire back, a beacon of incandescence, raw and jagged-edged, arcing upwards. The crystals themselves were filled with arcing bolts of violet and indigo, swirling within the gems.

There was something else. There were so many light sources in the sky it seems impossible that I'd notice one in particular, but this one was different. It was an acrid yellow, quite far from the palette of violet/blue/lavender that dominated here. While the crystals' light flowed and pooled, or formed jagged spikes when the storm was at its height, this light moved back and forth, slowly, carefully, a single sharp point that grew slowly in size and intensity.

A searchlight. I couldn't imagine what else it might be. Nothing about it seemed natural.

I pointed it out to S'zana. The pounding weather made it hard to speak, so I gestured at the light and looked at her questioningly. She studied it for about a minute, and shrugged. She also took the knife from her belt.

Even with the rain and mist and flaring crystal energies, we could make something out as the light source got closer. At first, it was simply a shadow in the fog, almost an illusion. It grew in solidity as it came closer, its outline becoming more clearly defined. Ovoid, with the main light source now one of many. Multiple lights formed lines that crossed the surface. The main beam swept along, forward and back.

It moved along the river, giving some sense of scale. I estimated it was perhaps the size of a delivery van. It had no support, wings, or propellers. Oval pods on the surface became clear as it moved closer still. Though smaller than the Aurora vehicle, it was definitely similar in overall design.

S'zana was transfixed, staring at it. I tapped her very gently on the shoulder, to get her attention, and she whirled, blade out, and would have easily sliced my chest open if I hadn't jumped back. She gasped, regained awareness of herself, and alternated pointing out the cabin window and shaking her head in negation or disbelief.

Point-and-wave wasn't going to get any kind of complex idea across. I took in air to shout over the storm, and S'zana shot forward to silence me. She locked her eyes with mine, made sure I understood, and removed her hand from my mouth.

This was something I'd trained for, and had done well enough to keep me alive. Patrol discipline. Behind enemy lines. Absolute stillness, absolute silence, no matter what. If S'zana considered this something worth being wary of, I was going to agree. All I needed to know about ignoring the opinions of the locals when it came to tactical choices, I learned from General Custer.

It passed along the river, at most thirty feet from us. The bright beam played directly into the cabin. I saw amber sparks surrounding S'zana, a flickering field of tiny points of light. The beam touched me, as well, but if I was subject to a similar effect, I didn't see it.

S'zana had held herself perfectly still as the light passed. It was a pretty impressive display of self control. I didn't know what the thing was, but she evidently knew enough about it to put the entirety of her will and focus on not letting fear overtake her. It's a lot easier to remain calm when you don't have a clue how bad it can get.

Time passed. We watched it go, then waited in silence until the raid faded enough that we could speak. By this point, the interior of the cabin was utterly drenched. Trying to start a fire outside seemed pointless. I resigned myself to a damp, miserable, night.

S'zana wanted to talk.

"That wasn't real. That couldn't have been real." She looked at me for confirmation.

"It *seemed* real. We both saw the same thing, right? Silver football? About van sized?" ('Football' wasn't translated; 'van' was translated to 'trader's wagon'. Close enough.) "Uhm, silver oval, pointy at both ends."

She nodded. "Of course. We both saw it. But it can't be real. It's like seeing a dragon."

(There was apparently something in their legends that was close enough to Earth dragons that the word-finder picked up on it. The "mythical" aspect was definitely conveyed.)

"Understood. Whatever that was, it was a thing of myth, legend, children's tales. But, what was it, in the stories? A... Guardian?"

"No. A servant of them. A hunter of those who broke the rules. It would find the criminal, and bring them to the Guardians for punishment. A seeker."

This "seeker" was so rare everyone considered it mythical, and then one shows up a few days after I crash. Coincidence seemed out of the question.

"It's probably looking for me."

"No. You saw it. The light... the seeker's eye... it touched both of us. Yet, it passed us by."

It had, at that. I wasn't going to let go of the idea I was involved with this, somehow, but there was something still missing. I tried to lighten the mood a little.

"Well, it passed you by, too. I guess you haven't broken any rules."

"I have broken thousands of the Guardian's rules. So has everyone. How can you not *know* these things? We are all guilty. But the seekers, in the stories, know everyone has broken the rules. They look for those the Guardians named. We weren't named." She shook her head furiously. "No, I'm being stupid. It doesn't matter what the stories say, the Guardians are gone, more years ago than anyone has counted. We... our ancestors.. were abandoned here, forever. The Guardians won't return."

She relaxed, or rather, half collapsed. The energy that had been driving her since the sighting had finally given out. She plucked at the soaking clothing she wore, as awareness of mundane needs took the place of wonder at dragons.

Searching through the cabin for anything vaguely dry, or at least merely damp, was clearly frustrating her. I found one of the spare jumpsuits I'd kept and tossed it to her. She thanked me, and began removing her tunic and the underlying armor.

I wasn't sure what she expected me to do, if her culture even cared about nudity, if she recognized me as male, or if her species even had the same sexes and associated plumbing that humans did. It didn't seem like a good idea to start asking now. I gave in to proper behavior as I'd been taught, and turned to study how the crystals' glow interacted with the swirling fog and mist, until I heard a few sharp curses and turned back.

Zippers, apparently, were not among the relics she was aware of. S'zana's technique of trying to stare balky objects into obedience was working as well as it usually did.

I stood, walked to her, and showed how it worked. It only took a little time, and she smiled at the simple cleverness of it. "I know some metalworkers who could make a thing like this, once they see one."

I noticed a few other things about her, as well. The ill-fitting armor she had worn all day didn't seem to have raised any calluses, but there was something odd where it had been scraping against her shoulders, a tiny pattern of white cracks, a spiderweb like you'd see in broken glass, and where the cracks were widest, slightly paler skin beneath. She scratched at the point of injury, and some bits flaked off. The flakes were transparent, very thin, and hard. Some kind of chitin? Or just how she produced scar tissue?

S'zana had taken first watch last night, so it made sense I'd take it now. This time, we'd both silently concurred that neither was likely to murder the other in the night.

No matter how often I reminded myself that I knew virtually nothing about her species, and how dangerous it could be to make assumptions, I couldn't turn off the part of my brain that responded to the fact she *looked* like a human woman, and all the different things that implied. So far, maintaining mission focus and thinking of this entire experience as being "behind enemy lines" had worked.

Several hours passed. The seeker never returned.

When sunlight came, we got a chance to inspect the raft. The mast structure had cracked, and was useless. S'zana said we could pole our way through the shallows, but that walking might be easier, especially if anyone asked why a craft sent out with three of Dolish's men on it was returning with a delnar woman and a man from an unknown land.

En route, we'd worked out other details of our story. I was "from beyond the Scour," sold as a young man and made to work as a rower on the merchant galleys that roamed the edges of the World's Wound. I spent most of the past decade without seeing much of the world, hence my ignorance of its customs and language. (S'zana thought it best if I didn't speak and was considered incapable of understanding.) A shipwreck freed me (I wanted to have strangled my master with my own oar chain, but S'zana felt that could make Dolish too nervous. I was to seem relatively docile. (That was going to be a challenge.) I scavenged the items we'd be showing off to establish my strangeness (such as the lighter and my other belongings), but I wasn't doing well on my own in a strange land. S'zana found me, taught me simple commands, and was making a little coin showing me off.

With any luck, Dolish would command an appearance, and then we could work out the rest.

The air was thick, heavy, and pungent. The downpour seemed to trigger a mass blossoming; to the normal autumn flame of the trees was added every other shade I could name. Flowers in mottled black and white like those tests where shrinks listen to what you say, frown, and make "Mm-hmm" noises while scribbling furiously and then tell you "There are no wrong answers." I eventually just said I saw puppies. There were flowers swirled in green and pink, others with colors that seemed to glisten with an internal light, even one tree that bore great, mirrored petals that reflected the sun's light with a painful glare.

The ground was even muddier than usual, and wriggling with masses of worms and bugs. It was not possible to walk without stepping on something that made a squishing noise, and after the first few minutes of trying, I stopped caring. We filled some of the time with rehearsing our story, and with S'zana teaching me certain basics, the things you're supposed to learn as a child -- how to greet people politely, how to talk to a merchant, how to show respect to a superior, how to show disrespect when you want the other guy to know it. My "spent his whole life chained to an oar, poor thing" tale was supposed to excuse my mistakes, and what I got right was to show how well I'd been taught. I kept reciting the tale: At the far side of the World's Wound, the Kingdom of Amareik was ruled, when last I left, by Niksa in the Sly. I was from the City of Five Burrows, a great port for trade, and that was all I knew of my homeland.

S'zana had filled in a lot of how we met, what we'd done, all sorts of things. She considered questions, composed answers. I wondered how many missions she'd performed as a "Listener", and how much was "Listening," and how much was "Silencing."

I should be clear: I was curious, not judgmental. My hands weren't clean. I knew what was happening below me, when I dropped flame on the jungles. I knew that planes I shot down in battle contained men who fought for their nation as I fought for mine. I didn't have the temperament for cloak-and-dagger work, but I respected that it had to be done.

"So you'd hurt your ankle when I found you. Left or right?" S'zana continued the drill.

"Left."

"Right."

"Sorry, right. Not left." I smiled, trying to make it plain I was joking. I was hot, tired, sticky, and bored. Anything to break my mood, even a wretched pun.

"Yes, left. You were right."

I laughed.

S'zana frowned and studied my expression. I probably had a truly silly grin at this point. "Do we need to rest? You're acting strangely. More strangely."

I thought of the words she said and the words I said. "*Zilar*" was "right" as in "right side". "*Consha*" was "right" as in "correct". The pun was meaningless; she wasn't even hearing it. That made me laugh more, which made S'zana frown more.

Then someone screamed.

It was a growling, deep, scream, a mixture of profanity and "Help!" and "No, stop, get away!", and then other sounds -- furious hissing, cracking wood, and large, dull, thumps.

Exploding out of the jungle was something much like the snorpion I'd fought days past. This one was at least twice the size, with skin covered in geometric patterns of red and black triangles. Its claws were wrapped in sparkling mesh cloth. On its back was a wooden howdah, fancifully decorated. Bags, boxes, and barrels were strapped along much of its body. A complex saddle arrangement was tied up just behind the head. The screamer, in the saddle, was a grazarn, dressed in loose wrappings of purple and gold, with tassels, fringes, and mirror-bright bits added to every seam and wrinkle. He kept screaming, and alternated hitting the beast on the head with a long stick, tugging at his own leg (tangled in the saddle), and waving the stick, extremely ineffectually, at the winged worms that had attached themselves, remora-like, to the sides of the great serpent, driving it to torment.

The mount was out of control, and would probably head for the river. The rider, imitating Captain Ahab, was likely to go down with it. All we had to do was stand back for a half minute, and then we could proceed.

As S'zana already learned, I'm not good at standing back. I'm better than I was, but still not very good.

1965. *Air Force Academy. The office of Lt. Col. Kendry.*

"Cadet Falconi, the APs say they're thinking of handing you blank reports when you go off base on a pass, so you can fill them in in advance and save them the trouble."

"They're quite clever, Sir. They should be commended for their effort to reduce paperwork and inefficiency."

"Do you want to be here, Cadet? At the Academy, I mean. Not this office."

"Yes, sir. More than anything else I've wanted in my life, sir."

"Then tell me why you decided to turn Cadet Brockwick into something resembling raw meat loaf."

"Sir, the report..."

"I want to hear you tell me."

I sighed.

"We were at the movie palace. We'd come out. There was an old man with a stand on the sidewalk, shining shoes. Cadet Brockwick wanted to look good for inspection. When the man was done, Cadet Brockwick refused to pay. He said it wasn't a good job."

"Go on, Cadet."

"I thought the man did a fine job. I told Cadet Brockwick to pay him. Cadet Brockwick informed me I was Italian, homosexual, and unduly sympathetic to Negroes, though those were not his exact words. For the record, I dispute the middle accusation. I repeated my demand he pay. Cadet Brockwick then challenged me to 'make him'. I did." I considered a moment, then went on. "In the interests of accuracy, I was the one who actually handed the payment to the man, though the money came from Cadet Brockwick's wallet. At the time, Cadet Brockwick was not capable of performing the necessary action."

"What was the total amount owed?"

"Twenty five cents, sir. I paid out fifty cents. I think Cadet Brockwick would acknowledge a tip was in order, given all the trouble."

"I am informed by the medics that Cadet Brockwick will be unfit to return to duty for two weeks."

"I am sure the medics have made an accurate estimate, sir. They're very good, sir."

"Do you think, Cadet, that the Air Force should lose a man's services for two weeks, because he wouldn't pay a Negro a quarter?"

"No, sir. I think that when Brockwick is medically fit, he should be discharged from this academy, sir."

"And why is that, Cadet?"

I pointed to a plaque on the wall. It contained the honor code that defined, allegedly, life at the Academy. It read 'We will not lie, steal, or cheat, nor tolerate among us anyone who does.'. He looked at it, then looked back to me. I continued.

"Brockwick lied by claiming the work was poorly done. He stole by refusing to pay the man. Sir."

"A quarter. Cadet, you beat a fellow trainee to a bleeding mess over a quarter."

"Sir, permission to speak freely."

"I don't see how you can dig a deeper hole for yourself, Cadet. Go ahead."

"When I... when some of us graduate from here, we'll be going to Vietnam, to risk, and sometimes give, our lives to stop Communism. Telling a man he should do his job, but not get paid for doing it... that sounds like Communism to me."

Lt. Col. Kendricks stared at me for a second in shock, then laughed. "So your best defense is that Cadet Brockwick is a closet Red?"

"No, Sir. My best defense, if I am still speaking freely, is that Cadet Brockwick is a grade-A asshole who is unfit to clean a latrine, much less become an officer. But if you think an inspection of his background and connections is justified, I would go on record with my suspicions."

"Confined to quarters, Cadet. I'll be deciding what to do with you soon."

I drew my sword and raced towards the writhing serpent-mount.

The things attached to it were much like the pests that were feasting on the spilled *klur* two nights ago, but many times larger. Four feet long, at least, they had leech-like bodies and three fan-like wings. Unlike a lot of the local creatures, they were fairly pale, mostly pink and white, with a few black spots. They didn't seem to have any claws or stingers.

I needed to get them off without injuring the snake-thing more than it already was. My hope was that if we could get the parasites off, its rider could calm it down. Doing this without being buffeted by the writhing thing, which must have weighed at least as much as an elephant, was tricky.

I skewered the first one near the neck, where it was attached. It made a nearly indescribable sound. Blue blood, very thin, thinner ever than water, spurted, followed by a gout of the thick, black, blood that I knew was from the snake. The winged leech detached itself, leaving a circle of tiny punctures on the red and black scales. I jabbed my sword into the ground, put my foot on its body, and pulled the blade free, then went on to the next.

This one tore itself loose before I could attack. It may have scented the blood of the first on me. It flew at me, maw open. I swung, hoping to kill it, but it twisted as it flew, and the edge missed. The force of the blow diverted it, but it reoriented quickly and came at me. This time, I was better prepared. As it swooped for the attack, eager to engulf my entire head, I ducked low. It passed over me, and a quick upward thrust impaled it. I spun the blade in a great arc, and the corpse flew off into the bushes. Two down.

I looked towards the front of the snake. S'zana had scrambled up onto the saddle structure, where she was sawing at the tangled leather straps with her knife. She kept glancing back at me and repeating "Stupid, stupid, stupid...", though I heard a variety of different words beneath the translation. Mr. Schenkle, the barber, once told me that his language had a hundred different ways to call someone an idiot. S'zana's language seemed similar.

After killing two more on this side, I had to move to the other. The rider had started to get his beast under control, but was still struggling, shouting out commands, hitting it, and tugging on reins, changing tactics moment to moment. I considered the best route to the other side, when the creature lashed the rear third of its body upwards. I kicked off against the ground, curled into a ball, and tumbled back to my feet just as the tail came slamming down again.

That was closer than I'd expected. It was still fun.

S'zana was on this side, as well. She had a less dramatic technique than mine. She simply grabbed one of the winged leech's tails, pulled it straight, then jabbed the blade into a darker spot near the front. As soon as she did, the thing dropped off. No gouts of blood, no ducking and weaving. She saw I was watching her. "Brain!" she shouted. "I can tell you'd have trouble finding it!"

I was planning an appropriate reply... then I saw the tail. The creature's stinger was sheathed in a leather scabbard.. which, in the course of the violent thrashing and writhing, had come undone. The enclosure flew off, and the tail twisted, seeking a target. It lashed down. I shot forward, under it, tackling S'zana and knocking her back into one of the many muddy pools that lined the river bank. The stinger impaled the winged leech she'd been about to debrain, and would have easily gone right through her.

She inhaled to speak, then looked past my shoulder and assessed the situation. "Thank you.", she said.

I stood up, and looked back. The tail had stung two more of the leeches, and the rest were detaching themselves. I suspect they had some kind of communication. The rider calmed the mount further. It eventually settled down, hissing softly, while the rider sang an odd, slow song and stroked the massive, scaly head.

"You're welcome. I wasn't sure if it was a good idea, though. I didn't want to interrupt a well-designed plan again. Glad I guessed right."

I can list excuses for hours -- hot, tired, hurt, frustrated, most importantly, resentful of being constantly reminded how out of place I was on this world and how much I still needed to learn to even reach the level of a small child on his first day of school. It was still a stupid thing to say, and I said it with somewhat more bitterness than I'd intended. Even then, I knew how much worse my situation would be without S'zana's help. I would probably have become the freak, or slave, I was pretending to be, and that would be the best of the likely outcomes.

S'zana wouldn't understand the metaphor, but she returned the volley with force. "Yes, thank you... for saving me from a situation *you* created for absolutely no reason. I put myself in range of the *ashagvar* to help *you*, and *only* because, having come *this* far, I need you for my mission. I had to choose quickly: To help you, or to make my way back to Krequel and report failure. Don't ask what I would have chosen if I'd had any time to think."

Even I know when to stop digging. It's usually when I hit magma, but still, I stop.

The merchant was an older grazarn, He looked at me curiously, then back to S'zana. He spoke to her. "Gratitude. Old girl and I, we ran over a nest. Terrible. Would have died, likely. Tragic."

S'zana smiled. "Yes, it could have been. Given that, we could use some help ourselves."

He made a series of chitters. "Poverty! It weighs upon me, but I can do something. Certainly."

Even a casual glance at the *ashagvar's* trappings, and the trader's robes, made the claim of poverty somewhat suspect. S'zana clearly knew this, and thus followed considerable bargaining. I wasn't sure I liked that... in fact, I was sure I didn't. I didn't rush in to earn a reward.

Being quiet was part of our agreed upon plan. I waited until they were done. S'zana took me aside.

"Shimgol can be a lot of help to us. He has fingers in half the drinking halls in Murz Ten, and his tail's wrapped around the other half. He was overjoyed when I said I didn't want a reward in gems or goods, just his help spreading word about our 'show'. He'll actually make some profit from this."

"Can we trust him?"

"To add to his own little mound of sparkling treasures? Of course. Besides, we did save his life."

"Alright. I got the impression... from you... that the grazarn were shiftless, greedy, and generally treasonous."

She nodded. "Well, yes, they are. No more than anyone else, though. *Delnar ta vril.*"

Literally, the phrase was translated as "Everyone is a person.", but the meaning was "People are people."

We helped Shimgol gather up some items that had come loose. Now that the leeches were gone, "Old Girl" was quite placid, and her hissing noises became a soothing purr. We did re-attach the tail sheath, of course.

It took most of a day to reach the city's gates. A few miles out, simple roads appeared, growing progressively broader and better-maintained as we neared the city. The final mile featured a convergence of paved roads, lined with ornate sparkling statues of prominent grazarn, as well as disciplined patrol groups marching up and down. There was no avoiding the attention I was getting, but Shimgol tended to smile or wave at the curious, and they didn't seek more than a quick glance.

Murz Ten had a broad gate across the river and smaller gates to either side. This close to the city, the river was congested with watercraft, from rafts to sailboats to galleys. There was a constant din of conversation and shouting, and I saw people passing on foot, on four-legged feathered things, on saddled lobster-crocodiles, on slow, hairy, beasts something like a giant yak and a tortoise, and some truly odd creatures I can't easily describe. Vendors, grazarn and otherwise, darted in and out of the crowd, offering trinkets, jewels, decorations, and highly questionable smoked meats, which S'zana refused to allow within five feet of her.

The area nearest the walls was a sprawling shantytown. Some of the buildings climbed up the walls, precariously piled upon each other, joined by ladders and ropes. A thousand chimneys and firepits streamed smoke into the air. Parts of the river traffic merged directly into the outer city, with boats permanently tied to each other and to the shore buildings. The main roads leading to the right and left gates were kept mostly clear by constant patrols of guards. I saw more than a few people, of a half dozen species, being kicked, prodded, or shoved off the road by these patrols, only to dash back in as soon as there was a break. S'zana kept close to me, intending to at least try to restrain me if I decided to run off on any more rescue missions.

I'd managed to learn a few things in my life, though, including making sure if I felt compelled to give someone what they deserved, to do it when there weren't a lot of people around.

Murz Ten's walls were incredible. At least a hundred feet high, and not made of any kind of stone or wood. They were of a dull-grey, dark metal, that I'd taken for granite at a distance. Seamless, bleak, and impressive, they would give any invader reason to reconsider their course of action, assuming the river gates were as solid when closed. Every few hundred feet, the walls bloomed into rounded towers, a bit like Russian Orthodox churches, and from some of those towers emerged skyward-pointing structures that screamed "Anti-aircraft emplacements"... if anti-aircraft emplacements sheathed themselves in red and blue lightning discharges every few minutes.

Shimgol was busily negotiating with a toll collector. I whispered to S'zana. "Did the grazarn build those walls?"

She replied with a too-familiar look of "What kind of a stupid question is that?", but failed to answer it. I guessed "no".

Inside the city, things were only slightly less chaotic. The main streets were well maintained... actually, they were of the same metal as the walls, laid out in strict, regular, lines. Lesser streets of fitted stone, or boards, or sometimes just trampled detritus, branched off. Stepped buildings, built from the grey metal, were placed regularly at intersections, but the bulk of the city was constructed of more primitive materials, sometimes partially engulfing the ziggurat structures. The dominant style of non-metal buildings were rectangular, with steeply slanted roofs.

Everything that could be made to sparkle, glitter, or shine, did. The cheapest pushcarts guided by the most emaciated vendors had chips of bright glass embedded in their rickety frames. Of the many things I knew I would regret not having when I left the wreckage of the *Bellerophon*, I had never considered sunglasses.

Trying to navigate the crowded, twisting, streets without Shimgol's presence -- the mob gave "Old Girl" a lot of clearance -- would have been far more difficult. I tried to point this out to S'zana, when I had a chance to speak, and she was unimpressed, finally noting that I'd hardly known my actions would have any such useful consequences. True, and all the more annoying because of it.

"Arrived!" Shimgol shouted. "My dwelling, humble though it is. Finally. I will give instructions, tell them to set up rooms for you."

Before he could move further, S'zana intoned, "Without witness by the Guardians, you have done as promised. I will let this be known."

"Truth. You took less than might have been yours. Told!" came Shimgol's response. He scurried inside.

Shimgol's "humble" dwelling was a three story ziggurat of well-carved stone, covered almost entirely with jade, quartz, and other brightly colored stones, set into complex mosaics. I spotted several well-armed guards walking inside or wandering the perimeter. A small wall, this one of stone and only ten feet in height, separated the house from the rest of the city. Old Girl was led away by a plainly-dressed delnar man, who cooed at her, and tossed small, wriggling, furry things into her mouth from a wooden bucket he carried. Given the size of her gaping jaws, I wondered what her primary food source was.

A grazarn in robes similar to Shimgol's, but simpler in design and with fewer glittering bits, came to lead us inside. I'd seen enough delnar now to see they had at least superficially obvious male and female genders, admittedly without being sure exactly who had which bits and how they might fit together. The grazarn, however... I'd seen hundreds in the last few hours, and I realized I had no idea if they had genders, or how to tell them apart, or if it could possibly matter. S'zana had used 'he' when talking about Dolish and Shimgol, but that might not be especially meaningful.

Given S'zana's general mood at the moment, I figured I'd save my stupid question allotment for something more important than "which ones are the girls?".

There was a quick exchange in hisses, snaps, and growls. The word-finder hadn't taught me grazarnish -- I wondered if it could be reset? How many languages could I get crammed into my mind? What could Air Force

Intelligence do with something like this? Not that I saw any way to even make a report, much less return, at this point.

S'zana had finished her conversation. "We've been given a room. I promised Colzhari you wouldn't make any messes."

"I'll be sure to keep that in mind."

After a quick exchange of level glares we followed the grazarn, Colzhari, down a spiraling flight of stairs. We were led to a large, circular, room richly decorated with glittering cloth hangings, an assortment of chairs and tables, and a broad steaming pool of slightly murky water set into a stone pit in the floor. The outer rim of the pit was lined with painted tiles, depicting grazarn in various states of activity. Oil lamps were hung around the room, casting light and creating a half dozen shadows. Colzhari and S'zana chittered at each other for a bit.

S'zana turned to me. "You still have clean clothing? From your ship?"

I nodded. "One left."

"Good." There was more chittering. "The generous Shimgol has offered to have his most talented and valued servants show their worth, and thus his, by cleaning what we wore. In the meanwhile, he can provide for me. You are more interesting, and thus more valuable, in your native garb."

"I could do the Twist. It is one of the dances of my people."

S'zana may have caught the sarcasm in my voice, but she ignored it. "That would be good, yes." She started undoing her tunic and removing her armor, while Colzhari waited patiently. About halfway through the process, she gestured impatiently at me. "You want that cleaned, right? We're not going to get a lot more opportunities to relax."

When in Rome...

Before I was finished, S'zana had handed her clothing to Colzhari (leaving the weapons and armor on the floor), and had submerged herself in the hot bath, with her gear in easy reach. I gave Colzhari my jumpsuit, and imitated S'zana with the placement of my gear. Colzhari left.

S'zana, I couldn't help but notice, was studying me. I got into the pool quickly.

"You're more hurt than I realized."

I tried to find a way to interpret that so it didn't sound particularly insulting. Before I could, she continued. "The long scars on your legs and arms. I hadn't noticed them before."

"The *Bellerophon* crash. Something about how it landed... anyway, the local plants fused into my skin a little. Then there were the wasp-things, more than a few cuts from your attacker. What I *thought* was your attacker..."

She made a very noncommittal grunt, then felt around on the bottom for something, found it, and pulled. Her hand emerged holding a bright orange sponge, speckled with a few blue-green dots. She squeezed it, and a liquid the same color as the sponge oozed out. Smiling, she began to scrub at her skin.

I tried the same. The floor of the bath, I discovered, was made from loose slabs of uneven slate, and there were several sponges growing in easy reach, as well as small eel-like creatures that darted about, apparently harmless. The ooze from the sponge tingled a bit when I touched it. Imitating S'zana, I rubbed it over a part of my leg that was particularly torn up, and I could feel each cut and scrape ignite. I refused to make any obvious noise, but my expression must have given it away.

"It's good. The *jors* blood cleanses the wounds. A pity it does not stay fresh long after being plucked."

Colzhari returned, without our clothes, but with two silver trays, which he or she placed next to each of us. The trays were identical, each containing a stoppered smoky-grey glass bottle, a small bronze cup, and an assortment of small bits of food, which could be partially identified as plants, meat, and something a bit like gelatin, but with a tough, rubbery, texture. The liquid was thin, very faintly red, and had a sour taste that became bearable after a few sips.

S'zana seemed almost relaxed. Her skin, scrubbed and cleaned, glistened. She scratched at her shoulder, where I'd seen the slight cracks before, and peeled off a large fragment, dropping it in the pool. The skin below was a slightly deeper color.

"It dissolves. The *jors* feed off it."

Her tone sounded oddly apologetic. I didn't have anything to say.

She laughed softly. "We... delnar... molt constantly. It's rude to just drop pieces of skin, especially in someone else's house. I felt I had to explain how I *wasn't* being rude tossing it in the water, then I realized you wouldn't know what was or wasn't rude at all."

"Everyplace has different rules. One place I was stationed, it was considered very rude to not take your shoes off in someone's house. Where I grew up, it would be rude, or at least weird, to do so."

After some time, a different grazarn, not Colzhari - different fur, a bit shorter - brought an outfit for S'zana. S'zana stood up, wiping the bulk of the water off her body. Chitin or not, she was definitely mammalian, by the very definition of the word. Her musculature, her proportions, were incredibly close to human... perhaps the tiniest bit elongated, very slightly stretched. Taut. Even relaxed, there was a sense of a coiled spring about her, energy stored to be suddenly released.

To be clear, my thoughts at the time weren't nearly so analytical. I waited until she had finished dressing to get out of water. S'zana, now wearing a tunic of shimmering green and yellow cloth over the armor, with bangled silver bracelets and blue walking boots, approached me and ran a finger along my chest and arm. "See?" she said. "The discoloration is gone."

She was right. It looked like days of healing had taken place. Useful stuff, *jors*. I dressed. S'zana kept frowning at her bracelets. "Noisy. I don't like them. But..." she sighed, "Shimgol looks like he's going to be a real aid to our plan, and if I complain, it looks bad. At least you get to keep your 'native outfit'."

"So, what is the plan?"

"Shimgol is having a feast at one of his taverns, announcing his triumphant return, showing off his wealth. We're somewhere between honored guests and the wealth he's showing off. I'm going to have to push him to agree to a Witnessed swearing, before we end up more permanent members of his household staff."

"What, he can just decide we're slaves? Good luck with that!" Instinctively, my hand went to the sword hilt.

S'zana gave me a warning glance. "Careful with your tone. He offered us hospitality, but he was a bit vague on specifics. He could claim some portion -- the food, or the pool, or the clothes -- were beyond a gift, and that we owe for them. Of course, we could dispute it, and force a confrontation, but I want as few questions about why we're here as possible."

"Understood." As least she was acting as if my ignorance was just that -- ignorance -- and not the result of being dropped on my head as an infant.

Across several nations on Earth, and many places off it, I've learned that every bar sounds, and smells, an awful lot alike. The details vary, but there's a commonality to raucousness that transcends world and species.

We were transported there in an enclosed rickshaw-like vehicle, so that my appearance would be partially hidden (never mind I'd already crossed half the city on the way to Shimgol's home). He'd sent a messenger ahead, so there were people ready to gawk as soon as we arrived. I *wasn't* happy. S'zana knew this, and kept giving me little "don't do what I know you're thinking of doing" looks.

I kept myself focused. I reminded myself I was on the job, that my mission strategy required me to play this part.

The tavern was built on three levels, following the stacked pattern of the city, and of course everything that could glitter, did. It was the most brightly lit bar I'd been to. Grazarn were not much for huddling in shadowy corners while they drank. The flood of light, color, and contrast provided nearly as much privacy, in its own way.

A large round table on the second floor was the domain of Shimgol and his chosen cohorts. All but one was grazarn; the last was delnar, a lighter purple S'zana, with blue-tinted hair, well past shoulder length, and pinned with several bronze clasps. He was dressed exactly like the grazarn, and they seemed, from what I could tell, to treat him as an equal. S'zana occasionally sneered when she was sure he wasn't looking. I never asked if it was a personal dislike of the man himself, or if he represented some faction or cultural choice she disapproved of. She seemed friendly enough with actual grazarn.

The tavern band was loud and a bit discordant. I had no idea, of course, if they were good or bad by grazarn standards. I'll assume good, since Shimgol wasn't going to cut corners when showing off. They were a strange mix, too. One was either wearing highly flexible full-body armor, or was actually a being with metallic skin. Three were delnar, or a similar humanoid species, two men and a woman, the woman being impressively well muscled. The fifth was a well-trained shaggy beast, vaguely doglike, that expertly plied the partygoers to deposit coins, small gems, and other trinkets in the gathering bowls set up in front of the band.

Partway through dinner, just before things began to go wrong, they stopped to talk with Shimgol. "Unexpected Meetings" was what they called themselves. I suspect something was lost in translation.

The meal was lavish. I got something of a free pass on rules of etiquette. I'd had the rules for formal Earth dining drilled into me as part of OCS, but they hardly applied here. I decided to follow them anyway, to give them a little show of my primitive native customs. They were amused.

They didn't toast as we do, but they had something similar. They pronounced something, and then swapped their goblets at random. Sometimes a swap was accepted, sometimes rejected, but neither seemed to be rude, and there wasn't any pattern I could see to how it was decided.

I can't describe the variety of things that were brought out and passed around. Flatbreads of various colors and textures were the base of many items. Meats were well-done, almost charred; fruits and vegetables were raw or pickled. One delicacy bears some mention. A platter of eggs, or so I thought, each about six inches long. When I was given one, I notice the "shell" was thin and elastic, and whatever was inside it was moving.

Through hushed whispers, S'zana explained that these were a kind of larvae, and that normally they were pickled, and even then, they were extremely expensive. Fresh was almost unheard of. It was an extraordinary honor to be offered such (and she'd made sure it was a gift, implying no obligation), but she could make excuses for me, if needed.

To hell with that. I'd eaten puffer fish when stationed in Japan, even after an hour of increasingly graphic descriptions of what happened if it was prepared properly. How bad could wriggling larvae be?

I kept it all down. If, by the time this has been received, there is a medal for "Most Horrible Thing Consumed In The Service Of Their Country," I demand to be nominated.

Shimgol and S'zana were deep in negotiations for their schedule, and exactly who would swear to what, as witnessed by the Guardians, when there was a ruckus downstairs that broke through the existing ruckus. I was seated near to a railing and was able to peer over.

A group of a half dozen grazarn, heavily armored, and armed with either short spears or swords, had entered. They didn't act like they were stopping in for a quick drink. The "Cheese it! The fuzz!" mood was evident in the room below, and it quickly spread to our floor. A few of Shimgol's closest friends instantly became strangers who accidentally wandered up here, lost, and had to be on their way. Others chittered back and forth. S'zana had gone into full-coil mode, but was holding back on action.

I shifted a little in my chair. If anything started, I was positioned to stand and draw with few obstructions.

The squad tromped up to us. Shimgol was smiling, or at least, I think that expression, on a grazarn, was a smile.

A lot of spitting, hissing, and chittering followed. S'zana remained ready to fight or flee, but I caught her nodding to herself, very slightly, as the

Fortress At The Top Of The World

conversation went on. She looked at me, saw me ready to draw, and gave me a quick "stay down" gesture. I didn't relax, but I moved my hand a bit away from the blade.

Shimgol came towards us, glancing backwards at the intruders. "Opportunity! We are requested to the Court of Dolish of the Unknown Reach, there to display the strange savage from across the World's Wound."

S'zana feigned some concern. "Are you sure? We have sworn some things within Witness, you and I, and you have done much without Witness, without giving us time to do likewise. Depending on what Dolish demands..."

Shimgol looked at the evidently impatient soldiers. "Witness! Under the Guardians, I forgive all obligation, witnessed or otherwise, by you. Reciprocation. None is asked from you; my promises remain witnessed."

That was one of the few times I'd seen S'zana truly caught off-guard. The seeker was a thing of legend to her, but she knew how to respond when a powerful enemy passes by. This wasn't a situation she had a ready reaction to, but she recovered quickly. If I hadn't spent days with her, learning her small quirks, I wouldn't have noticed the flash of confusion at all. "So it is Witnessed by the Guardians. Freely, under Witness, I give reciprocation without obligation. And your generosity shall be spoken of."

Shimgol tugged at my sleeve. "Hurry! They have little patience." He looked at S'zana. "Assistance? Can you hurry him?"

"Of course."

We left, with the guards forming a cordon -- three ahead, three behind. They did a good job of disarming us, too. Shimgol chittered nervously to himself, while S'zana made calming noises back. From this angle, I could see the guards also carried small crossbows, cocked and loaded, ready to be drawn quickly. There was something odd about the trigger for the crossbow, though. I wished I could get a better look at it.

Our escort's bearing and equipment indicated a professionalism that the raiders I'd fought -- had it only been three days before? -- lacked. Still, anyone could be trained to march. I wondered how well they fought.

Dolish's palace was located in one of the massive metal structures that were clearly built by some people or culture quite different from the current inhabitants. The ziggurat had four steps, with each step having two levels within it, judging from the windows. The third level was odd. Instead of the foreboding grey metal dotted with occasional amber windows, the north face of the third level was a huge, ornate work of stained glass, glittering from thousands of tiny facets.

An assortment of guards watched the front gate of the palace. Others patrolled the surrounding region. There was a clear zone around the building, with a few carefully tended flower beds and some walking paths, but with the beggars, merchants, and others kept well away. The main path was flanked with a series of squared archways, every twenty feet or so, linked by thick chains. Each chain held three large dangling oil lamps.

The lamps kept the path brightly lit, but much of the lawn and garden was dimmer. I heard noises from the cleared and tended swathe of landscape, moans, choking sounds, gasping wheezes. Despite the prods of the guards, I slowed, tried to look.

At first, in the shadows, I thought they were some sort of farm animal: About the size of a sheep, legless like a slug or snail, attached to a post by a short chain. Then, shifting light and darkness combined to give me a clearer view of the nearest one. It was a grazarn. What was left of one. His arms and legs had been sliced off, the wounds cauterized or sealed somehow. Hideous scarring surrounded the holes where his eyes and ears had been. I could easily guess why he couldn't speak. He moved by flopping forward, within the limits allowed by the short chain. A trough was set at the extreme limits of the chain. I saw him pull himself forward, choking himself to grab a bit of whatever muck the trough was filled with, then flop back a foot or so to swallow, and then repeat.

I must have seen at least a dozen such displays, just in the relatively narrow field of view I had while being marched along. How many might there be scattered among the grounds?

Until now, I had concerns about S'zana's mission and my part in it. Everyone paints the other side as the bad guy, and despite getting a sense of her character, I worried about just throwing my support to her, simply because the delnar looked more human than the grazarn. Even with just a few hours in Murz Ten, I'd seen enough to convince me that the grazarn were *people*. Soldiers and shopkeepers, beggars and merchants, this city of glitter and muck was enough like any city on Earth to make it impossible for me to consider the grazarn as innately inhuman or evil. S'zana herself had said as much: *Delnar ta vril*. Dolish may have been S'zana's personal enemy and the enemy of her nation, and I surely wasn't going to tell any soldier not to do their duty, but her enemy wasn't necessarily my enemy.

Until now. Shimgol looked as horrified as I was. Even a few of our escorts seemed very uncomfortable seeing this. This wasn't what passed for any kind of normal, not even here. Dolish was the local version of Caligula or Vlad Tepes.

The main door was made of the grey metal. Three guards on either side each took hold of iron chains hooked to the doors, and pulled. There was a grinding noise as the entrance parted. We went in. As we passed through the doors, I looked down. There was a two inch gap, and I could see hints of old machinery through it, frozen gears and corroded cables.

Inside was a large open space, perhaps a fifth the size of the building. A dozen passages led off from it. Our footfalls echoed dully through the room. Curving flat-topped structures, waist high, a few feet wide and five to fifteen feet long, were placed throughout the area. They joined the floor seamlessly. Most were decorated with sheets of shimmering stones or metal, sewn to layers of cloth. Many had busts or full size statues, in glass or jade or quartz, placed atop them.

We entered one of the outgoing passages, and threaded what could have been a complex maze. From somewhere below us, I could hear screams. There was a chill of horror as I realized that soon even screaming would be taken from them. Occasionally, we passed an open door, and I could see small rooms: Sometimes furnished, sometimes not. This looked less like a palace and more like an office complex, or an administrative HQ, to me. The elevator bank we eventually reached confirmed that idea.

Well, once it had been an elevator bank, or something close. I saw no signs of cables or machinery, but there were four tubes, spaced a bit apart, that reached up and down. A system of ropes, pulleys, and small enclosed platforms provided transit.

Shimgol had been looking increasingly nervous. He looked at S'zana. "Assurance? It does not make messes?"

S'zana spoke softly. "Assurance."

"Relief. Dolish is one of many moods." He considered the listening guards and added hastily, "Beneficent. All of his moods are that."

Yeah. I'd seen how beneficent he was.

The second and third levels were mostly merged into one. A portion of the second level ceiling stretched inwards, providing a third level floor, but the inner two-thirds were open space, so there was a cathedral-like aspect. There was no ceiling at all along the north face, which gave us an unobstructed view of the translucent glass mosaic that filled the upper half of that wall. Ten thousand points of color danced over the great hall.

Trying to take it all in while being hustled along by the guards was impossible. I got quick impressions. A dozen suits of ornate, glitter-studded, grazarn armor. Stuffed and mounted creatures of all kinds. Thick tapestries. A globe, a foot in diameter, hung suspended from nothing, slowly rotating -- it seemed to be a model of this world. A tiny crimson gem, near where the Arctic circle would be on Earth, flickered with an internal flame; a scattering of other gems shown only with sparkling reflections. Something best described as a glass rosebush produced eerie music as we walked by it, responding to our motion. Oval display cases held a variety of things, only some of which I could even half-recognize. Two of the things, though... I desperately wanted to look more closely to confirm what I saw, but the guards were insistent that we keep moving forward.

Then, there was the big one. The one I couldn't miss. Held aloft on lacquered wood poles, linked to the floor with a simple ladder, was a ship. It had the look of a Greek or Roman galley, forty feet or so in length. Along the edges, starting at the middle and trailing back, were chrome and crystal tubes, banded with occasional bits of darker metal. I could see, just barely, how the tubes crept over the top of the ship. I guess they ran straight to the prow. The tubes were fastened to the wood with copper braces, showing some faint hints of verdigris.

I recognized, sort of, the design and concept. Someone had taken the parts of a ship like the Aurora vessel, and attached them to a much more primitive craft.

For the first time since I left Earth, I had the feeling it might be possible -- however implausible -- to see it again. Obviously, this ship wasn't going to enter space. But if there were engine parts, who knew what other "relics" might be here?

I'd stared too long. Someone slammed at the back of my head, and there was a moment of darkness.

Chapter 6
Dolish

Only a moment, though. I caught myself as the floor came up, landing on my hands. I turned and stood, to get an idea of who was attacking me, while grasping for the sword I didn't have. That might not be a problem, I thought, if I was right about those display cases.

The attacker, unsurprisingly, was one of the guards. He's used the blunt end of his short spear to knock me down, and had flipped it around, hoping to goad him into using it. If I was some prize for Dolish, he'd be an idiot if he killed me, but he probably wasn't recruited based on his brains.

I stood up slowly, hands out, trying to look as non-threatening as possible. Since I was unarmed and unarmored, and he had many allies around him, this was easy to do.

S'zana and Shimgol watched me. Both looked worried, for different reasons.

That incident over, we continued to the far end of the room. Dolish didn't have a throne so much as an area scooped out of a mound of coins, jewelry, and other small, high value items, with the scooped area lined with multiple layers of padded cloth and thick pillows. He reclined in the center of it.

I'd imagined him as a bloated and dissolute creature, but I was wrong. He was young, lean, and keen-eyed. As we approached, he shifted from his relaxed posture to one of sharp alertness. He was wearing the usual sparkling cloth that denoted status here, in many complex folds and layers, but I saw glints of armor underneath it. Well placed among the treasures that served as his throne were several knives, a scimitar, and one of the small crossbows the guards carried. A steep incline split his throne-pile from the rest of the room, and there was no obvious way to sneak behind him.

S'zana's original plan gave her some freedom to move within the palace and to strike at her leisure. I wasn't sure how she'd handle this.

In addition to Dolish himself, the room had a good number of guards, including two huge ones in heavy armor that looked like slabs of jade and turquoise. There were servants carrying trays or flasks, a scribe standing behind a writing desk, and a few well-dressed grazarn that I guessed were officials of some kind. At the far side of the room was a partially enclosed area holding a dozen or so others, a mix of grazarn, delnar, and one of a species I hadn't seen before. It had an orange-furred humanoid upper body, balanced on four equally hirsute tentacles. Only the fact it was reading something from a scroll and interacting with a grazarn next to it made me certain it wasn't someone's pet.

Dolish studied the three of us. He issued orders. His guards obeyed, holding up my left hand, pulling back my sleeve to show my arm, then cutting off a hunk of my hair, and the cloth of my jumpsuit, and bringing it to him for inspection. Meanwhile, I kept my right hand clenched so hard I could feel a trickle of blood from where my nails dug into my palm. I locked two ideas into my mind: That I had made a promise to S'zana, and that there was a possibility for me to complete my mission and return home, and I had to keep myself alive to do that.

He said something to one of the official-looking types, who approached the three of us. "Elaborate. Tell Dolish of the Unseen Reach of your tale. Discovery. How did you find this oddity?"

S'zana relayed our well-rehearsed story. There were plenty of questions, prodding, and interruptions, but she did a great job, adding in details we hadn't considered and keeping them straight.

The translator, or inquisitor -- I'd picked up his name as Ormig, but not any title -- had one more consultation with Dolish, then returned to us. "Confirmation. You, of Krequel... you control it? Obedience? It heeds you?"

"Yes, mostly. It's ignorant of civilization, but it's learning. It isn't a beast, just a very odd creature from far away. I'm the only one here it knows or trusts."

"Preference. None would be able to claim knowledge of this but Dolish, but... Necessity. You are going to be needed." Ormig snapped out an order. Two of the guards lunged, one from in front of Shimgol, one behind. Spears impaled him from both directions. He barely had time to gasp before he slumped in place. The attackers pulled back their weapons, and he collapsed.

Shimgol had loyally obeyed every command he'd been given, and Dolish killed him anyway, because he didn't want anyone else to have a claim on me.

S'zana saw the look in my eyes. "Please..." she whispered. I got the message. "Please don't just charge in like an idiot, and get killed, and thus get *me* killed, with Dolish untouched."

I'd love to paint myself as the perfectly stoic hero. It's not as if anyone is going to verify this report. However, that isn't how it happened. I'd been holding myself under control, barely. Those poor things outside had shoved me teetering on the edge of madness, flailing my arms to keep my mental balance. Shimgol's murder crumbled the ground of sanity beneath me. I was just setting into motion, seeing, in my mind's eye, a path: Grab the guard's crossbow, hope I was right about how the odd trigger worked, spin and kick the guard out of the way, draw a bead on Dolish, fire, and to hell with anything that might come next.

It only *didn't* happen that way because of the brilliant light that came through the windows, the surge of the crowd in the room towards that light, and the rising sounds of panic from outside. The mad dash of people around me (including the guard I was targeting) broke me out of the red haze, for a moment, and in that moment, I managed to assert some control, claw my way back onto the cliff of semi-sanity.

S'zana and I stared at each other, both equally confused, and then we turned towards the brilliance from outside. The lower windows, the amber, glowed with a single tint, while the great jeweled mosaic filled the room with a brilliant mélange of colors. The sounds of panic were clear, as well. There was shouting in grazarn, in delnarian, in some others I didn't know. Out of the cacophony, I did pick up one word: Seeker.

Judging from the light there was either one big one or many smaller ones.

Dolish had a ladder set before his throne of wealth, and was starting to descend. The plan I'd formed just seconds before shattered, and a new one formed in its place.

I knew S'zana could adapt. Taking time to detail my idea, especially since it was in my mind more as instinct than thought, could cost us our window of opportunity. I dashed back, towards the display cases.

The grazarn couldn't work this metal. They put furnishings on it, or built over it. They couldn't shape it. The stained glass window covered a ragged hole torn by forces far greater than anything this King Arthur culture could produce. The cases couldn't be bolted to the floor. They couldn't be.

I reached my target, braced, and lifted. For a moment, I felt resistance... then it was free, tumbling over, and shattering.

The case had held two handguns. At least, they looked a lot like handguns. One had spun away from the case when it toppled over, but the other was close. I grabbed my prize. Silvery metal. A grip and two metal studs on the inner grip, where a trigger should be. A bulbous area above the grip, and a four inch long cylinder as a barrel. Set embedded halfway in the bulb, and sunk into the barrel, was a faceted orange gem.

Certainly, I was making assumptions. I took the chance because the stud pattern on the probably-guns looked very much like the crossbow's trigger, and the crossbows had decorative ovoids just above the grip, simple carved wood that added no function. The designers imitated these ancient weapons, even if it made the triggers more complicated, or added useless weight.

I'd bet my life on this. This time, I was right.

A guard had noticed my escape during the push to the windows, and had dropped behind another display case, aiming his crossbow. I pointed the silver gun towards him. It was light, less than half the weight I'd expected. The glinting of it caught the guard's attention. He shouted something, a loud chittering hiss, and fired his crossbow in panic as he tried to scramble backwards.

That was promising.

I fired.

Thunder. Not "a thundering noise", like a gunshot, but thunder. Like being caught right under the once-in-a-century storms that hit us every other year.

And lightning. A bolt, yellow-white, shot from the tip of the gun to the point I was aiming at, whiplashing all the way there, but ultimately hitting the target in a perfect line from the point of the barrel. The guard's mail armor probably didn't make him any deader than he would have been without it, but it surely didn't help. I felt a private, smug, "I told you so" moment, recalling my conversation with S'zana about armor. Admittedly, "It's not much good against lightning-guns" wasn't an argument I would have ever made before.

"Lightning-gun". An echo came to my mind, a pattern of sounds, instantly translated back to English: "stormfire bow".

If the room had been chaotic before, it was now, hmm, extra-chaotic. There were seekers outside, the city was in a panic, Dolish's new favorite treasure had run off, and now the primitive savage from the distant continent had got his hands on a firestick and knew how to use it.

The orange crystal had turned darker, changing to a deep ochre. Over the next two seconds, it brightened back. Battery? Building up a charge? Probably. One shot every three seconds. A little disappointing that a space gun had a lower ROF than a six shooter, never mind a semi-automatic handgun or an M-16, I thought.

To their credit, Dolish's other guards didn't panic. They were scared, but they turned that into a smooth response. They spread out, shoving anyone in their way out of it, regardless of apparent rank. One of the jade armored ones was escorting Dolish towards an exit.

I kept moving, as well. Their crossbows had one shot before a long reloading, while I had...

I had no idea how many shots I had. Was this a musket, or cowboy movie gun that only ran out of ammo if the bad guy was using it?

I dashed behind one of the armor displays. A metallic ring told me someone had just shot it. Peeking out, I saw the unlucky grazarn spinning a crank while holding a quarrel in his teeth. I rejected the impulse to shout out and let him know he was about to die. I simply fired, half expecting an empty click. Not this time.

Thunder, again. And a triple "twang" as three who had been waiting for me to expose myself took the shot, even as I threw myself flat and rolled to the next cover I'd spotted.

That move helped. Two of the shots passed over me. One pierced my left shoulder. The roll, which I'd already committed my body to, ended up putting all of my weight on that shoulder.

Those who survived that night would learn some exciting new words, even if they never learned exactly what they meant.

I was behind the scribe's desk. Fortunately for them, they were long gone. Two more guards were moving towards me, spears out, flanking. As soon as I turned to aim at one, the other would hurl and then charge.

I smiled and turned to the one on the left, taking aim carefully. He was watching me intently as he closed prepared to dodge or weave as soon as I fired, or wait for his comrade to attack.

I shot. Whatever tell or twitch he'd been waiting for, he didn't see it, because my shot caught him perfectly, and he collapsed, filling the air with ozone and charred fur. I turned to the one on the right. As I'd expected, he was dead as well, a quarrel through his throat.

S'zana tossed the bow she'd used aside and waved the bloodstained sword in her hand experimentally. She shrugged, deeming it tolerable.

"West hall!" she shouted, and pointed.

There was a glint of green. The jade-armored guards had gone that way, Dolish with them. The chamber we were in was clearing out rapidly; even with panic on the streets, the assorted guests and servants still wanted to be *here* least of all.

"Ladies first," I said sardonically, as if there was any element of chivalry involved in the mission we were on. Dolish was ultimately her target. I was backup. I wasn't going to do anything stupid, but if all things were equal, she deserved the first shot at him. As we approached the hall, she looked at my injured shoulder. "That looks bad."

I realized the pain of my shoulder injury was fading quickly. The wound may have been shallower than it seemed at first. "Looks worse than it is. Anyway, I shoot right-handed. I'm fine."

She accepted that without further question.

We were in another maze. There were well-placed lamps, but their light didn't completely fill the darkness between them. The grazarn love of all things sparkly meant there were uncounted small reflective surfaces, and so shadows and twilight danced around us, while the outside noises echoed. We moved carefully, wary of the occasional pools of deeper darkness that might conceal a niche rather than a wall. Once, following what turned out to be a dead end, we came upon a pit.

"Is it common to have open pits in buildings around here, just in case someone is wandering around who doesn't know where the pits are?"

S'zana shook her head, perhaps missing the rhetorical nature of the question. "No. Does it matter?"

Could we lure someone into it? Unlikely. They'd know where it was. "Probably not." We reversed course and found a different path. As with the lower floor, there were many doors here, sliding panels fitted into the metal. They were either fixed open, showing rooms fitted for different tasks, or shut, perhaps forever.

Our enemies were moving, too. The heavy armor that Dolish's elite guards wore wasn't intended for stealth, but the branching and intersecting corridors made it hard to pinpoint sounds. S'zana and I could move quietly, and did; signaling back and forth to each other, making sure that between the two of us, we could cover all possible angles of attack.

One of the flickering, dancing, shadows was moving with deliberation behind S'zana. I pointed. She spun, saw it, pulled back as the attacker turned the corner, swinging a broad-bladed axe, which clanged deafeningly into the wall.

This passage was narrower than the one he'd just left, however. He struggled to bring the blade back for another swing, and as he did, I got my shot. He collapsed to his knees, but wasn't dead. Shouting an alert, he forced himself to rise. I respected his strength. I shot him again. This time, he was either dead or wisely determined to make me think he was.

The double thunder of the blasts reverberated. Somewhere in this maze, we had at least one more guard, and Dolish, unless they'd reached an exit.

Exit...

I considered. Politics here were done at knifepoint -- well, all politics are, this place was just more open about it. The little I'd seen of Dolish made me doubt he was the kind to hide under his bed, or the equivalent, if someone was coming to kill him. Even if he survived, he'd appear weak in the eyes of his underlings and one of them would decide they were the better grazarn for the job. He'd been *arguing* with his guards as they left, not cowering behind them.

I was certain. He'd doubled back. He'd probably assemble more of his allies, and either wait for us to emerge from the passages, or storm back in force once he had the numbers. The stalking game had been to keep us distracted and penned in the interior pathways while he rearranged the board.

"S'zana... that pit..."

"No... it was flush against the wall. He is not beyond it, unless there is a hidden door. That could make sense...."

It would, at that. But that wasn't what I was thinking. "We didn't look above it."

"We also didn't... ah. The lift we took to this floor. You're right, it's about the same size."

I told her my plan. She liked it.

Flight requires thinking in three dimensions. Combat flying requires thinking in three dimensions faster than your enemy. I had a good mental map of where we were, and how the second and third layers of Dolish's palace linked together.

The pit was a shaft. We hadn't looked too closely at the walls surrounding it, but now I could see a rope, tied off to one side. They used this shaft, too, but not often. I couldn't reach it, but...

I said what are often famous last words, "Here, hold this", and handed the stormfire pistol to S'zana. Taking a few steps back, I ran and jumped, stretching forward to grab the rope. I felt a slight twitch of pain in my arm when I grabbed onto the rope, easy to ignore.

Scurrying up a few feet, I kicked away from the wall. As the rope arced close to the edge, S'zana leaped as well, grabbing it, with the stormfire pistol momentarily secured in her belt.

We climbed. I almost missed the exit; a tapestry had been hung over it, and only a few glimmers of light leaking in tipped me off. S'zana jumped first, landing in a roll, causing the tapestry to buckle and wave as she struck it. We both froze; anyone watching would know something was up. After a few seconds passed without a hail of crossbow bolts, she carefully peeled back the edge of the cloth to look around it, then signaled for me.

We were, as I'd thought, at the far side of the broad walkway above the gallery below. From the ground, we were invisible. Lights were still blazing outside the windows. There was still noise coming from the city, but I tuned it out to focus on the room itself. Voices speaking in grazarn, the clank of metal.

We moved cautiously to the edge. A low wall, two feet or so, and set a few inches back from the edge, provided protection from casually falling off. We knelt and peered down. Yes. There was Dolish, and at least a dozen more soldiers. He was busy giving instructions, hissing and pointing, waving his arms. The soldiers' curt, clipped, replies were pretty obviously grazarn for "Yes, Sir!".

I tapped the gun in S'zana's belt, and pointed to Dolish. She drew the gun, turned it over in her hands, ran her fingers along the metal body and the inset crystal. Reluctantly, she handed it to me. "You know this weapon, I don't. Success is what matters."

For the second time that night: No speeches, no dramatic moment of revelation. Just a shot, lined up, and taken.

And missed.

Sort of.

Instead of the single flaring line that reached from barrel-tip to target, there was a splaying web of a half dozen bolts, leaping and arcing across the room. Some found living targets; others smashed furnishings or left jagged, twisting scars along the floor. The thundering noise stuttered, as a series of near-simultaneous shockwaves warred with each other for dominance.

I had about two seconds to try to form some thoughts. Was there a "shotgun" option I'd somehow set off? I tilted the gun to look at it more closely. The gem on the surface was fractured. Small chips had flaked off, and...

S'zana grabbed the pistol from my hand, hurled it over the wall, grabbed me by the shoulder and pushed back, throwing herself down as well. Both of us were flattened behind the wall when there was an explosion of sound and light.

Stunned, we worked to regain equilibrium and stand; or at least get up enough to peer down at what was left below. Ears ringing, I tried to talk, but I couldn't hear much but a dull buzzing.

Below us was a blasted mess of rubble, body parts, and sparkling things. It looked like someone had dumped a mountain of glittering dust on the aftermath of a major earthquake. The ship hanging in the center of the hall, fairly far from the main blast area, had sunk somewhat in its wooden cradle. It was tilting backwards, slowly cracking the supports.

I didn't see anything moving. S'zana was stalking along the edge of the balcony, constantly checking below. She made her way towards some hanging cloth displays that were only slightly shredded, and began climbing down. I followed.

My hearing began to return. "You knew that would happen."

"Well, yes."

"Some warning? 'Hey, that thing explodes at random moments, be careful?' Were you worried I'd stop using it if I knew how dangerous it was, lose the advantage we had?"

I'd expected an angrier reply. Instead, she was subdued. "I thought you... You were so adept with the stormfire bow, I thought... that when we'd talked about weapons, something must have been confused or misunderstood. When you kept holding it after the shattering, I realized you didn't know the danger. I'd been trying to... "

We were half down the precarious climb. I heard the sounds of ripping. The tapestry would not hold for long.

S'zana continued. "I know how frustrating it is for you to be constantly told the most trivial things, so when I saw how well you wielded it, I thought, 'Well, this is something he knows well, I don't need to constantly gnaw at his wounds.'"

We both heard the final rip as the cloth gave way, and jumped back to avoid being caught in the folds as it fell. She kept scanning the rubble, gore, and sparkle filled room. You report a confirmed kill, or you report failure. No middle ground.

We moved together. She studied a torn and blackened body on the ground, shook her head. Not Dolish. "You're *kalveer* on your world. When you said that, I laughed a bit. Anyone can claim a rank, especially when meeting strangers. You proved me wrong. You're skilled, brave, clever..."

"Clever?" I interrupted. "That's one word I haven't been called yet by you."

"I'm trying to apologize. Don't make it more difficult than it has to be."

She pointed to the scattered remains of Dolish's throne. I nodded, and we headed that way. "Clever, yes. If you were my enemy, I would still owe you respect. Do you think I enjoy correcting you, telling you simple things, treating you like a fool?" Before I could answer, she caught my look, and cut me off. "Maybe when we first met. I was angry. I learned better. It cut at me every time I had to do it. You deserve better. Usually. I saw you struggle with anger. You volunteered to put yourself up as something to be stared at and insulted, so you could correct a mistake you made out of an instinct to help. I'm used to wearing masks in my work, knowing whoever people think they're dealing with it, it's not really *me*. You're not."

We'd approached the scattered mounds. Coins, jewels, small statues, goblets, unnamable treasures, all charred, blasted, and molten. "So, if you'd think I'd put you at risk by not telling you about the dangers of stormfire bows, just so that you'd be of more use to me... I understand why, and I'm sorry that's what you've come to expect of me. You've already walked *knowingly* into danger. I know I don't need to trick you into walking into it unknowingly."

"So, what you're saying is, you don't need to lie to get me to take foolish risks, because I'll do it straight up?" She looked upset for an instant, then saw my smile, and returned it.

"Something like that, I suppose." She idly poked the end of her sword at a pile of fragments of red and blue stone, the remnants of a statue, then turned back towards the main hall, looking for a likely spot to search next.

I thought I saw motion. I kept talking as I looked more closely, trying to confirm. "When we're done here, we..."

There was thunder. I saw the flash, saw a blue-white bolt connect to S'zana's leg, saw the skin blacken where it hit, saw her collapse, jerking as the current rampaged her nervous system. Traced the line back. Dolish had found a spot far from our initial search pattern. He'd also found the second stormfire bow.

Nobody here, it seemed, was inclined to make dramatic speeches when they had their enemy in their sight.

S'zana was gasping, shaking, but still alive. I bent, grasped at the sword she'd dropped, and headed towards Dolish, thought not in a simple straight line across open terrain. "Run away from a man with a knife, run towards a man with a gun." Sometimes good advice, sometimes fatal, but right now, it was the best plan I had. I kept moving. Left, right, duck, behind this, over that. I tried to keep my him in sight. I couldn't let him melt back into the shadows. If my hand found anything small and vaguely heavy, I pitched it.

Dolish wasn't a great shot. He overcompensated for my motion, forgetting that a beam of lightning travels a lot faster than a crossbow bolt. He also seemed to be tapping the trigger frantically, not waiting for the recharge. Not knowing if a trigger pull would get a response made his aim worse.

One came close enough to hurt. I saw the flash as the bolt struck near me, felt a sharp sting that faded quickly, smelled burning flesh.

By then I'd crossed the gap. When I closed with him, I could see Dolish's robes were torn, and so was the underlying armor. Blood seeped in a few places, but the wounds didn't seem mortal. Score a point for armor vs. shrapnel, I admitted.

Dolish tossed the weapon aside and drew a thin blade of ebon metal. Looking at it was painful. It was like looking at a hole in space. The blade was defined by where it was *not*.

"Vengeance! Gibbering *chirk*, you will be a special prize! Forever! Limbless, eyeless, legless, caged by my side!"

He stepped forward, slashed. I parried... nothing. His blade went through mine, slicing it cleanly.

Well.

What was left in my hand had an edge, and an uneven point. The angle of the sliced blade did still give me a thrusting tip... just half the length it was a second ago, and useless for parrying.

I had to keep retreating, trying to think of something. Obstacles and cover were nearly useless. He ignored them, the strange sword moving through rock or metal as if it wasn't there. Only once did I see the blade deflect, when he struck the floor, but even the grey metal wasn't entirely immune. His rebounding blade actually sliced out a small shard.

His attacks were not aimed at my vitals -- he was very determined to keep me alive, and I was very determined that only one of us was going to be that way when this fight was over. He was, however, quite good about not giving me an opening, using his reach. He swung wide, but he had time to get his blade back before I could step in with mine.

One option came to me. I shifted my dance of avoidance, tying to lure him along. Meanwhile, more noises were being added to the ongoing din still coming from outside. As we turned in our battle, I could see one of the entrances to the hall. A few more of his soldiers were there, looking worn and battered, some sporting obvious wounds.

Dolish saw them, too. "Hold! I've killed the other, this one must remain. Promise! Any who might take him from me will share his cage!"

He didn't know S'zana wasn't dead. Thank God, or the Guardians, or whatever might be watching this world. I knew how she'd want me to react to her being treated as a hostage. I wasn't sure I'd react that way. Taking that possibility off the table, even for a moment, relieved a pressure I hadn't realized I'd felt.

Dolish kept his eyes completely on me. Nothing distracted him now. I was tired from many fights, and knew that if I lived, I'd be in severe pain once the adrenaline wore off. He hadn't done much fighting, but was still a bit sliced up, and showed it with occasional winces. He continued with threats and enthusiastic descriptions of the things I'd suffer, telling me he might let me keep one eye, or maybe my tongue, if I just submitted now, the usual blather. I kept replying, mocking him, threatening him, because I wanted him looking at me, always at me.

Not up. Not to where I'd led him, into the lattice of supports of the ship. He'd spent the whole fight recklessly hewing through any barrier I hid behind, any momentary obstacle.

He didn't disappoint me this time.

He swung, slicing apart the strained woodwork. He looked past me, and shouted. "Alert! The other one!"

Other? S'zana?

Before I could check behind me, before anything else, there was a terrible, wonderful, creaking noise, and Dolish looked up. He saw the ship looming, barely a few feet over his head, and gasped. The wood splintered around him. Awareness came too late.

I jumped back. He tried to do the same.

In the roar of the collapse, I almost certainly couldn't hear the squishing sound. I like to imagine I did, though.

The ship ended up listing downward, the edge of the deck less than a foot from the floor. I wanted to look closely at it, but there was the small matter of the last loyalists at the door, following their final orders.

"R'yan!"

S'zana was staggering towards me, limping badly. She kicked an intact sword across the floor. I grabbed it. She took two more steps, bent, and took one for herself.

At least four more guards. She could barely walk; I was gasping. I saw streaks of blood everywhere on my body, a dozen slices inflicted by Dolish's near misses. I should have been in far more pain.

"Just wondering. What was your original exit strategy, if I hadn't interfered in your mission?"

"After I killed Dolish, kill as many of his people as I could before they killed me."

"Well, we're still on-plan."

If we could scramble onto the boat... get through the hatch, into the hull... we'd still die, but they'd have to come at us one by one.

I climbed on, then pulled S'zana up, using the support ropes that had fallen across the deck as handholds. The silver piping of the engine structure led to a stand perhaps a third of the way from the bow.

S'zana was bracing herself with one hand, her weight on one leg, and swinging at the guards as they tried to get a foothold. They'd evidently run out of arrows. I pushed myself up further, found a way to wedge myself into position, and examined the controls.

There were a few embedded crystals arranged on an ornate length of carved wood, and beneath that, a large bronze disk with a sapphire globe in the center. The disk spun around the globe, and could be tilted in any direction. At the moment, it was perfectly perpendicular to the floor.

Well, why not try?

I touched the first crystal, a dull green. It did nothing. I touched the second, a similar shade. It came to life, building to a serene emerald glow. The first crystal wasn't glowing, but it had brightened, and I saw, very faintly, a thin line of pale lime stretching to the left.

There was a vibration now. It was familiar. It was the feel the *Bellerophon* had, when it was trying to align itself.

"Drop the sword! Hang on to anything you can find!"

I pushed the crystal left, slowly. It slid through the wood. There was no groove or slot, the wood just flowed around it.

The ship twisted, tearing itself free of what remained of the enclosure. I heard something fall away. Looking over my shoulder, I saw it wasn't S'zana. She was clinging to a now-vertical mast, still battling one of the guards, who had managed to grab the edge of the deck and then climb onto the surface. She saw me looking, and shouted, "Fly!"

Never argue with a lady when she's holding the sword you told her to drop.

I pushed gently on the disk. The ship shot forward with gut-wrenching lurch. No "gravity compensators" here. I took my hand away. It stopped.

An arrow shot past me. More troops were arriving, perhaps unaware of Dolish's death. I tried to nudge even more gently on the bronze plate, generating another surge of thrust. Easing off, I tried not to dwell on why demolitions training wasn't one of the MOS' my aptitude tests pointed me towards.

More arrows. OK. This wasn't working well. Maybe it wasn't really usable, that's why it was a museum piece. Still... the far right crystal was very far to the right, as if it has been slid there, just as the left crystal had. I touched it, and it flickered to life. I pushed, and yes, it slid through the wood. I tried again, pressing on the disk.

We began moving forward slowly. I pushed harder, and speed increased a little. I nudged the rightmost crystal back towards its original position, while keeping the disk in place...we accelerated.

Suddenly, a shadow darkened the controls. I turned in time to see a snarling grazarn face an inch from my own, then it flew back, like someone had just hurled a grappling hook into its shoulder and pulled. *Exactly* like that.

S'zana was straining to pull it towards her, but she needed one hand to grip the mast. The grazarn was doing its best to tear itself free. Its blood spattered the deck, flowing from the gouging wound where the hook had dug into flesh and bone, but it, like us, had decided that if it was certain to die, it was going to take its enemies with it. I couldn't hate it for that, but I certainly wasn't going to make it easy.

"Grab on tight, then let go of the rope!" I yelled back, then turned my attention to the controls. We couldn't just hover and drift. Another few arrows flew past, thunking into the wood.

I tipped the ship left, and heard a dwindling scream, followed by a crash. Then, I straightened it, and spun it towards the north wall, towards the great stained glass mosaic filling the gaping emptiness created by an unknown and ancient event. "Flat! Now! Eyes closed!" I pushed down on the disk, and the ship bolted ahead. As we hit, I dropped behind the partial shield formed by the control stand. It might have been spectacular to have seen it, a storm of brilliantly colored shards, but I likely wouldn't have seen anything again.

The thousands of pieces of falling glass sounded almost like static, and then the sound faded, and the formerly muffled din of the outside grew to an immense roar, becoming the only sound we could hear.

The streets below us were mobbed. Multiple fires blazed throughout the city. Drifting through the air, oblivious to the arrows occasionally plinking off them, were at least a dozen seekers. Our spectacular exit from Dolish's palace was one more thing for the throng below to scream at, and our ship was one more thing to shoot at.

Seekers were so rare that S'zana compared them to dragons, to things of myth, and now we had two confirmed sightings, both where I happened to be. "Coincidence" was implausible at the first sighting; now it was ridiculous.

A burst of thunder, far louder than the stormfire guns, was joined with a glaring blaze of energy that left afterimages for a good minute. The things I'd taken to be some kind of anti-aircraft guns mounted on the towers were exactly that. Someone had fired one. It might have taken time to get them working, or perhaps no one could give the right order and no one wanted to take responsibility. If they'd fired earlier we would have heard it even inside the palace. It hit a seeker dead-on. The target lost stability, shuddered, and dropped, then slowly righted itself and began to rise again.

The others reacted. They spun as one, their primary "eyes" focusing on the source of the attack.

The gun tower exploded. I saw no weapon or beam, didn't hear a missile. There was just a cold attention, then devastation. The metal of the wall where the attacking gun had been blazed white-hot and melted.

How many people had just died? How many people were dying in the madness below me?

I didn't know how or why, but I knew this was happening because I was *here*. Because I *existed*, this city was being torn apart, and the only question was if it were the seekers or the panicked mobs that would do the job first.

S'zana had hobbled forward, and leaned on the panel, next to me. "Fly this thing. Any direction."

"I... no. This is somehow my fault. I don't know what's going on, but they want me." I stepped away from the controls, shouting and waving. "Hey! Yeah, you! Big floating eye! Over here! You're looking for me? The invader from space? Here!"

A heavy chunk of wood, something left over from the old support structure, was at my feet. I hurled it at the nearest one, and it clanged off harmlessly. The seeker did, at least, turn towards us.

As at the river, something passed over us, illuminating S'zana in golden sparks and doing nothing to me. Satisfied, it drifted off again.

"Get! Back! Here!" I looked for something else to throw and was nearly flung to the ground as the ship shuddered and twisted.

S'zana was trying to work the controls. She looked at me. "If you won't fly this, I'll figure it out! They don't *see* you, R'yan. I don't know why, but if they're looking for you, they can't find you, even when you stand in front of them." She gestured in a downward direction. "*They* see *us*, though. We either move or they bring us down and we die. Look at yourself! I don't understand how you're even still standing!"

"I brought those things here, somehow... I have to..."

She smashed her fist on the panel, jarring the disc enough to shake the ship. "I keep being wrong about you. You're *not* clever. If the seekers are looking for you, and you die here, they will *never* find you. They will keep *looking*, and whatever is happening here will happen everywhere. We need time to understand what they want, and stop them. If your sense of duty and responsibility demands you risk your life, do it when it will *mean something*."

"God damn it.", I said, spitting resignation. Returning to the controls, I asked, "Where?"

S'zana pointed somewhat northeast. With a few movements, I turned the ship in that direction, and accelerated away.

The seekers didn't respond. It was insane.

As the burning city dropped away behind us, I finally had sense enough to ask, "What do you mean, you can't understand why I'm still moving? I took a few scratches, nothing serious. I barely feel them." I continued to accelerate the ship, getting a feel for how it responded, making it an extension of my own body. The wind was oddly muted as we picked up speed. A side effect of the engines?

"You're covered in blood. I can see several deep wounds. My leg's injred much less than any limb of yours I can see, and I can barely stand, and don't think for an instant that I don't know how to handle pain."

"It's all someone else's blood."

"No." She touched my shoulder, the one I'd taken the bolt in. I felt a slight pressure. Beneath us, the glow of the forest was fading into darkness. No crystals here. Starlight revealed the shadowed outline of a mountain range growing as we moved towards it. Gently, I kept increasing the speed. There was only the slightest sense of acceleration now, but the occasional dots of light from the ground below appeared only as blurred streaks.

"You should be screaming."

"Why?"

"Because I'm squeezing an open, bleeding wound, and tugging on a jagged, splintered piece of wood inside it. Yes. That's what I thought. We need to stop."

"Why?"

"Inside the wound there's a grey-green residue. I recognize it, a poisonous paste of *jolik* root. It causes numbing, paralysis, then death."

"But I'm *not* numb. I feel your hand, I feel my arm move, I feel the wood beneath my fingers. I've *been* numb. We have drugs that do that. This isn't that feeling."

Far beyond the deep shadows of the mountains, I thought I saw a few glimmering lights. Other cities?

Then dizziness came. The world spun for a few seconds, then seemed to stabilize. S'zana must have seen me waver. "Take us down! Unless you think you can teach me to control this thing before you collapse!"

"I..." Yeah. Something was not right. How did I not even suspect this? What kind of poison makes you fight *better?* If it dulls pain, but with no... a second wave of dizziness, and then, the pain *undulled*.

I tipped the ship downwards, tried to bring it in, but it felt like every muscle was tying itself into knots. The dizziness became permanent, and then there was darkness.

Chapter 7
Dureen

Cold.

That was the next thing I clearly remember, being cold.

There was brightness, too. Painful. I was afraid to open my eyes, as the light was too bright even with them closed.

I tried to move. At first, nothing happened. Then, like a wave spreading down my body, I felt awareness of my body return.

Then I tried to scream, and what emerged was a raw, empty whistle.

Everything hurt. I couldn't piece together every source of pain. Each time I considered moving a limb, the pain would burn itself along every muscle involved, and I'd give up, and gasp, and the gasp itself was painful. Even lying still, breathing very shallowly, there was constant pain.

Was our escape an illusion? Was I feeling phantom limbs? It might be that I had no eyes, just raw optic nerves.

I shoved that out of my mind. I concentrated on my hand. There was wood beneath them. I could twitch my fingers a little.

I forced myself to roll over. The light faded as I did. After a minute or so, waiting for the pain of that motion to die down, I dared to open my eyes.

I was lying on a wooden board. Above me, light -- very bright light -- poured through a square opening. I saw curving walls, some crates and boxes, and more light, this time through a jagged tear in the wooden wall. Through that... blurry shapes. Some still, some waving slightly.

I tried to talk, or cough, but there was just wheezing.

A shape grew outside the torn hull, passed into it. As it neared me it resolved. S'zana.

When she turned towards me, she gasped, then ran forward, knelt down next to me. She patted at my forehead, neck, chest... gently, but each touch still felt like a slap in the face. She breathed in and out a few times, trying to relax, clasping my hand in both of hers.

Then she slapped me in the face. "Idiot!" She stood up and walked back out the way she came. I wanted to call after her, but I still couldn't manage a noise beyond a rasping wheeze.

She returned with a cobalt-blue ceramic bowl, tipped it over my mouth. "Slowly... you don't get to choke to death."

Tepid, sulfurous, and slightly rancid. Still wonderful. I took a small swallow. It felt like what I imagined drinking battery acid must be like. The second sip was easier. After a few more, S'zana helped me sit up, as gently as she could. I tried for perfect stoicism. I failed.

I managed to finally choke out a word. "Where..."

"Later." She reached for my shoulder. "This will hurt."

(I ought to say here that I made some kind of really deadpan comment in reply. Actually, not only was I far too blurry-minded to think of one, I couldn't have managed to say it if I'd had one to say. Instead, I just grunted when she poked and pressed on my shoulder, which I imagined must have looked like raw hamburger.)

"Good. Better than good. Better than I'd realistically hoped. You were so close... I've been watching you, doing what I could, although it seemed pointless... How can *anyone*, no matter what far-off land they claim to be from, not sense that something is wrong when they stop feeling wounds? How did your people not die from stupidity a thousand years[2] ago?" She stood and left again, then returned once more, this time with a green-glazed bowl containing a cold, sickly-white vegetable (I hoped) mash. I tried to reach for it, but that was more than I could stand. She sighed, scooped some with her hand, and placed it in my mouth[3].

Growing up, if I made a fuss over food, my mother would tell me of the Depression, of the things she'd had to eat, of trying to turn the most barely edible scraps into something that could be swallowed. I envied her those fine meals after tasting this. I guess my expression was pretty clear. S'zana responded with a smile that was somehow both cruel and caring. A neat trick. "I've been eating this for three days. It's about time you had to, too. Finally managed to catch something closer to meat. Two or three *more* days, maybe you'll be ready to chew it. If I feel like sharing." She sighed, and her smile lost most of its cruelty. "I probably will, but I'm not saying that under witness of the Guardians."

---

[2] The common word for "year" was literally "a thousand days", closer to three years for Earth.

[3] The hold of the ship had not been empty. Some valuables had been stored there -- expensive bowls, for one, a few ornate weapons, and some bolts of fine cloth, and the normal things found in ships, like spare canvas, utility tools, and rope. No spoons. Or pinup calendars.

She helped me finish the mash, then gave me more water. "Sleep. You'll rest better now, I think."

I tried to get my mind focused enough to form a reply, to start asking questions... and the bits of words I was trying to piece into sentences fell apart as I fell back into slumber.

So passed two or three more days of gradually increasing consciousness. Each time, I was able to stay awake a bit longer, move a bit more without biting back a scream. When I actually asked for a second bowl of Wallpaper Paste And Cardboard Surprise, S'zana decided I was recovered. Also, masochistic.

She helped me to my feet. I still grimaced a bit, but I managed. Putting weight on my feet triggered another bout of pain. Forcing it to pass, I gently pulled away from her, and did a classic "3 AM stagger home from Clancy's Bar" to the gap in the hull. Clinging to the wood for an instant, I let the fire in my soles die to a few embers, and stepped out.

White dust. Grey and white and tan rocks, jaggedly spearing from the ground. Some plants, best described as albino cactuses that had performed illicit relations with weeping willows, grew in clumps. A fire pit, below a makeshift spit formed from a grazarn spear and some crudely shaped planks as supports. Blackened somethings roasted on the spit.

S'zana's voice came from behind me. "There's a spring about ten minutes from here. Not much else. This has been the dullest nine days of my life. My only distractions have been wishing you wouldn't die, and plotting how I was going to kill you."

I walked towards the firepit and found a semi-flat rock. The air was cool and dry. Very dry. It was much more what I was used to than the sweltering jungle I'd crashed in. "I've put it together. The poison... it didn't just remove pain. It gave me a kind of high."

"High what?" S'zana sat down and removed the spit. She pulled off a Blackened Something, and handed the spit to me.

"Wrong word. Drunk, I suppose. It made me not care. I repeat, that's a really stupid poison." I removed a Something of my own, bit into it. The inside was moist, runny, and disgusting. I finished it in two more bites.

"It came close to killing you. I could treat the wounds easily enough. The toxin, I had to simply let run its course. Either the Guardians don't want you dead, or you're too stupid to know when you're supposed to die."

"Too *stubborn*", I responded.

"Stupid." It was almost a term of endearment. I'd take it.

I shrugged. "Something that's poison to some creatures can be food to others. I reacted differently to it." A somewhat troubling thought. I'd been blithely eating anything that didn't kill S'zana, and so far, it was working out. What if it didn't?

"When we return to Alsoria, I know some herbalists who would love to see how you react to any number of things the Listeners use. Also, I'm going to spread my arms, catch the wind, and follow the Guardians to where they've gone."

Huh. I'd been so focused only on staying alive that I hadn't thought about what might happen if I managed it long enough to get to think about anything else. S'zana was joking about using me as a guinea pig, or the local equivalent... I hoped. Did I want to go back to her country and be a freak there, instead of being a freak among the grazarn, or among any of the other peoples of this world? Besides that...

"About that, about Alsoria... do you think you could get home without me?"

Her look dropped the local temperature even further. "I don't know," she said, "I suppose I *could* try making my way without someone completely ignorant about the lands we're passing through and who draws attention wherever he goes, but it would be very, very difficult. Still," she sighed dramatically, "I can attempt it." She looked more serious. "Why? What are your plans?"

"Figure out what the seekers want. Make them notice me. Maybe contact the Guardians, if the seekers serve them."

"Alsoria has scholars, lorekeepers, storytellers. You'd be better off coming back with..." she paused, looking suddenly worried. I guessed what she was thinking.

"And the seekers will follow, cause panic, maybe even attack as they did in Murz Ten. I don't want to lead them *anywhere*, but certainly not to your home."

"Yes...," she nodded slowly. "Yes, of course. That's what I was worried about. Good point. Hmm. We'd better figure out where we are and decide where we're going. Assuming you *want* me to help you."

"Of course I do, but not if it conflicts with your duties."

S'zana smiled, a bit sadly. "My last mission was expected to *be* my last mission. I'm glad it's not, but no one's expecting me home. There's nothing waiting for me. No missions or duties, save this new one: Determine what is causing the seekers to return, and how to stop it. To do that, I will need to work with you."

"Right. So, what facts do we have? What do we know? Who, what are the Guardians?"

"Ask a dozen priests, get a dozen answers. I can't count how many different truths I've heard concerning them, and that's just in Alsoria. Go to Zulsair or Freshar, and get even more truths, and those are delnar lands. Go to any of the grazarn lands, and there are still more."

"Anything in common? Anything everyone, or almost everyone, agrees on?"

"Everyone agrees that everyone else is wrong." She took the last Something. "Beyond that... ," her voice became flat, ritualistic, as she recited tales she'd heard countless times. "Ages past, all the peoples walked with the Guardians in the sky. But some among the peoples were evil and disobedient. From each of the stars, the Guardians took those who would not repent. Because the Guardians are wise and merciful, they gave the evil ones another chance to rejoin the Guardians among the stars. Here, under the witness of the Guardians, they would work and perform the tasks the Guardians set for them and so show repentance. Their children would be born here and do the work of their parents and the Guardians would watch them all, and those who showed true repentance, and who did all they were asked, would be returned to the stars."

She continued: "And then, after more ages, the Guardians grew weary. The evil became worse. The children of evil learned only evil and taught only evil to their children. The people fought the Guardians instead of heeding them. Seeing that there was no true repentance, the Guardians drew back. No more would they give the people tasks; the people must find their own tasks. No more would the people of different kinds be kept apart, but all would be free to take the lands of others."

"They no longer walk among us as flesh to hear our disputes, to enforce our promises, to punish and reward, but they still watch, and listen. If the world shows signs of true repentance, they shall return. If the world shows itself beyond hope, it will be destroyed."

She stood and began to search for bits of wood for the fire. "Even that tale is told in different ways. Each of the people says it was some other people who truly angered the Guardians. Usually, whoever they're currently at war with." She tossed a branch onto the dwindling flame and set the rest down. "Others say the Guardians themselves warred, all taking different sides, and left because they realized the evil of the peoples had infested them."

I thought of Asgard and Mount Olympus. "Was there a place the Guardians lived? Or left from?"

Shrugging, she gestured for me to be silent and still. Following her eyes, I saw a pink-and white creature, with the bloated body of an albino spider three or four inches in diameter, and at least fifty legs, scurrying along near me. Metal glinted in the flame's light, and the crawling thing emitted a small *squiss* sound as a slim dagger impaled it. S'zana retrieved it, slid it off the knife, impaled it on the spit, and set the spit over the fire, where the spider began to blacken and sizzle. One mystery revoltingly solved. Others remained. "Anything? Any legends of the 'Home of the Guardians'?"

S'zana cleaned her knife, tapped her fingers, and began to intone, "And when the working was complete, each Guardian went to the places of the people they had chosen, bringing their servants of glass and iron and light, and built in each place a palace to hear the people's disputed among themselves. But the peoples disputed with each other, as well. So that different peoples might plead for resolution without entering each other's lands, and so that the Guardians might have a place apart from the peoples, a city of palaces was built where none of the peoples dwelt." She turned the spit, and there was another sizzle and some popping sounds. "Does that help?"

"Not much, if we don't know *where*. Where does no one live?"

S'zana laughed. "I'm feeling like you must all the time. I never thought about these questions. 'The Stranger And The Sword'." She saw I had no idea what she was talking about. "A child's story, one Listeners tend to remind each other of. The essence of it is that in an unnamed town in some unnamed delnar land, there was a legend of a magic sword. All the people had heard of it, but no one knew where it was. A stranger came into town one day, and realized the sword was in the hand of a statue in the main market square. Everyone in the town looked at it every day, but only the stranger saw it for what it was." She went silent for a moment, thinking. "In the north, perhaps. There are many places you'll hear that someone is from, even if you never actually meet anyone from there, but I've never heard of anyone claiming to be from beyond the Ebon Jungle. Sometimes, someone will claim to have been there, but they are always quickly proven to be liars."

"It's very little to go on. Hmm." The globe in Dolish's hall... many dim gems scattered around the world, but one still glowing. "More than a little, maybe." I shared my idea with S'zana. She considered it possible. "You think the light means the Guardians are still there?"

"Their servants could be. You said 'glass and iron and light'. Machines. Devices. We have a word that means 'a man of metal', a servant made to look like us."

She was impressed. "Your people have built such things?"

"No, but we have stories."

"Hmm. Maybe the Guardians abandoned your world, too, so long ago you have no stories about them, but you still have stories of their servants, who stayed behind... if that's true on your world, why not here?"

"It's a goal. North, in search of stories!" I looked for something to toast with, but all we had were ceramic bowls of sulfurous water. I offered it to S'zana, as I'd seen the grazarn do.

She seemed bemused, but accepted it, and handed me hers. I had the distinct impression I'd just done something slightly silly, like eating a hot dog with a knife and fork.

"In a few days. You're still weak, and I'm not sure what might lurk between here and anyplace with people. Do you think you can get the ship to fly again?"

I looked at the huge hole and was about to say something sarcastic, then thought a moment. It didn't need an intact hull, after all. The machinery created some sort of bubble around itself. As long as it was intact enough... "Possible. I'll check it tomorrow."

I tested it while S'zana was gathering supplies, for a few reasons. First, I hoped to have it working when she got back. Second, if anything went wrong, I didn't want her on-board with me.

It turned out to be a good choice.

My guess on the hull and the machinery was half right. The flying mechanisms were mostly intact, but it seemed the shape and structure of what they were attached to mattered. My attempt to force the ship to lift itself created a... I'm not sure what to call it. It was a lot like two giant, invisible hands grabbing the ship and wringing it like a dishtowel. I think my position at the controls, the "center" of the bubble, put me at the eye of the storm, so I ended up merely bruised in a dozen places, lying in a mound of splintered wood and assorted other detritus, a mix of what was still in the hold and parts of the flight mechanism in varying states of ruin.

I'd pulled myself free by the time S'zana came back. Once she was certain I'd only set my healing back a day or two, she became much more focused on the ship's corpse.

"How many of these kinds of flying ships exist?" I asked her.

She was looking at the remains with the same resigned "Getting angry won't fix it" look my Dad wore when contemplating what Uncle Sal's towing company deposited in our driveway in 1963. "Not many, and now there's one less."

"Turning a one-of-a-kind aircraft into a pile of smoking wreckage is what test pilots do. The lucky ones get to do it more than once. Twice for me, now."

"You should have waited for me. I could have..."

"What?" I knew I held the high ground in this fight. "As little as I can understand about how these things work... in this at least, I know more than you. If you'd been standing on the ship, except right where I was, you would have been hit much harder than me. And if you'd been standing anywhere near enough to the ship to scream suggestions at me..." I pointed to the willow-cacti, most of which were skewered with foot-long bits of wood.

She started to form a counterargument a few times, each time stopping before she finished her first word, realizing some obvious flaw. Finally, she simply dropped the conversation altogether, and proceeded as if the ship had always been a non-issue. "I took a different route to the spring this time. I spotted some trees over that ridge, growing fruit. *Tzurr*. Green and yellow, about this big." She formed a sphere a half-foot across with her hands. "I've been hauling the water since we crashed here."

"Sure." There were still many fragments of tarp from inside the hold of the ship. I cut one into something I could use to carry the *tzurr* in, double-checked the directions, and went off.

"Bleached" was the best word for this area. After the wild colors of Scarmallor and then Murz Ten, this was like going back to Kansas after Oz. I followed the path I'd been given, saw the slightly more lush area around the spring, and turned towards the promised trees. There might have been more water there, too, a second oasis. That would be good.

I made it up another incline, and saw a clear path to the grove. A dozen or so trees, their bark white with grey-green mottling; the fruit, a lemon-yellow sphere upon which someone had dripped blue paint, hung like a beacon to whatever creatures ate it.

Despite the moisture-sucking dryness of the air, this had been an easy climb up, and it would be an easier climb down. I moved forward.

The ground beneath me felt oddly springy, for a moment. Then it was oddly *gone*, and I plunged.

I landed on something soft, sticky, and damp. The impact knocked the wind out of me, and it took a second to figure out what was going on. Sunlight leaked in from above me, beams some passing through the hole I'd fallen through, but more were filtered by white-grey sheets covering a larger hole in the cavern ceiling. The walls of the cave were made of rounded, fluting, columns of a stone that shimmered and glistened like wet mud, but a dull white in color. The floor was of the same material, relatively flat, with a few blobs and growths scattered across it. The scene trailed off into darkness, so I couldn't judge the full size of the place. If I looked in the direction I'd seen the grove, above, I could dimly make out a thick tangle of roots that reached from the cavern ceiling and into the stone below.

There was a clinging, all-encompassing odor of rot and decay. If you'd ever had the misfortune to be around at the excavation of a mass grave, you'd know it and never forget it.

Draped across the walls were hanging, flowing, curtains, along with misshapen, darker colored spheres and tapered cylinders, all of the same substance that I'd fallen through. I was lying on...

I shoved myself up and away, getting to my feet while staggering backwards. I'd landed on a cluster of the spheres, breaking them. The resulting mess was a soup of retch-inducing liquids, sickly grey, ochre, and hospital green, with puddles of other colors... and fragments of bone with threads of tissue dangling loosely. It had soaked into my clothing, and it was hard not to just strip naked right there... but the crystals of the wall and floor looked sharp, and I didn't need another round of wounds.

Getting back?

The opening was out of reach, period. Maybe I could climb the walls, a little, but there was no way I'd make it to the exit unless there was a radioactive spider somewhere nearby. In time, S'zana would follow my trail, see the tear, and we could figure something out, but I didn't think I'd have a lot of time. The corpse stew was fresh. Whatever lived here was home, and it surely took the sound of my fall as the ringing of the dinner bell.

Drawing the sword from my belt, I carefully scraped the bulk of the glop from my clothes and started to explore. The spot I'd fallen was near a corner of the cavern. I made my way along the wall, trying to avoid heading too far from the light. There were sounds. Dripping water. Echoes of my own footsteps. Clattering. Distant clicks and scrapes, hisses. Something else. I inched into the darkness, wary of a sudden drop in the floor. Sweeping my sword before me like a blind man's cane, I felt it hit a wall. The sound of the impact was different. I tapped it a few more times. It was striking a surface with a bit of give to it. I heard small bits of something fall to the ground, then I felt a much more solid substance beneath the blade's tip, and heard the sound of metal hitting metal.

Running my fingers along the revealed surface, I discovered I'd chipped away an encrustation of soft rock over a flat metal plate. I worked at it more and found an edge. Shoving the blade in, I twisted, and with an extremely loud creak, I felt the plate give way and slide back, revealing a dim light coming from somewhere far ahead. I turned back to see how far I had come from the entry, and then saw the looming thing behind me.

It was a lot like the Blackened Somethings we'd been eating, in a pre-blackened state, inflated to the height of a man and somewhat stretched out. Mostly silhouette, it had come to within a few feet of me before I turned. Producing a noise like a lion coughing up a hairball, it fired a spray of webbing. I shielded my face instinctively, and that was good, as the exposed parts of my arm went momentarily numb where the sticky threads touched them. With light behind me, and this thing in front of me, I chose the light.

I jogged down about a hundred feet, nearly tripping once or twice on the irregularities in the floor. The walls scraped my skin where I brushed by them. The light brightened. I found the source of the illumination as I entered another chamber, at least as large as the first. The glow came from a partially overgrown mechanism of some kind, a column of polished stone, metal, and crystal running floor-to-ceiling, ten feet in diameter. The light, a baleful lime-green, spread from those parts of it not covered with rivulets and blobs of the shimmering white stone that formed the bulk of the cavern. Some of them glowed steadily, while other flickered or pulsed.

I spun back, prepared to strike first against my pursuer. It came to within about twenty feet of me, then chitter-screeched and danced backwards on its dozens of tiny legs.

It didn't like light, which was great. All I had to do was sit near the column of light until I died of thirst.

More sounds, coming from deeper in the darkness. They didn't fit the rest of the noises in this place. My mind kept snatching at them, trying to make sense of the bits I could barely hear. I moved in the direction I thought they were coming from, something of a guess given the cavern's echoes. As I got closer, I could start to piece things together. It was a voice.

Drazk flug ke var! Mallig ve klorg ig kar, flug! Vor jal ve drazk ig!

The language, and voice, was neither delnar nor grazarn. The voice was hoarse and scratchy, and it sounded female, but I wasn't going to make bets about how the different peoples of this world sounded. There were chittering and spitting noises as well. Whoever the voice belonged to it, it was *probably* fighting the spider-things. Unless it was their king or queen, telling them to enjoy the yummy snack. I decided to take the chance.

"Hey! They're scared of light! Lead it my voice, there's light here!" (The person I was shouting to, I realized, might not speak delnar, but hopefully, they'd figure out a non-spider voice belonged to at least a temporary ally.) I was ready to slash at it as it came by, or bolt back to where the light was brightest, if I had to. I wasn't a big fan of running away, even when it was smart, but forcing the fight to take place on my terms wasn't running away.

"*Ve norg jal* I'd *frarg* love to run that *gravgar kler* way, but there's a *drazk klorg* wall in my way, ya *grek*!"

(As this is a formal report, I will save the Air Force some amount of redacting fluid by leaving certain vocabulary untranslated. The meaning should be clear.)

So, they did speak delnar. It may have been a common trade language. The word-finder seemed to erase some aspects of accent and dialect, but the words I heard underneath, the true sounds being made, definitely had a different tone and emphasis to them than the same words spoken by S'zana.

The wall couldn't be too thick, I realized, since the voice was coming through clearly. I moved towards the voice, feeling ahead. Ah. Wall. Another white-stone structure. On the other side, there was hissing, spitting, and a ceaseless stream of angry-sounding syllables. I swung my sword at the wall, feel it crack a little, then again and again. Finally, it shattered.

"Ha! *Frarg* yourself, *klug*!" said someone as they barreled past me, shrouded in darkness. The sound of dozens of clicking, segmented, feet followed. I pursued one shadow towards the light, while another shadow pursued the two of us.

Fortress At The Top Of The World

In the green glow, I got a better look at the source of the voice. About four feet tall, and broadly built, a build amplified by thick armor of metal-reinforced leather. Facial structure and what I could deduce of general build, under armor, reinforced my initial guess as to gender, which was later confirmed. She was carrying an array of tools, weapons, and things I couldn't entirely identify. Her skin, the little of it that was exposed, was covered with very short fur -- mostly grey, with some white patches. There was some blood smeared on her face, and I could see tears in the armor. She had a short hatchet in her right hand, and two more looped on her belt.

She kept a watch on the shadows, waiting for the spiderpede to clatter out of them. I was checking the other known passage.

"Dureen. Do ya need the entire *grelf* rest of it?"

"Probably not. I'm R'yan." I decided to also leave off "the rest of it".

Something moved in the darkness. It spit, but the glob didn't hit either of us. It splattered against part of the light, and dripped, and dimmed the illumination further as it hardened. I was going to write it off as poor aim, until two more followed, from different angles. One moving around, or several taking position... it was hard to say.

"Is there a way out, back the way you came in?"

"If there was, would I *krel kar* have come this way?"

Another splat. We'd be without the light quickly. Maybe the two of us could fight back to the place I came in. They couldn't block the sun. Probably.

"That passage -- kind of a slightly less dark patch -- if we can get through it, there's someplace a bit better than here." I considered. "If we..."

She'd already started running, screaming a battle cry in her own language. I suddenly had more sympathy for S'zana.

I charged after her, catching up quickly. A shadowy mass bulked before us. I could sense its bulbous head twisting left and right, trying to decide who to target. I was more aware of how it attacked, now. I danced a bit in front of it, jabbing quickly, striking a few times, not deeply, but enough to hurt. As it prepared to belch its webs, I feinted left, then moved right, and slashed down against the thin neck that connected head to body. Dureen, moving an instant after it had fired, jumped *onto* its head, then rebounded onto its broad, quivering, back, and hurled one axe, then a second, then a third, down the passage ahead of us, as the beast she was standing on began its death spasms from my attack. I heard two solid thumps of axe into flesh, and one clang of axe into floor.

"*Frarg!*"

"Two out of three..."

"Is *zum ka* worse than three out of three!"

We continued. There was clattering behind us, and just enough of the light left to see fragments of what was around us. I was focusing my attention backwards, trying to see what might be following, while Dureen reached to retrieve her weapons from the creature they'd struck. I caught the motion at the edge of my vision. I was starting to turn and shout when it lunged suddenly, its mouth engulfing Dureen's arm. Her roar of battle fury turned into a scream of pain as the fangs sunk in. As I completed my turn, I thrust the sword through its head, hoping that I was missing her arm.

She pulled her limb free. In the dimness, I had no idea how injured she was. Her status report was a stream of untranslatable words. There was still noise behind us, growing louder.

We kept moving, passing out of the door I'd pushed back. The shaft of light from above was clearly visible. We headed for it.

The sun had moved, of course. The light was angled differently. Eventually, it was going to fade completely.

Dureen did not look well. In the light, I could see her injured arm more clearly. The armor had kept the fangs from sinking too deep, but they didn't need to do more than break the skin.

She grunted as her arm spasmed. If her internal anatomy was anything close to human, basic first aid should apply. "Let me see if I can deal with this, before the light fades or they get too hungry to care."

"Can't make things... augh... *frarg* worse, can ya?" She held out her arm, then told me how to detach the armored sleeves. She was wearing an ornate wristband, made from a dozen beaded strands. It was attached with an intricate geared locking mechanism.

I tugged at it, seeing if I could break it. Seconds counted.

"No... *frarg*... way. Top latch, left, bottom, right, middle two, left, up..."

I followed her directions, removed the band, pocketed it, then tore off part of my own sleeve, a part that hadn't soaked in gore, to form a bandage. "That should slow it down a bit. I know someone who is pretty good with poisons. She'll help." *If she gets here before it gets too dark. She has to have noticed this is taking too long.*

"You planning to sit here and *drakzig* wait for her?"

"Any better ideas?"

"Left side. Fourth... *drelg ka zrak*, that *frarg* hurts like a *krel va*... pouch. Rope. Grappling hook. Where are you *drelk* from, anyway?"

I retrieved the items. I wasn't sure what the rope was made from, but it seemed strong. "Uhm... across the Scour. The western shore of the World's Wound."

"The local *klef* buy that pile of *grelg*, huh?"

I stood, studied the gap above for a good place to hurl the hook. "Why not?"

"Because I'm from *frarg* Drolg Gor Kra, which *is* west of the Scour, and I've seen every kind of *grak* come through there, and nothing looks like you."

I sighed, and hurled the hook. Fell short. How long until the spiders came back? How smart were they? Could they talk to each other?

"So, how did *you* get here?"

She was silent a bit while I tried again. Closer.

"Long story", she said at last.

Toss. There. Perfect. I tugged. It was set firmly in the rock.

I started to climb. She asked, "So, where are you really from?"

"Longer story."

"Everyone's a *ka frarg* jester."

Climbing shouldn't have been too difficult, especially since I'd done very little physically for many days. The way my muscles burned by the time I'd reached the top reminded me how much I'd damaged myself. My first plan was to run, find S'zana, get her to help... but this wasn't the spider's plan, and they outranked me here.

Before I'd taken even a handful of breaths, I heard cursing. I peered back down. Dureen was standing and moving deeper into the circle of light, and she kept looking around, trying to keep more than one thing in her sight at once. "Grab the rope!"

She did. I started to pull. I told myself that I'd climbed with a 50 pound pack, and if I could pull myself and 50 pounds up, I could pull her up. I figured if I told that to myself enough, I'd believe it.

"*Ja klur ga vrak*! One arm's *drazg* numb, and I can't let go with the other!" Halfway up. I could hear a rising chorus of clicks and hisses.

"What's... the... problem?" Each word I spoke made my lungs burn. Pull. Don't think. Just move. Pull. Don't think beyond each motion. Repeat. No pain. Just move.

"Great shot at the *kulg*, and I can't take it!"

I didn't reply. Her arm had hurt before; it was numb now; whatever the poison was, it was progressing.

Finally. She was up. I fell back, gasping. I had to stand. Poison. She shouldn't move. She'd be dead before I found... I found... someone. I had to... something. Stand. Yes. Stand.

I turned my head. Dureen was sitting next to me. She was pointing back towards the ship. "Is that your friend?"

I managed to sit up enough to look back where she was pointing. Approaching us was a seven foot tall, green-furred, gorilla. It had a longbow in its right hand, and when it saw us, it swiftly nocked and aimed an arrow.

"No." I told her.

"*Frarg.*"

The gorilla -- gorilla-like biped -- was dressed in loose, folded garments of white cloth trimmed with bands of gold and black. I saw an immense scabbard at its waist, and a quiver strapped across its back. It was barefoot, but had heavy bracers on its calves, matching those on its arms. It had a crested skull, larger than that of an actual ape, and that skull was covered with something between a helmet and a headdress -- a cage of iron bands wrapped in silver wire and set with small discs of hammered gold. Its face, other than the pine-needle green color, could have come from any of those movies with Heston.

Dureen's good arm was slowly moving towards an axe. I was running through every plan I could think of, but each of them ultimately had me being cast as "Sheriff's Henchman #2" in a Robin Hood movie a second after I started.

It looked at Dureen, and held the bow to cover both of us. "Now, nothing unbalanced. Is one of you Kaveel R'yan Fallingstar?" His voice was surprisingly soft and calm.

"Me." If it knew that name, it must have spoken to S'zana. Had she sent it? Or was it an enemy, hunting both of us, for some reason? I couldn't imagine how our names could have come this far, this fast. Then again... how many days had we been camping here? Many. Long enough for word from

Murz Ten? Did they have carrier pigeons here? Giant mirrors? A whatever-they-used-as-ponies express?

"Ah, great!" He released the tension on the bow and returned the arrow to its quiver. "She said I'd know you because you wouldn't look like anyone I'd seen; and then, there's two people who don't look like anyone I'd seen. Not balanced, you know? So, you're alive. That's good."

I stood. "She... Dureen. Poisoned. She needs help." I realized Dureen had gone at least a minute without shouting at anything. She needed help *badly*, if what I'd seen of her behavior until now was normal for her.

The green ape tilted his head curiously. "Poisoned by the *zelk*?" He saw my blank look. "Oh, of course, you wouldn't know what to call them. They live in the dark? Lots of legs? Spit nasty glop?"

"Yes! We were down there. She was bitten. I'm just... tired. She's..."

Dureen had been supporting herself by leaning on a rock, but was slipping off.

The gorilla bounded forward, caught her, and scooped her up. "Mmm. Her health[4] is greatly unbalanced. Not good at all."

Whoever he was, his gift for the obvious was amazing. "S'zana... the one who sent you here... can help, probably. If you can help me take her back... to our camp..."

"Sure, sure, but you have to come with me. I agreed to find you and bring you back. I want to help this other one, but I can't go back without you. Witnessed and everything."

"I'll come back with you."

"That's good! We have to move quickly. You should have just said that earlier."

He moved quickly. Even if I wasn't running on pure "too stupid to quit" at this point, I wouldn't have kept up with him.

I arrived a few minutes behind him. S'zana was kneeling next to Dureen, and engaging in some kind of debate with two more green gorillas, while the one who found us (I could tell them apart, at this point, solely by their differing clothing patterns) was perched on a rock, looking down the slope

---

[4] The word he used was *ickhin*, which meant something like 'vitality' or 'life essence', and also 'sap'.

and toward the plains beyond. A group of three six-legged reptilian beasts was tied up nearby, fitted with riding saddles.

The others saw me approaching. I moved to the firepit and sat, trying to make it look like I wasn't just collapsing into a sitting position.

Dureen was unconscious, and she spasmed with each breath. Her arm was swollen and discolored, with patches of grey and white fur falling off, leaving bare and diseased looking skin beneath. Her helmet and most of her armor had been removed. This revealed something like a mane of red-gold hair along her head and down her back.

"Will she live?"

"I don't know. Krer and Quarrin, here, both of the Fourth Rising, have given me some advice, and some of their own supplies for which I promised them information of value. If she lives, what you did to slow the flow of the poison probably saved her. I'm not sure of the arm. I don't know her people, I don't know how fast they can heal. This isn't what I *do*. Who is she, anyway? Where did you find her?"

I related what happened.

"Now, your turn... who are these people?"

"Krer of the Fourth Rising, Quarrin of the Fourth Rising, and Cherrik of the First Rising. They're Border Walkers, Second Gathering.. scouts, patrollers... and they're from Hreek, a city a day's walk or so from here, bordering on the Solid Sea. None of which were more than names to me until now."

That wasn't especially helpful, but I could understand she wouldn't want to give a more detailed opinion when they were standing right there.

S'zana looked at Dureen and frowned. She ran her finger very gently along Dureen's wrist where the poison had entered, and her body spasmed violently even at that slight touch.

Her voice carefully measured, S'zana asked me: "Do you know anything about her people? Her beliefs? Would removing her arm be worse than letting her die?"

I'd known too many who'd lost limbs, or eyes, and who couldn't adjust, who drifted off into one kind of self destruction or another. Others made it, decided that they weren't going to fold after a few bad hands. I knew what S'zana was asking. How well someone adjusted depended on who they were and how they were raised. The kind of guy who thought it was hilarious to trip the kid with braces on his legs wasn't going to last long if he ended up in a wheelchair himself.

S'zana was watching me, waiting for an answer.

This wasn't what *she* did, she said? It wasn't what *I* did, either!

Could Dureen, who clearly enjoyed how well she could fight, be who she was if that was lessened in any way? I barely knew her at all, knew nothing of her people. We'd exchanged maybe a few dozen words in our time together. I couldn't make that decision, and that's what helped me make it.

"Save her," I said. "If she doesn't want to live after that, she'll have to be alive to let us know."

It was not a good night. I wanted to stay up in case Dureen awoke; she deserved to have someone with her when that happened. S'zana was insistent that I rest at least part of the night, pointing out that the journey to Hreek was dangerous. The Border Walkers had set their camp a short distance from ours. S'zana wasn't going to have both herself and me asleep at the same time when they were so close, despite the fact we all seemed to be getting along. "New friends in the day can become new enemies at night" was the moral of a favorite childhood story.

I'd heard such stories as well... the farmer and the snake, for one. I told that one to S'zana, and she wanted to know if I knew any other tales or legends. Our guests made me immediately think of King Kong, but I considered their hearing might be acute. Most of my stories were from TV or Sunday School. She seemed to like tales of betrayal, so I told her about Samson. She considered it to end poorly. Delilah was the true hero of the tale, who eliminated an enemy of her people.

"I may tell portions of it to D'valya. He may reshape it." For a moment, her eyes focused on the past, and she laughed slightly. "If she commands it, I suppose he'll have to."

"Who?"

"Hmm? Who... ah. I must be tired, if random thoughts leave my mind and pass into speech. Fortunately, this was no great secret to keep. D'valya constantly bemoans an invisible tormenter, his... artistic spirit? Inspiration?"

Muse, suggested the word-finder, or maybe it was my own mind at this point. Its translations and my thoughts were mostly one. I spoke that word, and heard echoed a delnar word that seemed to match closely enough.

"Demon-muse, or muse from hell... that seems right," S'zana continued. "She is responsible, he claims, for late nights working, for days where no one sees him, screaming tales into his ear until he finishes them and makes her go away, for a time." She shrugged. "Storytellers are strange. I've never met one who wasn't at least a little insane."

Hard to argue with that.

I slept, or tried to. My mind wouldn't stop circling around things I could have or should have done differently. I couldn't think of a choice I might have made differently that wouldn't have ended up with things being worse -- if I hadn't been in the cave at all, Dureen would most likely been killed outright. Such reasoning felt hollow and self-serving.

When S'zana woke me for my watch, I wasn't sure if I'd ever fully fallen asleep. The rest of the night passed uneventfully.

Dawn's light glared off the glistening wastes spreading out below the crash site. Quarrin and Krer came by to keep speaking with S'zana, their prior negotiations cut short by my arrival. I barely listened to what they were discussing; the worth of information, the laws of Hreek, what might be promised, what might not. Quarrin and Krer seemed fairly easy going, though not entirely without concern that one person of a people they knew mostly by tales, and two people, neither known at all, had all shown up on their border. I heard the word "seeker" more than once, and noted S'zana deftly saying nothing specific while hinting she had information worth trading for.

I was focused on Dureen. S'zana had made the cut below the elbow, where the rot was at its worst, figuring that if it came to that, it was easier to take more than to return what didn't need to be taken. They had good techniques here, even with their technology. They knew about sterilization, cauterization, proper bandaging.

I didn't notice Cherrik approaching until he sat next to me. Closer than I liked, but I didn't say anything. His fur wasn't fur. It was very fine, thin, blades of grass. I watched in momentary fascination as a small flying insect landed on Cherrik's arm. The grass sweated out drops of sap, and the bug was trapped. The sap rolled down the blade, taking the unfortunate insect with it. I assume it was digested over time.

Cherrik looked down at Dureen curiously, as if he had never seen her before. "She's not good," he stated as if this was a conclusion he'd pondered for a long time. "She's unbalanced."

I tested the platform we'd strung together to use as operating table and bed. It was stable, laying flat on the rock. "No, it looks good to me."

Cherrik laughed, a hooting sound. "No, no. Not like that. Unbalanced. You know. The world. In balance, out of balance. When it's all good, when the world's what it should be, it's balanced. When it's not, it's unbalanced. You have to keep the world balanced, to do what should be done." His eyes drifted out of focus, then seemed to lock on something a few yards away. I looked, but saw nothing out of the ordinary, when the ordinary included green gorilla-plants spouting philosophy. He wandered off to examine whatever, leaving me alone, which was preferable.

Dureen moaned, coughed, and tried to move. She'd been tied down during the surgery, and S'zana was worried about her wandering loose in the night, if the poison caused confusion or other impairment.

"*Va kraj frelg nakir ca vla... grazgar... klar bel kiz...*" She pulled at the rope again.

"Easy... I'll let you loose. What do you remember?"

"*Frelgin...* " She looked at me, squinted, frowned. "You weren't a dream... *krav*. Stuck... still in *frarg* caves?"

"No." I started working on the ropes, releasing her good arm first, then working on the main body. "Just relax. What do you remember?"

"A whole bunch of *krel*. Not sure what was real. Green guy?"

I nodded. "Real."

"Iron snake?"

I shrugged. "I didn't see that one..."

She managed to partially sit up, flexing the fingers of her right hand. "I remember my *frarg* left arm feeling like someone stuck a dozen knives in it. It still *drazg* does."

I'd heard a lot of advice on how to give bad news, most of it contradictory. I felt it was more respectful to cut to the chase. "Uhm... no, it doesn't still hurt. The point of injection... where the poison was concentrated... by the time we got here and could treat you..."

She grabbed for her left arm with her right, felt down to where the amputation had taken place, closed her eyes, and lay back down with a quiet "*Frarg.*"

I kept talking, mostly on autopilot. "We call it phantom pain. It's..."

Fortress At The Top Of The World

She turned her head slightly to look at me. Her eyes glistened, but her voice was controlled. "I *frarg* know what the *krelf* it *gramal* is, ya *ka frarg dretch*. Second husband lost both legs to a *drivk*. *Drelks* about it almost every day, too. Now we'll have something new to talk about."

Talking about going home was a good sign, probably.

"*Frarg*!" she shouted, sitting upright, as much as possible. She cursed again, and tugged at the remaining ropes, then tried to find one of her axes, or knives, or one of her countless unidentifiable sharp things. We'd put them all out of reach. I cut the rope myself. She looked at the bandaged stump for a moment, closed her eyes, breathed deeply, then opened them and look around her. "My wrist. I had a *frarg* bonding band. Where..."

Taking it from my pocket, I handed it to her. "Here. Your arm was swelling, you told me how to remove it." She clutched at it desperately, then closed her eyes and breathed deeply a few times. She lay back down again.

After a few minutes without anyone speaking, I felt obliged to say something soothing or inspirational. "Uhm... I know this isn't a good thing, but, uhm, with time and, the..."

Despite her obvious efforts to avoid it, her voice still cracked with emotion. "You *frarg* say any *krelf* about bright hopes and *ka vrak* shiny days and *frarg drazk* plans of the Guardians, I will shove the one fist I've still got so far down your *frarg* throat that I will rip out your *grach* and show it you."

I still don't know what part of my body my *grach* is, and I've never asked. "I'm actually glad you said that, because I had no idea where I was supposed to go with that speech. Now. We have vile white mashed something, and grotesque fire-blackened something for food. Any preference?"

"Not hungry. Go away. If I *frarg* want something, you'll know."

I went away, but not so far away I couldn't keep an eye on her.

S'zana saw me leaving Dureen, and joined me. We were far enough away it seemed unlikely she'd hear us.

"How is she?"

"Angry. Sad. Not hungry. In pain. I don't know! Do you want me to sit next to her with a little pad, ask her to look at inkblots, and try to get her to tell me why she hates her mother?"

"She hates...?" S'zana began. I interrupted. "Never mind. Ignore me. What I mean is, I'm not a..." this language had no word for 'psychologist', which was a point in this world's favor... "...healer of minds. I don't know what she's feeling or *should* be feeling."

"Neither do I. I'll speak with her in a moment. I can ask her about her body, if not her spirit. As for us, for now, I've made some bargains with the Border Walkers. Fortunately, the two of the Fourth Rising are in the cycle of celebration, so they're easy to deal with. I'm to give news to a Drawn Council -- I'm not totally sure what that is, but I think that's their city leaders -- of everything happening in Murz Ten, and some other things they'll want to know. Krer has given us marks of passage, which will give us ten days of time to stay in Hreek, and as much time after that to reach the northern borders of Cal-Hreek, their nation. That should be enough to plan our next action."

"What about Dureen?"

"I named her in the bargaining, since I knew you wouldn't leave until she was healed. I guessed she didn't tell you what her plans were, but I doubt they're close to ours. If she's not lying about where she comes from, she's very far from home. Did she tell, or even hint, at her purpose here?"

"No. We were a bit busy not being eaten."

S'zana's expression told me she considered that a poor excuse for not conducting a proper interrogation. "I'll learn what I can from her. You and I are still going to Hreek. I.." she paused. Her voice softened. "I bargained for you, without your permission. You were busy, and they took it for granted I could speak for you. If I promised anything you don't agree with, there's still time to change our terms. I made sure of that, as part of the bargaining."

I waved it off. "I appreciate the apology. Yes, in the future, ask me first if you can. For now," I sighed, "I could probably justify getting angry, but given the decision *I* had to make for Dureen, it's not worth it. I'm too tired. Uhm, before I get too calm, exactly what *did* you promise for me? More sideshow acts?"

"No. Hreek gets so few distant visitors that we're all equally strange. I promised you wouldn't attack anyone, mock the Guardians, break any other major laws, that you'll make appropriate penance if you do break them, the usual. You don't have to fertilize anyone or put out your eye or profess a belief you don't share, as long as you don't condemn *their* beliefs. We're going to be limited in where we walk within Hreek. There are only a few places we can go, there are many more restrictions than in the cities of the

Klurish League, but we're more likely to be warned of those restrictions than be allowed to break them and then be punished. "

"Seems as fair as we're going to get. You said you wanted to talk to Dureen. I'll gather what's left of the supplies. I don't suppose your bargain included anything to drink?"

She smiled. "Two barrels of *clean* water, and a small jug of something fermented. It tastes like... hmm, it tastes like you'll stop caring after one or two drinks. Not too bad, really. I also received advice on locating water in the wastes between here and Hreek."

S'zana managed to convince Dureen to eat something. Both were hoarse from shouting at each other by the time it was done, and my vocabulary in delnar was expanded. I'd scavenged rope from the ship's ruins, cut some clean bandages and boiled them, blackened some *chulg* (the little spiderpedes had a name), made some mash, cleaned our weapons, and otherwise did everything I could think of with the limited supplies at hand. The Border Walkers were long gone, Cherrik taking time to remind me to stay balanced, and to tell me that he had a dream about one kind of beast I'd never heard of transforming into another kind I'd never heard of and that meant something I didn't understand.

Dureen was going through the wreckage on her own. There was a sound of triumph, then a stream of increasingly frustrated exclamations.

S'zana and I walked over. Dureen, kneeling over a portion of the alien machinery she'd unearthed, looked up at us. A number of the tools she'd carried were arrayed around her. She was holding one in her right hand, muttering quietly, looking fixedly at the mechanism. It could best be described as multiple rectangular units crammed together, at odd angles, embedded with crystals and interwoven with cables of flexible glass, the whole thing the size of a suitcase. It looked intact -- no burns or marks or obvious jagged edges. A section of gold, silver, and translucent purple cable, as thick as my arm, was hooked into it. There was blood on the connection, and, I realized, on Dureen's hand, matting the fur.

She knew we were there. S'zana was about to talk; I put my hand up. She stopped.

Silence, for a minute. Dureen looked at me, spoke. "One of ya, hold the *drazk tiluvishal*." I guessed she meant the central portion. I knelt opposite her and gripped it. She took the tool in her right hand and began to apply it to different parts of the mechanism... *tiluvishal*... engine block. Her left arm kept moving to grip or adjust another part, and each time it did, she cursed again, then barked at me to grab, turn, or twist something. I tried to follow how she used her tools. She would sometimes swap out one for another, but each was uniquely odd. They kept bending in her hand, which didn't seem right, and then I noticed they reshaped themselves as she worked, the metal flowing to a new form, then solidifying. Like having a screwdriver that changed itself to fit whatever screw you were using. Useful.

Eventually, she got the *tiluvishal* free of anything hooked to it, and removed and discarded a few parts which were, I supposed, extraneous.

I avoided any kind of pep talk about how you can do anything if you set your mind to it. If success just took determination, there would have been a lot fewer washouts as the Academy. I just asked, "That's valuable on its own?"

"Would I *frarg* slice up my *krel va* one good hand if it wasn't?" She stood, then bent over to lift it, and cursed again. I tried. It was lighter than it looked, weighing about 20 pounds, and humming slightly. It was easy to transfer it to Dureen, balancing it on her right shoulder.

S'zana had quietly observed this entire process. "Your tools are unusual relics."

We were all walking towards the gear I'd stocked. Dureen nodded. "Yes. Whole *klar* set of them. Bond gift from those before me."

"Did you travel here to meet the mreech? Or are you going further?"

"Ah, *frarg ka vral*. I can't take this *krelf* any longer. I have no *drazk* idea where I am compared to where I was. When R'yan pulled that *sreg* about being from the western shore of the World's Wound, I knew I was far from home, 'cause where I'm from, someone who doesn't want to talk about where they come from says he's from beyond the e*astern* shore. I left seven, maybe eight *drazg* days ago. No place anything like here is seven or eight days away."

"How did you..."

"Look. You got two *frarg* choices. You take me at my *kla vrag* word I don't know how I got here, or you can decide I *do* know but I've got my own *frarg* reasons to not talk about it."

I started splitting the supplies between S'zana and myself. Dureen insisted she carry both her share and the engine block. It took a little rigging, but we managed it. S'zana picked up the conversation.

"The Klurish League is south and east of here. The mreech trade at the fringes of the League. You could probably join a caravan to there, make it to any port on the River Tendran... hmm, you'd better avoid Murz Ten if you can, it will take some time for things to settle there... then find someone planning to head to the World's Wound. It will be long and risky, but it can be done."

Dureen looked at S'zana with outrage, then her eyes widened and she laughed. "You've never met anyone from Drolg Gor Kra. I thought you were *frarg* insulting me there. But you don't know... ah, *kreg*."

We began walking down towards the wastes. "Go on."

Dureen sighed. "It's a bunch of *fralk krev,* honestly. Old ways, traditions, stupid *drazg*. You two saved me, *and* you're strangers, *and* it was with cost or risk to yourselves. So I have to repay that. I keep you alive when it's sure you would have died without me. Until then, I'm stuck here, wherever *frarg* here is and it's *krel va* going to be *var kleg* for me to be sure I've paid off my debt."

The grey-white plains sparkled in the sun. I was already getting thirsty. "I'm happy to swear to whatever pledge or oath you need in order to call it even." S'zana nodded in assent.

Dureen shook her head resignedly. "Nope. Sorry. *Frarg* tradition, culture, rules, all that *krelf*. I can't do that."

S'zana tried again. "You don't seem to think much of the tradition. I would swear, under Witness, never to speak to anyone of this. No one would know. You'd face no dishonor."

Dureen looked suspiciously as S'zana. "Does that work for you? Do you only care if you get caught?"

"No! I..." she stopped. "I'm sorry. You're right. My work requires a special *kind* of honor, and I often deal with those who have none of *any* kind. I'm more used to those who loudly proclaim the rightness of their ways, and then quietly ignore them, than those who do what they must no matter what. Nothing you've done makes me think you're one of the former type."

Dureen spoke to me. "How about you? Got any *frarg* clever ideas?"

I'd learned quite a while back that the only answer to that question, in all of its many forms, was "Sir! No, Sir!". That's what I went with.

Chapter 8
Hreek

The wastes were dry, flat, and dull. The directions we had were mostly those needed to keep us pointed the right way, checking every so often that a distant mountain or other marker was where it was supposed to be. Near early evening, we saw a large obelisk of black marble, with writing carved in each side. None of us could read Mreech, but this matched with what the Border Walkers had told S'zana. It was heartening enough that we decided it was worth trying the contents of the jug. It had a small copper cup attached by a leather strap, clearly the intended serving size. I'd been carrying the thing, so I decided I deserved the first try.

I'd call it caffeinated, garlic-flavored, moonshine. (The locals called it *skreej*.) The bit of a morale boost we had from reaching the marker was undermined by Dureen's realization she couldn't hold the cup and pour from the jug. She didn't want to ask for help, she didn't want to be offered help, she didn't want to make an obvious excuse about "not wanting anything, thanks". I made the decision, pouring a cup for her and handing it to her. She accepted, drank, handed the cup to S'zana, and poured for her. I'm not sure if it was a statement, a rebuke, or just her people's idea of how to do things. I didn't ask.

Shortly after passing that marker we started to see occasional signs of civilization. At first, I thought they were odd natural formations, then it was clear they were buildings. They were slope-walled structures formed of slabs of the same substance as almost every place else in this region. Their angular asymmetry was attractive.

Night came, and we chose to camp rather than push on in the dark. We made our campsite quite visible, just off one of the markers that were now appearing every few miles. During my watch, a patrol came by. I showed them the marked clay shards Krer had given us as signs of passage, and after a few pointed questions from them and an offering of *skreej* from me, they warily accepted my story, though all three made it clear they thought I was a suspicious type, clearly up to no good, and that they'd be watching me.

Some things are universal.

The land to our south became more jagged, rising in sharp, irregular tiers. Activity was increasing constantly. The marked path became a road, and there was a flow of mreech, on foot, on reptile-back, and in hauled carts and wagons, moving south and back again. We were noticed, of course. Most avoided us. A few waved jovially, unconcerned at how odd we were.

We passed a good-sized cluster of buildings, crowded with green apes in a variety of clothing and styles. Dozens of different stands and stations were set up. If there was a set order in which the locals passed through them, it wasn't obvious to me. Making it clear we'd truly reached civilization, there were also a good number of soldiers walking the perimeter and keeping an eye out for dangerous vagabonds, such as ourselves.

The main substance being handled, exchanged, weighed, and packed was salt. There wasn't much else here to trade.

"The mines are mostly to the south, though there's small outcroppings all over." S'zana explained. "So I've heard. I'd never seen a mreech before we met the Walkers."

"Who works the mines? Slaves, criminals?"

"The mreech don't take slaves. At least, this nation doesn't. 'Unbalancing', Quarrin said, whatever that means. They claim they don't have many criminals. Those few they do have are exiled or killed. When it comes to the mines, almost everyone does some of the work, and this earns them some kind of say in the local politics. I think the oldest are excused from the labor. After you've done enough in your life, you earn a permanent rank or title. I didn't press them for more details. I was more interested in finding out what we might get in trouble for, not in government procedures we won't be here long enough to get involved in. I do plan on learning more when I can. The Listeners will want to know the finer points. It's the kind of lore we collect for future use."

Dureen snorted. "Visit the far side of the World's Wound. Learn *frarg krev* about *grazk* salt, and get your *krel va* hand bit off by a *grek* spider. So, since they don't sell the *frarg* stuff here, what are you two here for, anyway? Long story, fine, so we got anything else to *drazg* talk about?"

I sighed. "You won't believe a lot of it."

"Is it a bigger pile of *krev* than the first one you tried?"

"Yes."

"Now I really want to *frarg* hear it."

S'zana first extracted a Witnessed promise that, in exchange for the tale, Dureen would not speak about it to others. Then I related it all, as the outer borders of Hreek grew more visible. When it was done, we'd reached the city.

Dureen looked at me as if deciding just how mad I was, then spoke to S'zana. "*Frarg*. So, how much of that *krev* do you believe?"

She considered this. "All of it that I've seen, I believe. As for the parts of it I haven't seen, I can't find any explanation that isn't even more unbelievable, and lying isn't one of R'yan's skills."

I decided that was a compliment.

Dureen accepted this. "Heading to the 'Ebon Jungle'. Fine. I've heard of it, or how you describe it. It's called other names, but it sounds like the same *frarg* place."

We reached the outer wall of Hreek. We'd been stopped by four different groups of mreech between when I started telling Dureen my history and now. So, of course, we had to go through it all a fifth time. The mreech who checked our marks did so quickly and casually, and would have waved us through, but another insisted on repeating the work, this time much more thoroughly. The device Dureen had scavenged from the crash got a lot of attention, in particular. After much arguing, it seemed to boil down to an inability to find a law *against* it. When he finally gave up, he directed us to "The Dwelling Of The Lost" -- the closest thing they had to an inn or hotel.

The city was of the same general construction as the outlying buildings. Most of the buildings were crystalline structures following a "flowering" pattern of increasing size. Some others were wood, metal, or a mixture of materials. A host of cultivated gardens, parks, and terraces, so colorful as to seem alien among the shades of white and grey, surrounded buildings or lined the roads. Insects, and things that weren't insects but seemed to do much the same thing, swarmed among the plants. Most of the gardens or displays contained pillars of twisted blue-grey stone which "sweated" liquid. I couldn't tell if they were condensing it from the air, or drawing it up from a deep aquifer.

Crowds, of course. They mostly parted around us. About one mreech in four or five would stare at us, or follow us for a bit, or sometimes offer some inane or irrelevant comment and then ignore our reply. Only a few guards or soldiers kept order inside the city itself.

I whispered to S'zana, "Why are some of them so... strange?"

"The mreech have cycles of mood they go through. Something about how they're born or budded or however they reproduce links groups of them in each cycle, so around a fourth of the population is in the same cycle at the same time. I think each cycle lasts twenty to twenty five days, and it takes only a day or two to shift to a new cycle."

"So, if I meet Cherrik again, he could be almost a different person, depending on when I meet him?"

"Yes. That's a big part of why they don't welcome outsiders. The mreech are used to the cycles. It's normal for them. They find other people's fixed personalities confusing."

The Dwelling Of The Lost was near the eastern edge of the city. There were extensive flower beds around it, leading to equally extensive swarms of things that seemed unsure if we contained nectar but were willing to sample us a few times in order to find out.

The innkeeper (I never did learn a formal title) was surprised to see us. He (the mreech reproduced sexually, sort of. I never learned the actual mechanics of it, and it was a coin toss as to which partner would carry the offspring. I'm using 'he' because it's more convenient than 'he and/or she at the same time but also not really either') was surprised to see *anyone*. He was elderly, his fur fading to the color of dried pine needles. During our stay, fortunately, he was in the cycle that brought with it a genial, outgoing mood, but without the distracted randomness of the 'dreaming' cycle Cherrik was in.

Food consisted of things which could be stored for extended periods. Dried meats, pickled vegetables, some grains that attracted few pests or rot. It wasn't exciting, but there was variety, and none of it was wriggling or interested in eating us first.

Our rooms were basically one large room, separated by curtains mounted on mobile wooden frames that we could arrange at will. Furnishing consisted of folded mats covered with padded cloth, and some simple tables and chairs made from a mix of wood and the crystal slabs that formed so many of the local structures. Spartan, but not uncomfortable, not after days of sleeping on rocks.

The first few days were peaceful. S'zana talked, bargained, and fulfilled her promise of information. The "Drawn Council" was a kind of emergency government randomly selected from those older citizens momentarily in the cycles appropriate to making decisions. They were satisfied with what S'zana told them. Some were angry that the deal was made at all, because Krer and Quarrin were in their "celebration" cycle and hadn't bargained nearly hard enough, but that wasn't grounds to negate the agreement.

Shortly after we'd settled in, Dureen asked me: "So... if the *frarg* seekers are hunting you, why *krel kar* haven't we seen anything, all the *frarg* time I've been with you, or before that, when you and S'zana were *drelg zak* sitting still day after day?" Obviously, she didn't believe at least that part of my story, and I didn't blame her. Would you believe someone who claimed they were being chased by dragons?

It was a good question. The first two times had only been a day apart. Much more time had passed, we had been in one place for many days, but the seekers hadn't appeared. Maybe it *wasn't* me? *Was* it a coincidence? Was this whole "find the Guardians" thing an astounding waste of time?

The fifth day we were in Hreek we got the answer: No.

S'zana spent her time mostly outside the Dwelling. Dureen and I, mindful of the various agreements she'd made in our name, didn't go out much. What we did do was work on the "engine block," what she called a "*tiluvishal*," a word not from her own language.

It was complicated. She had her relic tools, but told me she'd never seen an intact example of this kind of thing before. Combine that with her having to work one-handed (frustrating, slow, and sometimes sending her into periods of seething darkness), trying to give me instructions when she wasn't even sure what instructions to give, and it added up to slow progress. On the other hand, tinkering with engines was something I'd enjoyed for a long time. I wasted a lot of after school hours at my uncle's garage, doing odd jobs, learning how to break down and reassemble almost anything that came in. When my Dad and I tore into each other about my decision to join the Air Force, it didn't just split the two of us; it pretty much cut me off from the entire family, both sides. It got that bad. Sitting in an inn run by a grass-furred gorilla, tinkering with a space-twisting engine I'd stolen from a megalomaniacal lizard-rat is what made me feel a sense of fond nostalgia for my carefree youth.

Dureen's ability to swear like my Uncle Sal added to the atmosphere. Her frequent shifts from "loud and cranky" to "frustrated and bitter" didn't.

On the fourth day of work, we managed to get the block split open, revealing the inner workings. Looking inside it hurt my eyes. It contained a space seemingly impossibly large, far larger than the frame it was contained in. Imagine Yankee Stadium in a shoebox; not *shrunken* into the box, but somehow full size, as if you were flying over it in a helicopter, and yet at the same time all of it in the shoebox. The headache you have now is a hundredth the size of the one I had, seeing the real thing.

A few hours of cursing, fumbling, and mucking about later, Dureen got what she wanted. A yellow and blue striated gem, plucked out of the maze of the inner engine. She extracted a few more jewels of different colors and sizes. We reattached the lid. I tried to get the world back in focus.

"Useful?" I asked.

"No, they're *frarg* garbage. We just spent four *krel va* days getting worthless rocks. Would have been under a day, if... *frarg*. Never mind."

"Fine, it was a dumb question. Better question: What are they good for?"

"Hopefully, some *drazg* merchant in this *vrek* town wants them. These are pretty *klurg* quality, ancient relics of the *frarg* Guardians. Gonna' get *grazk*-all for them, I'm sure, but it's better than nothing."

"I meant, why are they valuable? Do they do anything, outside the engine? Or are they just pretty?"

Dureen looked at gems in her hand, then dropped one, a brilliant sapphire with tiny sparkles of green-gold light floating within it, in my lap. "You ever find another stormfire bow, this'll probably work *drazg* better than whatever *frarg* might be in it already. Those *joziv* stones S'zana says her family carves, they're *klef* versions of these. There are the real thing, the Guardians' own pretty *drazg*. Don't ask me *how* the *klar* they work. They hold stormfire. Just make sure they're not cracked."

"Noted. I've seen what happens."

"And you're still alive," she sighed. "It's going to be a huge *krarg hav kla* saving your life. You're too *frarg* lucky for my own good."

All my bad luck seemed to hit the people around me. That was how I got through life. I charged forward and never looked back to see what was in my wake. Depressing. Time to change the subject.

Based on what I learned from S'zana, general trade here was limited. The whole city was more-or-less a big gorilla commune, with fewer sitars. The majority worked in the mines at least part-time, except the young, old, or injured. Most had secondary jobs. A few did specialized work and got credit for it as if they mined.

"What do you plan to buy *here*?" If Murz Ten had been a street bazaar worthy of Cairo or Tokyo, Hreek was barely a kid's lemonade stand.

"Get someone to make something." She left, which left me alone to think, and it didn't take too long before I started pacing.

I needed something else to do. I'd reached the point here in Hreek where I was getting bored and frustrated as soon as I didn't have something occupying my immediate attention. Yes, there was something calming about the work we'd been doing, but I'd about hit my limit for calm. I'd rested, I'd recovered, and I needed to get back to active duty.

Exercise could distract me for a time. Our allowed travel areas were good enough to run some laps. I'd been healing. Now it was time to start pushing myself to see how far I had to go.

By the fourth circuit I'd attracted some curious onlookers. By the fifth, one mreech was running alongside me, driven on by whatever impulse had seized his mind for the moment. By the seventh, he'd abandoned me to clamber on top of a building and draw lines in the air. At any time, a quarter of the city was like him, I thought, and somehow they still managed to make it work. On my eighth lap, I glanced up to see if he was still there, and then caught sight of something else. A glinting in the sky, a tiny sparkle in the clear air.

I kept glancing at it, trying not to draw anyone else's eyes to follow mine, not breaking my stride or slowing down. In the small space between looking ahead and scanning the sky, S'zana managed to step into my path. I ducked around her as she started to talk, then waved for her to fall in besides me. I didn't feel like stopping; the exercise was needed, I was falling into a familiar rhythm where my body just ran, with my mind simply along for the ride.

"Northeast." I said. "Sky. Sparkling thing. See it?"

"Yes..." She had the same worry I did. "That could be a problem."

"Could be. But they. Seem less panicky. "

"Since I told them about the events in Murz Ten, if the seekers come, they're going to assume the same thing we did. I don't know how they'll react. *Frarg*! I'd just reached an agreement that would help us move onwards!"

I didn't comment on the fact she'd picked up some of Dureen's extensive vocabulary. "Dwelling. Of The Lost. Coming up." The sparkling wasn't noticeably larger yet. "Inside. We'll talk."

Dried, thinly sliced bits of some fruit, along with a sour, scarlet, juice, was what the old mreech operating the place had dug out of the random stockpile maintained for the occasional guests. We returned to the rooms we'd been given and went over what we knew, waiting for any sound from outside that would indicate others had noticed what was coming.

"I think any hope that I'm not connected to these things is gone, not that there was much."

S'zana agreed. "Yes. The first time may be chance, the second time may be coincidence, but the third time..."

"...is enemy action", I interrupted.

She smiled and laughed. "*Delnar ta vril.* So, what now? Fleeing gives us nowhere to go. Waiting means that whatever happens, we will probably be blamed."

I sat there for a few minutes, bouncing from one useless answer to another, growing more frustrated. S'zana's slowly tapping fingers and fixed expression showed her mind was working through the same circles mine was, but with more external calm. I cracked first, slamming my fist against the crystal tabletop. "To hell with this. If they're looking for me, I'm going to find some way to make sure they can't ignore me." I left, ignoring the stairs to the lower level. Instead, I headed for a window, reached up, grabbed onto the rough edges of the slanted stones, and pulled myself to the top of the frame, then on to the flat roof. The glistening in the sky was closer, taking on a familiar shape. Some below seemed to notice either it or me.

S'zana's voice came from the window below. "R'yan! What are you planning?"

"I don't know! Something!" Admittedly, that sounded stupid. It was stupid. I was raging against an unknown enemy, full of an impulse to *act* but with no idea what action to take.

She uttered a sound of pure annoyance. A moment later, I saw her on the street, running. She headed directly for a group of mreech, got their attention, gestured at the sky, at me, and was clearly arguing with them over something. Others were drawn to the debate, and this spread. The few soldiers in the city started to take up positions.

From my vantage point, I saw a part of Hreek I hadn't noticed before, that no one bothered mentioning to me. About a half mile from the western wall of the city was something very like a series of piers and warehouses. Roads ran to and from the city. I could see some traffic along them, beasts bearing cargo back and forth. Next to two of the piers were ships, sails furled. They were identical in design: Two masts and catamaran-like outriggers on either side.

The only thing missing was any kind of *liquid*. The entire structure -- apparently still quite active and used -- was set directly on the shore of nothing but a vast, white, expanse of *not water*.

Increased noise from the city below drew my attention back to the sky. The seeker was clearly visible now. Soldiers had their bows ready, but held their fire. S'zana was still rushing from group to group, sometimes shouting, sometimes imploring. Whatever message she was sending seemed to be getting around.

The seeker drifted through the city. Its beam played across the mreech, lining each with golden fire and passing on. Maybe, if no one did anything foolish, it would just leave Hreek in peace.

It slowed down when it drew within fifteen feet of the roof. Its beam passed over me, and again I was invisible to it. For all my determination to make it notice me, no brilliant idea exploded in my mind. I tried to keep myself calm. If it was going to move along harmlessly, then let it. If the mreech could keep from attacking it...

It stopped where it was, hovering over a street near the Dwelling. A violet light flicked on from its "belly" and shone downwards. That was new.

"New" was probably "bad." The mreech seemed to agree. Whatever S'zana had been trying to tell them, they'd decided not to listen. Disorder, dissent, and desperation rose and spread through the crowds below.

Beneath the seeker, where the beam touched the land, something was forming. Either the beam was pulling the ground upwards, or it was creating a structure out of the air. "How" seemed less important than "what" and "why." A column of multicolored shards of stone took shape, growing upwards and outwards, pulsing with energy. Static crackled through the air. A spark snapped against my hand when it brushed near the hilt of my sword.

One mreech ambled curiously towards the column, ignoring the increasing discharge of power. He reached forward, screamed, and pulled back, clutching at a charred arm. The scream acted as a signal to everyone else, shattering their indecision. Archers fired, choosing targets at will -- the column, the seeker, me.

The seeker and the column ignored their attacks. I dodged back and crouched. Unperturbed, the seeker continued its work, rotating slowly in place, gradually altering the width, color, and angle of the beam, shaping the growing structure beneath it. I didn't know what it was making, or what it would do when it was done. I did know I didn't want to find out.

It was "facing" me now, the central lens clearly visible: A ruby with a thousand facets, set into a circular frame. The crimson eyeball hung suspended by nothing, rotating freely inside a socket of silver metal.

More arrows clattered uselessly against the seeker's armor.

S'zana was still arguing with the crowd below. Rather than actively running from group to group, she was now holding her ground, as the small clusters of mreech converged around her and merged into a crowd that was well on its way to becoming a mob. None had drawn weapons on her yet, but that couldn't last. *Delnar ta vril.* Eventually, someone would give up on attacking what they couldn't hurt, and focus on the strangers who'd brought this thing to their city. That they hadn't done so yet (other than a few arrows shot my way so half-heartedly I couldn't be sure they weren't just badly aimed) was almost more amazing than anything else I'd encountered.

The seeker rotated in place again, turning the scarlet eye away from what I knew had to be its objective -- me.

I jogged back to the other side of the roof, ran forward, reached the edge nearest the seeker, and *leapt.*

Impact.

The upper surface was smooth, but not frictionless. There were small protrusions and ridges I could use to get a grip. Splayed on top, like a desperate monkey clinging to the back of a flying metal tortoise, I pulled myself towards the front, towards the eye.

It didn't react to me as I inched along. When I made it to the forward edge of the upper dome, I reached into my pocket and pulled out the gem. I studied it for a moment, noticing how its sparkling came from both refracting the outer light, and from the swirling lightning trapped within it. I smashed it against the metal skin as hard as I could, wondering what the line between "too hard" and "not hard enough" might be, and if I'd live to find out.

Fractures appeared along the sapphire facets. Almost like a liquid, the energy within the gem seeped out and flowed around its outer surface, flaring and forking.

I had probably no more than a few seconds to complete my plan, reciting it in my head as I acted.

Reach forward, down, around. Force the crystal into the space between the ruby lens and the socket in which it floated. Then roll -- slide off the metal surface, try to get my feet under me before I hit the ground, call back training in how to fall, how to land, how to not end up screaming with bones sticking through my skin...

I hadn't quite hit the ground yet, then...

Explosion. Too near. My hearing went. Flashes of fire and sound, of lightning and thunder. A summer shower, brief but intense, of metal rain, changing to blizzards of crystal flakes as the tower disintegrated. Then, a thousand voices, heard from a great distance. S'zana next to me, helping me up, her voice lost in the silence. Dureen, dimly seen at the edge of my vision, bashing through the crowds, heedless of who she was knocking aside.

Whatever the seeker had been creating, all that was left was a charred black stump that crumbled to ash as I watched.

Chapter 9
Across The Solid Sea

The next few hours blurred. S'zana did most of the talking. However little S'zana knew about local traditions and politics, it was more than Dureen or me. Periodic status reports kept us informed. A quarter of them wanted us dead; a quarter wanted to make a deal; a quarter were spinning the conversation into a hundred random tangents, and a quarter wanted to either get back to work or to analyze the situation further. A Drawn Council was formed quickly, and more words were exchanged. S'zana kept hammering on the deal she'd made with Krer and Quarrin. I considered it like trying to hold up a bargain a POW had made with two corporals as binding on the President, but the mreech seemed to be considering it. "Unbalanced" was the word S'zana reported they kept using. There had to be balance. Things had to be restored to their natural and proper way.

Dureen and I were waiting in the Dwelling. A good number of mreech, all in the cycle that kept them locked onto their task, were stationed around us. This cycle also made them extremely touchy if drawn away from their duty, so we didn't try to talk with them too much. They stood there, green and implacable, while we chatted in delnar. They probably understood us; it seemed everyone spoke it, or some variant of it.

Dureen was optimistic. "If they *frarg* decide to *grazg* your *grach*, there's no way you'd win. Not even you, Kruzvahko," (Dureen had, over the past few days, started calling me that. The direct meaning was 'fortunate stumbler,' a "Tall Tales" character from Dureen's childhood, but the more meaningful translation would be "lucky bastard".

I'd been called worse.

"And with my death near-certain, you could claim to be saving my life, or dying in the attempt."

"Yup. Rather not *frarg* die, but the way *krelf* happens around you, it's going to be *drazg* doing enough to save you without getting killed. Even if I weren't..." She looked at the bandages on her left arm, went quiet for a moment. Then she chuckled humorlessly.

"Ya know, I told Sarell a dozen times that if it *frarg* came to it, I could *grazg* beat her in anything one-handed. Might not get a chance to prove it."

Her right arm moved towards her left and she cursed softly. "Kruzvahko. Do me a *frarg* favor. Touch the blue beaded strand, the one with the ovals." She held out her right arm, bearing her bracelet. I did as she asked. "Sarell," she said, then pulled her arm back.

"Stupid *frarg* tradition," she muttered.

"What is?"

"You mention one of your spouses, you touch their strand, so they know you're thinkin' of them." She smiled wryly. "Either none of 'em have *frarg* talked about me in days, or it's *krelf* nonsense."

There were a lot of strands on the bracelet. "How many people are you married to?"

"Four wives, five husbands. Just before I left home the last time, Grezak told us he'd met someone we were supposed to meet. Probably *frarg* happened by now. Hope they don't hold out for my say on it. How about you? How many?"

I wasn't sure I'd followed her line of thought. "How many people am I married to?"

She nodded.

"Uhm... none."

She seemed a little confused by that. "You're a *frarg* adult, right? I mean, however you people make your *krel va* soft-skinned hairless stretched-out babies, you can do your bit?"

"Yes...," I replied, trying not to be too insulted.

She mulled this over a second, then continued: "So, are you ugly? A criminal?"

"No!" She wasn't making the "not be insulted" part easy.

"Then what's your *frarg* problem? You fight well, you're some kind of *klem va* officer in your Sky Army, so if you're not lying about how ugly you are, someone should've snapped you up by now."

"We do things differently." I really didn't want to give a lecture on the quaint mating rituals of Male, Human, American, one each, especially after a few days of *not* having to fight full time for raw survival had let me remember there were needs that may be less immediate, but just as vital.

Fortunately, a ruckus outside ended the interrogation. If it had been the formation of a lynch mob, it still would still have been a relief.

S'zana entered, flanked by two very serious looking mreech, their green, apelike faces set in hard scowls. They wore hard leather armor and helmets, and held spears tipped with *joziv*. Brightly colored sashes crossed their chests.

"I've managed to restore the original bargain I'd made. Barely. We need to go *now*, and we have to leave behind what's left of the *tiluvishal*."

I stood and gathered what I had, which was the grazarn sword, the word-finder, a knife and pouch we'd found in the ship's hold, and that was about it, other than my jumpsuit (Days earlier, we'd bargained for some reasonably fitting local clothing, which allowed me to clean my other gear). Mostly done, I asked, "What was the original bargain?"

"We were interrupted before I could tell you. The mreech trade to the north, too, to lands I've never heard of. It's a dangerous trip. The mreech of Cal-Hreek dislike fighting. They consider it unbalancing, though they do it when they must, to restore the balance. I volunteered our services as guards in return for passage as far north as they sail."

Well, that explained the docks and the boats, if not the lack of water.

Dureen was nonplussed. More than usual. "Hey! *Frarg* right now?"

S'zana nodded, while making 'hurry up' gestures. "Yes. They really don't want us around. Do you blame them?"

Dureen stopped moving. "Don't care. I traded a *klem va ilinash* for some work I needed done. I'm not leaving without it."

S'zana's voice remained calm and precise, though I saw a few hints of frustration in her body language. "That has been dealt with. The smith was very insistent that he finish his work, because he already had the *ilinash*, and the balance would be upset otherwise. It was discussed at length." I got the distinct impression from S'zana's tone that she would have been happier without that addition to the bargaining. She continued: "The first one is made, and it's on our ship. If we make it back, and if I can promise the seekers won't follow us, you can claim the others. "

Dureen was not happy with this outcome, but pragmatism beat out rage. "*Frarg.* Let's go. I'm tired of this *drazg*."

We were escorted to the docks.

It was dark now, and a cold dry wind, laden with slicing dust, blew from the docks. Torches set far apart along the main road provided a dim light, casting long, flickering shadows across the smooth white plain.

The docks had more extensive lighting, extending my vision. Lines of marker stones, fifteen feet apart and about a foot high, formed a clear line demarcating nothing obvious. White and grey rock and sand on one side, the same on the other. Mostly. The boulders and outcroppings faded out quickly, leaving nothing but a flat expanse.

Our ship was tall and narrow, with a thin, iron-sheathed bottom. It clearly rested on the stone, not in it. Twin outriggers, also terminating in iron blades, kept it standing. The masts were complex. I was not an expert on sailing ships, but while the basic design looked normal, there were details of it I didn't understand. I figured I'd learn if I had to.

"Do either of you know how this *works?*" I asked.

Both shook their heads.

It was named *Sails To Far Shores*, and it was under the command of Balancer Yeeak Of The Seventh Rising, a mreech of middling years. The left side of his face and much of that shoulder and arm were furless, or grassless. Covering the exposed skin was a black fungus that occasionally puffed clouds of spores into the air, and leaked a thin, oily liquid with a sulfurous odor. Yeeak wore a uniform of black and tan cloth, minimally decorated, and I never saw him without a heavy, curved, cutlass-like weapon strapped to his waist.

He looked at the three of us with cold contemplation. "You placed great weight on Hreek. I am charged with bearing you off, to restore balance. I accept that charge. Know that on this craft, I am the Balancer. I will decide all things. The balance is mine to measure, the balance is mine to keep."

Our guards departed. Yeeak immediately shouted commands, and the crew, perhaps twenty in all, obeyed.

Observation: Having four functional hands is especially useful on a ship. Recommendation: Get the Secretary of the Navy to look into it.

Sails unfurled. A slight vibration passed through the ship, and the wind against our faces picked up. Looking back, I saw the dock starting to move away. The three of us strode to the railing and looked down.

In the flickering light of the ship's lanterns, we could see well enough. The left blade had passed into the smooth surface, sliding in only an inch or two, but clearly embedded. It left no trail behind -- it wasn't cutting into it like a skate, but sliding through it, the same way the stones in the word-finder slid, or the controls of the ship we'd stolen. As my eyes adjusted to the light, I saw strange shadows below the ship. At first, I thought we were passing over embedded boulders or differently colored patches of rock. Slowly, awareness arrived: The shadows moved on their own. Fish, or something like them, swam through the translucent white substance of the sea.

One of the sailors perched on the rail next to me. "I like looking down," he said.

"What are they?" I pointed to a pattern of shadows that darted under the ship, then back out.

"Fish that swim in the Solid Sea." He pondered the question more, then announced, "I wonder what they call us? We have a name for them, so, they must have a name for us. Unbalanced otherwise." He looked over at me. "You're the one who brought the *treakk churr*. How do you call one to you?"

"I don't."

"Oh." He seemed disappointed. A moment later, he bounded down the rail and scampered up some ropes, where he adjusted the sails with what appeared to be competence.

Balancer Yeeak had completed two circuits of the ship, making sure everyone was doing what they were supposed to do. "You three. You are here to battle, but unless we have enemies, you have other work."

I spoke. "It would be unbalancing to have some work and others not, right?"

Yeeak nodded and smiled. "Exactly."

When not on a duty shift, we all shared a small area in the hold, separate from the mreech. Hiring foreigners as mercenaries was somewhat common, we learned, though usually they were hired from the northern nations and were rarely seen as far south as Hreek.

Dureen's purchase was a cap for her arm, a metal sheath of iron, leather, and bronze that she could strap on over the scarred stump. It ended in a sharp blade.

"This *frarg klef* happens a bit in Drolg Gor Kra. I've seen how people deal, described it to the crafters in Hreek. Paid for a *klar* more than one of them, but we had to go *frarg* running off. They better have them ready when I get back, or there's going to be some *drel grazk* unbalancing going on."

I didn't comment on "when" being a lot more optimistic than "if", in terms of getting back.

One of my jobs was applying a fresh coat of a lacquer to the parts of the ship where the raw wood had been exposed, thanks to the constant spray of skin-scraping dust. It was every bit as tedious as it sounds. We did minor repairs, we helped with tangled ropes, we patched sails, we learned how to repeat working chants without ever learning the meaning of the words. I assume they were raunchy, for whatever counted as raunchy to a half-vegetable.

Balancer Yeeak began to warm to us, somewhat. He was used to dealing with non-mreech, and once he was certain seekers would not just swoop down and attack, he became... not friendly, but more willing to think of us as part of his ship's own balance, not a source of imbalance he would have to constantly compensate for.

He was one of the few from Hreek who never worked in the mines. The mreech had a word that meant "the single-passioned," a rare few who were so dedicated to a job that changing work as the community needed was hard for them. Yeeak had first been called to work on this ship when he was "barely sprouted," and he had never left it for long. "Planted seeds in a dozen ports along this Solid Sea," he told us, "Never saw them bloom. Three I saw blossom here, on these decks, but they were drawn to the mines and the land."

Days passed. Once I thought I saw the silver gleam of a seeker in the distant sky, but it never drew close and vanished quickly, so I concluded it wasn't a seeker or hadn't found me.

There were other moments of interest. Islands of pale blue, green, or aqua crystal, ranging from about the size of a shed to one over a mile long, appeared occasionally. Once, a sub-surface shadow at least the length of *Sails To Far Shores* was spotted following us. Yeeak ordered a series of desperate maneuvers to avoid it.

The lookouts spent little time watching the sea, though. They watched the sky. That, we were told, is where the enemies came from.

The navigation device Yeeak used was a cross between a compass and a mariner's astrolabe, with the addition of an abacus and long lists of calculations and observations stored on scrolls which could be unrolled to specific points marked on their edges, said points determined by other readings. There were no planets in their night sky, and the stars drifted over time as the world moved, slowly enough that generations of navigators had determined angles and offsets and worked forward, year by year, to know where a star should be at a given time. (This told me the world followed a straight path through space. Did the path bend slightly as it went past the gravity of a star? Could it draw near enough to a star to be pulled into an orbit? Questions without answers.) The more distant the star, the less it moved, relatively. Standing on one leg, Yeeak turned and adjusted three controls simultaneously on his tools to get the correct bearings. I didn't envy this world's two-handed navigators.

One day, after doing a noontime check of the ship's heading and location, he called us from our jobs.

"Two days, perhaps three, until we reach the Edge Of Flight. That's when things will become truly dangerous. We..."

He stopped as a loud cry came from the crow's nest. Looking upwards, Yeeak said something in mreech which needed no translation.

Expecting a seeker, I followed his gaze. It wasn't a seeker. It was something dark and bulbous, distant, but moving slowly towards us across the sky.

Hastily, he pawed, and sometimes footed, through his navigation documents, muttered in mreech, then turned to us. "This has never been. They've never come this far southwest. I know I'm right, we are where we must be, but they are not!"

"Unbalanced!", he shouted in frustration, telling the universe that it had got things wrong.

I watched the approaching thing in the sky. "Who is attacking us, anyway?"

"The Concord of Yerritt. They hope to convince us to trade them our goods not for anything we need, but for safe passage alone. Those of Kreak-Fa," he spit," has claimed they see balance in doing this, but we of Cal-Hreek do not."

He drew his cutlass and began issuing orders to the crew, then focused on the three of us. "Show me the weight I lifted from Hreek will bring balance here!"

Green furry gorilla or not, I saw a commander preparing to lead his men into battle, and I reacted the way I'd been trained. I snapped to attention and saluted. "Yes, Sir!"

S'zana and Dureen, both warriors in their own right, though from less formal traditions, looked at me like I was even crazier than they'd already concluded. They took up battle stances just the same.

Yeeak continued. "We'll take shelter until they land. They have the advantage in the sky, but they can't steal what they can't grab! Once they reach our deck, we fight back!"

We moved to positions shielded from the sky, mostly on the lower deck. There were small slits in the planking that could be used as viewports from below. Others jumped over the side of the ship opposite to the direction the raiders approached from, easily clinging with multiple limbs, able to leap back to the deck.

I heard a thunking of arrows into the wood. The attackers weren't aiming at anyone, that I could tell, just using suppressing fire so that we couldn't strike at their people. I guessed the thing I'd seen was a flying ship, though it wasn't shaped like any craft I'd seen on Earth or here. Who or what was piloting it? If it landed next to us, perhaps we could seize it.

I risked a glance through a gap in the deck above me. It would be particularly ridiculous to die from a lucky arrow shot -- I didn't much trust in Dureen's name for me -- but I had to see what I'd be facing.

A swarm of giant birds had descended from the flying ship. No, not a ship. It was a living thing, the size of a jetliner, red-orange, with hundreds of waving tentacles. Call it the offspring of a jellyfish and a blimp. The birds weren't birds. They were obviously artificial, very similar to the earliest airplanes: A two-man crew, the craft itself having a light body formed from canvas stretched over a frame. No obvious propellers, no engine noise, and lift and thrust provided by single set of flapping wings.

I'd seen all the math and all the physics and knew how ridiculous it was to make a plane that could fly like a bird. I then considered my companions and my situation and decided not to worry about it.

The pilots looked... well, at first glance, they looked to be delnar. I mentioned this to S'zana. "Will this be a problem? Fighting your own people?"

"They're of my people, maybe, but not from my land or any land near mine. Certainly, they are no one we have treaties with. You've said that in your land, you have only one kind of people?"

I nodded.

"And you're a soldier. You fight, and kill, your own people, if they're not of your land, when it's your duty to do so. Why should we be different? This isn't a war between peoples, it's between lands, and it's over wealth, not survival. The attackers are warriors who enter the battle knowing the cost. I'd rather do my fighting from the shadows, but if I have to fight in the light, I'm not going to hold back because my enemy looks more like me than they look like the people I swore, under Witness by the Guardians, to defend."

"You *frarg* talk too *ka vral* much. Get out there and get in serious *grazk* trouble so I can save you already! I got a *frarg* family to get back to!"

The bird-planes... ornithopters was the right word, I guess... were landing. The clatter of arrows stopped.

With an assortment of war cries, screeches, and howls the mreech charged to defend their cargo. We joined in.

The attackers wore leather armor reinforced with wooden slats. They had helmets of similar design, some crested with brilliant feathers or strips of snakeskin covered with colorful, geometric patterns. Others had belts and gauntlets of smooth hide, painted in mad, colorful, designs. They used slashing, single-edged blades, similar to cavalry sabers. Judging from facial structures, there were a mix of men and women among them, but it was hard to be certain at that point. Their armor hid any other distinctions.

As spotted a shadow, too thin to be a mreech, lurking as I ascended the stairs onto the deck. Someone was on the roof of the deckhouse above the stairs. I ducked low as I came out, and the Yerritti pirate overreached himself, tumbling to the ground. I dispatched him quickly, then moved away, trying to take in the battle as a whole while maintaining situational awareness.

The ornithopters were not on the ship. They circled above, artificial vultures. Each had deposited one raider, then retreated. Next time, I thought, I'll talk with Balancer Yeeak about striking at their landing craft as soon as they get within range. There must be some way to target them without exposing ourselves. The Yerritti warriors were likely much more expendable than their planes, and it could make raiding much too costly if the planes went first. If there was a next time...

Following the flow of battle, I saw instantly why the mreech needed mercenaries. They fought randomly, with no coordination between them. Some fought with surprising viciousness, while others exerted only the effort needed to defend themselves. I saw one so intent on a single enemy that he ignored the multiple wounds he took from others. He could have avoided being surrounded if he'd backed off just a bit, but his focus didn't let him, and he went down. His foes cheered, then scattered to find other targets.

Yeeak was a whirling green fury. Maybe it was his "cycle", maybe it was his status as a "single-passioned", but he was very unlike his fellow mreech in this. He leapt across his enemies, pirouetting on one's head in a handstand, tossing his cutlass from hand to foot to hand and slashing with consummate skill. He had only one weapon, but it seemed as if he had four, one in each limb. If I could have sat back and just watched him fight, it would have been a worthy spectacle.

I didn't have that option.

The raiders had slightly more discipline as the mreech, but far more savagery. They slashed wildly, with little thought to defense or positioning. If anything, they seemed to be showing off for their companions. (Some were quite good, I had to admit, but none could match Yeeak.) I took down two more before the rest noticed the battle was more serious than they'd expected.

Dureen lacked reach, and half an arm, but she was still terrifying in combat. She was using her axe for her attacking blows, easily cutting through the Yerritti armor. She was still getting used to the prosthetic blade, and found it more useful for parrying than attacking. Mostly. I saw her hack at one foe's knees, and, as he fell forward, she swung her arm up and across his throat. I think he was dead before his head hit the deck.

It seemed she was quite used to fighting enemies almost twice her height, and using their unfamiliarity with fighting her to great advantage.

S'zana had her own fighting style, one I was becoming used to and learning to work with. She flowed from place to place, moving through a dance, taking whatever opportunity presented itself to make an attack before getting out of the way of the response, all as part of a single, seamless motion. She kept me in sight, and we worked together. She would attack a limb, cutting deeply, drawing attention to her, then I would take a full swing, putting all my strength into the blow, while my target was distracted and couldn't take advantage of my lack of defense. Then we'd switch off, with me keeping an enemy focused on parrying and trying to break my guard, while she moved in for a lethal strike.

Three loud, blaring trumpet calls came from the ship above. The circling vultures broke formation and began to retreat, flying away and outwards from our ship as they ascended upwards. The remaining Yerritti screamed and howled and raged at the fleeing craft. Evidently, this wasn't the usual plan. There was no attempt at retrieval; they were being abandoned.

Yeeak shouted above their protests. He spoke in delnar, but with a thick accent -- the dialect of Yerritt. After a few sentences, I started to get the essence of the translation. "You give up. Weapons, down. Treated with law of north lands on Solid Sea. Balanced. Otherwise, death. Choose with speed."

They looked around, saw the odds. No one wanted to be the first to surrender, but no one wanted to be the first to die. Finally, one tossed his sword onto the deck and placed his hands outwards, palm up. The rest moved to do the same.

Then the arrows came.

Not from the mreech, though they had bows drawn and ready if the Yerritti decided to go down fighting. The arrows came from above, striking the surrendering Yerritti and the mreech equally.

Chaos erupted. Some of the Yerritti who hadn't yet dropped their weapons, and had been missed by the original volley, attacked the mreech, perhaps not realizing who had attacked them. Others ran for cover, which got a response from the mreech. The archers couldn't decide who to aim at -- the Yerritti on the deck, or the flying creature above. (The attacks were coming from a wooden gallery hanging below the thing's belly. It looked as if was fused with the flesh somehow. I couldn't see any straps or ties.)

The casualties we were taking meant that if we retreated below, they could land a second wave, and then there'd be little hope of winning. If we stayed above, we'd just be picked off one by one. Their advantage was overwhelming.

Time to deprive them of it, or at least try.

A mreech lay dead next to me. I grabbed his bow and a few arrows. If I was right about how the "carrier" flew...

I moved next to one of the ship's lanterns, dipped an arrow in the flaming oil, and fired it upwards, aiming away from the gallery, towards the main body of the sky creature. It still hit on the bottom half, and bounced off harmlessly. Maybe, I thought, it's more heavily muscled on the underside. All those waving tentacles have to attach to something.

A perfect shot would have been from high above the thing, but none of the ornithopters were conveniently in reach.

S'zana caught my eye. Her expression said, quite clearly, "What the hell are you doing?"

I had to answer in words. "Just hold them off!"

She shook her head in disbelief, but did as I requested, focusing on those who tried to move towards me. I could hear her mumbling, as she intended me to hear it. "Insane or idiot or both..." There was no rancor in her voice, though.

I'd gotten off two more shots during all this, getting the range, getting a better feel for the pull of the bow and the quality of the arrows. Neither hit, but neither was expected to.

This time, I took more careful aim. I knew I needed to hit above the ring of tentacles, where I hoped the outer skin thinned enough to penetrate.

Clean miss.

I couldn't keep ignoring the fight going on around me, but I had a belief... a hope, really... that I could end the battle early.

Last shot.

It hit.

Nothing happened.

I sighed, let the bow drop to the deck, reached for my sword...

Then *everything* happened. The sky brightened as roiling orange flame erupted across the creature's skin. It took seconds for it to ignite completely, and then it began crashing downwards.

"Oh, the delnariti..." I mumbled as softly as I could.

Any fight left in the Yerritti left them. Some tried to surrender again. Others just stood there stunned, letting themselves be disarmed, or in some cases killed by attacks the mreech had begun before they realized their enemy had stopped fighting.

The few ornithopters lucky enough to be last on the list for landing clearance flapped away. Given that they'd had to bring their career in dangerously close, I guessed they were short range. If there was no base very nearby, the pilots were flying to their deaths. Did they assume the mreech tortured or killed prisoners? Hmm. *Did* the mreech torture or kill prisoners?

I realized I was gasping for air. I'd taken many cuts and scrapes -- and there was no poison dulling the pain now, just the normal rush of combat, rapidly wearing off. Allies and enemies were scattered around me. Some dead, some dying, some trying to figure out which category they were in. Dureen, as I watched, delivered a powerful kick to one of the Yerritti who was a bit slow in removing all of his weapons. His reaction to the attack told me some anatomical traits are shared.

S'zana... I didn't see her among the standing. I had a moment of panic. I'd been intent on taking down the flyer. She'd put all of her effort into guarding me, and I had assumed she was doing well because I wasn't being attacked. If she'd been overwhelmed while I wasn't paying attention...

Before I could finish that thought, she climbed up from the lower deck. She was as cut, scraped, and bruised as myself, and just as tired. "It seemed wise to make a quick survey of the lower decks. The last thing we need is to head below and find an ambusher, waiting to take vengeance when they can, killing as many as possible until they're stopped." She grinned ferally. "It's a common tactic used by the desperate and determined."

I smiled back. "Such as yourself."

"I didn't say that it was wrong, merely that I didn't want to be on the receiving end." She looked appraisingly at me. "You live for this sort of thing, don't you? Taking risks. Pushing yourself. Fighting someone worth fighting."

"Mostly. I'd say, 'Fighting for something worth fighting for'. Alright, both. So? I've seen you fight. You're the same way. You have a gift, you know it, and you enjoy using it."

"To repeat myself: I didn't say that it was wrong."

I'm not sure, at this point, which of us moved first, or if it was simultaneous. We had been a few feet apart, and then, we were together, holding each other, embracing. It may have lasted a few seconds, or a minute, I certainly wasn't keeping track of time. For the first time in weeks, I let go of alertness while I was still conscious, giving myself up to a tangle of sensations. The feeling of her hair, almost like flexible glass. The skin along the back of her neck, smooth and cool as polished marble, but flexible and alive. Her hands grasping at my back, then one roaming up to travel through my hair, tracing the outline of my ear and down along my cheek and then neck and shoulders, the tip of one nail drawing a thin line along nerve and muscle, pressing on my skin just hard enough to invoke passion, not pain. The defensive lines of mental resolve I'd constructed were overrun, the barbarian hordes of emotion running unopposed across the placid and defenseless fields of reason.

We finally pulled apart, a little, our faces still only an inch or two apart, our arms still wrapped around each other. I had a conviction that I had to say *something*, and that my future here, or at least my future with S'zana, was going to depend on it not being incredibly stupid. Naturally, my mind was completely and utterly blank.

If I thought she would have accepted, I would have told Dureen her debt to me was paid in full when she broke the silence and saved me from having to do so. In a voice they could probably have heard back in Hreek, she said, "Hey! It *frarg* looks like I'll be real *grazk* busy helping repair the *drakzig* damage up here, so I guess I won't be back in our cabin for a *long time*. Maybe you two should go *inspect it* or something."

Our cabin did get a very thorough inspection. Any details beyond that are on a need to know basis, and no one reading this has any need to know.

The voyage continued. If the mreech noticed any change in how S'zana and I were acting, they said nothing. I think Balancer Yeeak was the only one who had enough experience with other peoples to do so, and he seemed to think it was none of his business. Dureen, naturally, rarely missed an opportunity to make some sort of inappropriate comment, many of which were ruined for me by overly-literal translation.

I did learn a few things. First, most of the concerns, issues, and thoughts I'd been having involving S'zana were mutual. She too had been wondering about taboos, about what might give offense, and so on -- perhaps more than I was, since a lot of her training had involved learning how ignoring subtle differences between one culture and another could lead to grave insult, or to breaking her cover. Second, she'd been holding back a lot of the same needs and desires in the name of professionalism as I had been, and was very enthusiastic about finally being able to express them.

Third, she really didn't want any discussion about what might, possibly, happen if we both somehow survived, solved the problem with the seekers, and went on to live happily ever after. If I tried to walk any conversation in that direction, she led it away -- something she was professionally good at doing. Pushing at the topic was not going to do any good, and I decided that given the long odds ahead of us, I'd wait until we had *actually* both survived before really thinking too much about what might happen after. Another complex problem tossed in a shoebox and shoved under the bed to be forgotten about.

It had always worked for me so far, depending on how you defined "worked."

Sails To Far Shores had a long and complex route. The nations on the eastern shore of the Solid Sea didn't have the equivalent of the Klurish League. There were no main ports that served to sell bulk goods to many buyers. While any city on the route might have taken all that the mreech had to offer, none offered everything the mreech needed, and so, many stops would be necessary, trading here for one thing, there for another.

The first port was a town called Roan Spenstar. "Town" may be an exaggeration; it was mostly some docks and warehouses and guard posts, lacking even the kinds of places you'd expect sailors to patronize when they got a moment on shore. The locals were hard-shelled beings a bit like lobster-centaurs. According to Balancer Yeeak, they had a fairly extensive kingdom stretching back from the shore. They offered sacks filled with long green rice, barrels of chopped blue alligators in brine, and finely carved amber gems. S'zana, Dureen, and I spent a long, dull, night standing near Balancer Yeeak while he haggled and bargained, none of us understanding a word of the conversation.

Going north didn't seem to affect the temperature as I'd expected. Conversations with S'zana, Dureen, and Balancer Yeeak, all of whom knew something about large areas of the world that the others did not, taught me that the temperatures didn't change along the north/south axis, but were instead based on distances from a few areas of extreme geological activity. Not quite volcano belts, but rifts that poured heat out into the world. The Scour, cutting through the World's Wound, was one of them, and everything bordering that ocean, which stretched pole to pole, was lushly tropical. Another, much smaller, rift was northwest of Cal-Hreek, but we were sailing towards it, and the heat was increasing.

The plan was to leave us at the nation closest to the Ebon Jungle, and then let us make our own way there. While sailing to the jungle's borders was possible, Balancer Yeeak was not about to do so. On his maps, the narrow offshoot of the Solid Sea which reached farthest north was labeled "The Fool's Passage". Our route cut across the mouth of it, but not into it.

When *Sails* reached that point in its journey, the storm started.

There had been storms earlier in the voyage. Balancer Yeeak and the crew handled them expertly, and cast out empty barrels, on a line, to catch as much water as possible, then hauled them in when the rain ended. The water otherwise sank into whatever the Solid Sea was made of without leaving anything on the surface.

This storm was different. It came on us suddenly, with none of the signs the crew normally looked out for. It brought wind that drove the rain so hard that crossing the deck was like walking through the sandstorm. Lightning struck all around us, some bolts close enough that when the flash blindness cleared, we looked out at the surface of the sea and saw twisting paths where the substance of it had boiled and refrozen, like streak of foam turned to stone.

Even with the sails struck, the ship was pummeled and shoved by the powerful winds. *Sails To Far Shores* careened out of control.

Balancer Yeeak shouted orders, commanding all hands to get below. Most complied quickly. One of the crew, trying to finish tying down the sails, got caught up in the winds and was carried off, a desperate effort to hold onto the rail lasting barely seconds. His screams as he was dropped back to the sea, then slid out of control across the nearly frictionless surface were lost under the far louder screams of the wind. I started to move towards where he'd been working, intending to finish the job, when Yeeak grabbed me and almost threw me through the door leading to the lower deck, then followed after, slamming the door behind him.

"You're very good to have around," he told me. "You've been keeping things balanced, no doubt, but when I give a command, it's to be obeyed. Nothing is more unbalancing here than not listening to me. Is that clear?"

I nodded. Yeeak had moved into the "dreaming" mood of easy distraction and random inspiration between the raiders attack and our first few trade stops, and was now in the "gregarious" mood.

Flashes of light. Shrieks of wind. Ceaseless creaking as the ship was driven along.

If anyone survived to tell about this, I might become a legend. A dark omen, a Jonah cursed by the Guardians to bring doom wherever he travels. "If you take him aboard your ship, it will surely be ruined before your voyage is done."

Hours passed. We could hear pieces of the ship tearing themselves free. We wondered if we'd know the final moment when the ship shattered and have time to see each other hurled away into the storm, or if the killing strike would be so powerful and sudden we would have no awareness of it until we reached whatever afterlife there might be.

It turned out to be the former, minus the being hurled onto the sea. The ongoing roar that outmatched everything else shifted suddenly, and new sounds, a dozen different kinds of scraping, cracking, and breaking, changed the wind's howling solo act into a choir. In an instant, we went from being inside the hull of a ship in a storm to being inside a collapsing pile of wood rolling across something solid, as those inside tried to keep from bouncing around, something the mreech had an easier time of than the rest of us. Finally, there was a sharp shock as the ship hit something solid enough to stop the roll. The winds faded and died; the machine-gun staccato of the rain slowed and stopped.

Ever-widening beams of light began to drift in as the clouds scattered. There were more holes than there was ship at this point, though the fact there was any ship at all was a statement about mreech construction. I was bruised and slightly scraped. Dureen wasn't much worse, despite having only one hand to grab with. Whatever she was made of, it was tougher than human, mreech, or delnar flesh. Three of the mreech were badly injured, one was outright dead, the rest were taking stock of themselves. Balancer Yeeak... I could see bone, or something close enough to bone, sticking through his arm. Rechir, the ship's surgeon, was working on him.

S'zana was limping slightly, using a splintered bit of board to support herself as a makeshift crutch. "Twisted ankle. I'll be fine, as long as we don't need to run from anything."

I looked at her and smiled slightly.

"You tend to run *towards* things," she replied to my unspoken comment. "Especially when they're things any sane person would run away from."

I couldn't deny it.

The mreech who were able to do so were making their way out of the ship. One had found a rope ladder, and tossed an end down. I went up, with the others following close by. I reached down and tried to help Dureen. She glowered up at me and muttered something. I got the message, and left her. It took her a while to manage it, but she did.

We were on a beach, if you can have a beach without any water. The Solid Sea stretched away to the south. The ship was leaning against an immense, freestanding boulder of dark rock, basalt-like in texture but veined like marble with rust-red lines. Behind us and stretching to either side was a jungle formed of shadow.

Chapter 11
Edge Of The World

It took a few minutes to start seeing the details in the landscape. The darkness was not absolute. There were transparencies, and shades, and different textures of midnight and void. Pitch-colored vines striped with hints of the deepest possible purple wrapped the midnight and asphalt trees. Reflective, glistening, obsidian leaves contrasted with dull, rough, bark the color of old tires. The closest tree was a slender charcoal thing with layers of black vinyl triangles at the top of its twenty feet of trunk. Beneath the spreading leaves hung clusters of tapered black glass spheres. The storm had knocked some loose, cracking them open near the base of the tree. Pooled around the shattered husks was a silver liquid with the texture of mercury.

Things moved within the jungle, chittering, crawling, slithering. Hoots and cries began to fill the air as awareness of the storm's end spread.

Looking at the ruin of *Sails To Far Shores*, Yeeak wept. "Out of balance... clearly... we are out of balance... the world tilts, trying to find its center..."

The survivors were wandering around, acting according to their personalities and their cycle. Rechir was the only one who had a solid idea of what to do in the face of disaster. Others waited for orders, or acted independently, sometimes at cross purposes.

"Balancer Yeeak?"

He turned to me. His arm was wrapped in bandages cut from what was left of the sails. The growths along his face and shoulder seemed like they belonged in this jungle. His voice was distant. "I think you're where you should be. Yes, it's good for you. You should leave now, spinning off, find what balances you. Your duty is ended with the ship. Leave freely. Shattered. There isn't balance or imbalance, just floating motes."

The dreaming cycle did not combine well with stress.

"And you?"

"I am finished. That is me." He pointed to the broken hull. "I was the ship, the ship was me, we were one thing. It's broken, I'm broken. We will rot here together. Things will grow from us. The balance will be restored."

Things the AFA does not prepare you for: Dealing with a plant-gorilla with Combat Stress Reaction.

"No, it won't. Not if you choose to lie down and... go to seed. Look behind you at your crew, Balancer Yeeak. That's your job, isn't it? Your role? *Not* to command the ship, but to *provide balance*. You said it to me: 'The Balance is mine to measure, the Balance is mine to keep'. Fine. The ship is gone, things are unbalanced, everything is out of control. Bring it back *under* control, or it just keeps getting worse."

Yeeak looked down at me. I remembered what he was like in the combat, how he went ap.. berserk... when fighting. I *thought* I knew how the mreech cycles worked by now, that in this dreamy state it would be impossible to move him to violence, but I could be wrong.

Finally, he gave me a small nod, then turned back to the milling crew. "Attention! We are without balance now, our old tasks and goals flung away. We must find the new pattern, find our place in it, and then rejoin the larger pattern. Hoyak, Gream-Clar, tally what food we still have. Yes, that will be good. That's one step towards balance. Chirr, Hajrik, find all you can of the skids. Rechir..."

S'zana stepped from the shadows near the boulder, still leaning on her makeshift crutch, and sheathed the dagger she'd been holding. She had quietly positioned herself to attack Yeeak if he had attacked me. "Well done. You told me you don't like giving orders."

"I don't. That's why I got him to do it. It's his job, not mine. Now, I'm free to recon the area, find out what might try to kill us next."

S'zana surveyed the beach. The mreech were definitely getting organized. "They likely won't need me for a while, either. I will..."

I shook my head. "Your ankle. There's always the chance we'll need to run *from* something, after all."

She didn't waste time arguing a point she knew she couldn't make. "Dureen..."

"...has a lot of talents. Being quiet? Not one of them."

S'zana considered and discarded a few more replies, then relented. "Be as careful as possible for you." She went to rejoin the others.

We were in a small bay. I walked carefully, making sure not to wander onto the Solid Sea. You couldn't drown in it, but you could easily slide out of each of anyone on land and meet some unknown fate. There was about a mile or so of shore where I could keep the wreckage in site, then the land curved away.

If what I sought was within the Ebon Jungle, it wasn't obviously *where*.

Around a quarter-mile from the camp, the growth thinned. There was, if not exactly a trail, a twisting path where the plants grew less closely together. A few mreech could cut a route easily. I followed it until it reached a clearing surrounding a small lake. Five or six three-legged near-tortoises, walking pyramids half the height of a man, bent their snakelike necks to drink, while two others stood apart, keeping watch. My approach set off a high-pitched barking alarm, which ceased when I didn't draw closer.

Assuming the water was drinkable, this would be good news. I returned to tell Yeeak.

Yeeak heard my report, and had me show the way to some scouts. By the time the sun set, near-tortoise meat was roasting for S'zana, Dureen, and myself over a firepit dug near the lake. At a second fire a few yards away, Rechir was boiling water to use for bandages and some of his surgical tools. His medical kit consisted half of things a ship's surgeon from Napoleon's era would recognize, and half of a collection of living sprouts, moss, and fungi.

Outside the small circles of firelight, the darkness was astounding. There were no glowing crystals here. In full daylight, the Ebon Jungle seemed to be made of pure shadow until you looked closely. At night, it became almost invisible, its few distinctions of color and texture swallowed completely.

Invisible, but hardly inaudible. There was the usual litany of wilderness sounds, calls for mates, howls of rage, declamations of territory. Dureen had taken it on herself to teach two of the "Celebration" cycle mreech a game involving tossing small rocks at an upended tortoise shell, the prizes being cups of the surviving jug of *skreej*. From what I overheard, she was constantly altering the rules to suit her results.

S'zana and I sat by the fire, occasionally tossing on another bit of wood. We didn't talk much, preferring to just enjoy the other's nearness. If you didn't look too hard at the shapes of our companions in the shadows, it could have been any summer cookout. That thought tipped a few dominos in my mind, making some connections, and a vague concern started to form.

S'zana had been almost dozing as she lay next to me, something I took as a compliment. Through most of our journeys, even when she was asleep, she always seemed to be on the edge of full consciousness, ready to shift to high alert at the first unexpected sound or breeze. Her current state of relaxation was not one she entered easily.

Nor did she stay in it long. As soon as my own thoughts drifted to how worrying it was that nothing worrisome was happening, she sensed it. A muscle twitch, a slight shift in my posture, a change in my heartbeat... I don't know what it was, but I felt her reaction. She didn't move either or take any obvious action, but I could feel her becoming completely alert.

"What's wrong?" She wasn't asking in the tones of a lover trying to share their partner's troubles. She was asking for a situation report.

"I don't know." I tried to force myself to articulate whatever my subconscious had picked up on. "This is supposed to be a place of legendary dangers. So far..." I shrugged slightly.

She considered that for a moment. "Old legends. Perhaps exaggerated stories. The storm may have driven some of the dangers further inland. Maybe we've been lucky." She contemplated each of those concepts, one by one. "You're right. We should be more cautious."

"Balancer Yeeak has posted guards, here and at the wreck. We're not being completely careless."

Our eyes met. There was no need to say the words; we were both thinking the same thing. In her language, the idiom translates as "So he said at the end." In mine, "Famous last words."

We stood. This motion got Dureen's attention. She walked... well, staggered... away from her game. "Hey... so... *frarg* are you two... oh, really? In the jungle, with all the *klem var* thorns and *grazk* bugs and *krelf*?"

"Wrong guess. We're just going to do some additional patrolling."

Dureen laughed. "Oh, sure. I used that *frarg* a lot when I was young. I did all sorts of *grazk* 'patrolling' back then. Still do, but only with my family." That thought instantly took her mood down about twenty notches. The last thing I needed was her wandering off alone, drunk, and depressed, if we were right that there were more dangers here than we were seeing.

"Come with us," S'zana said, then, seeing Dureen's expression, added, "Not for that. We actually are going to explore somewhat. Your people have the same legends we do about this place. Consider this: Jungle isn't what the mreech have experience with. They're using the same procedures and rules they use in their own territory, or on the Solid Sea. Balancer Yeeak has learned every trick there is to surviving on a flat, featureless, expanse of white. How applicable can that be here?"

The words took a bit to penetrate Dureen's *skreej*-saturated mind, especially since she kept going over them for possible double entendres. Finally, she assented. "Sure. Maybe you'll be *frarg* right, and something will try to eat either or both of you. Then I can *grazk* split its *krel va* head and start home. Let's go. We'll try to get in trouble."

Despite Dureen's hopes and I and S'zana's shared disquiet, we didn't get in trouble. The night passed quietly.

As long hours passed without anything noteworthy happening, I became more and more determined to *not* be the guy in the movies who, as soon as the gunfire stops, decides it's safe to light up his cigarette. At least none of the mreech had any photos of their sproutlings back home.

The convenience of the almost-path nagged at me.

The next morning, I decided to look at it more closely, as part of the general patrol duties I was assigned to. It was difficult, given the "black on black, with highlights of black" color scheme, but I did find what I vaguely expected to. There were signs of sharp, straight, lines cut into the trunks of trees, places where I could see that old growth had been cut back and that new growth had followed. Sometime in the past, this had been cleared deliberately, probably within the last ten years.

Was it just from the shore to the lake?

I conducted a more thorough check of the jungle surrounding the clearing. Yes. There was a hint of a trail leading from it, deeper in. It might be nothing but the remnants of some other unlucky bunch who eventually succumbed to whatever gave this place its reputation. Given the legends, it might also be that someone else had come looking for whatever the Guardians left behind.

I considered going back to get S'zana, or Dureen, or Hoyak, or anyone Yeeak could spare. Actually, no. Later, I realized I *should* have considered it. In reality, I just went ahead.

Distance was hard to measure. The path meandered. Whoever cut it, long ago, had tried to follow the road of least resistance, and that road was not a straight one. Two miles, perhaps three, and the jungle grew a bit more sparse. It opened onto a small meadow, covered with knee-high grain stalks and tangled vines. Breaking up the meadow were copses of large trees. In the distance, I could see a small group of creatures, at least the size of bison, gathered around the stands. There was something else, though. Something colorful.

I approached it.

Caught in a bulbous tangle of thorny vines were the shredded remains of brightly colored cloth. It didn't look like the mreech's style of clothing, at least not the ones I knew. They might have been Yerritti, or something unknown. I kept looking. Near the far edge of the meadow, I found more scraps, and here and there some bits of rusting metal and rotting, but obviously shaped and carved, wood.

So, now what?

It looked unlikely there was anyone nearby now, but someone had come here before. There was no sign that this was a camp, or any other place where people might have *chosen* to abandon gear. I kept looking, kicking around in the dark soil where I'd found most of the detritus. It took me a while to realize I'd located what I was looking for. Bones. Human, or humanoid, bones, all as charcoal colored as everything else around here. I tried bending one of the longer pieces, and it snapped, revealing a much lighter-hued inside. My fingers were covered with soot rubbed off the remains. Burned.

No indication there'd been a major forest fire through here. Despite the Mother Nature of the Ebon Jungle being a bit of a Rolling Stones fan, the area was lush, alive, and healthy. The scraps and bones were near the surface; there hadn't been time to erase a disaster so completely.

I reconsidered the idea of a camp. A small one *could* be overgrown in a short time. I felt that was a reach.

Cannibalistic locals? Was this where they dumped some table scraps? Not impossible. Not necessarily cannibals, either. They might just have burned him, or her, as a witch... or maybe they just burned bodies after a natural death. No reason to jump to the most morbid possible conclusions... but a little paranoia could be a good thing. (Please note, as far as I'm concerned, if you eat something else that thinks, you're a cannibal, even if it's not the same species as you.)

It was at this point that I finally realized it would be a good idea to alert the rest, show them what I'd found, maybe do a wider sweep of the area. If the bones were from a prior storm victim, we might find supplies or other useful things. If they were from any locals, well, just about *anyone* else from our group (except maybe Dureen) would be a better diplomat than me.

Balancer Yeeak, S'zana, Dureen, and two other mreech accompanied me back. The grazing animals were more numerous now, and I got a better look at them. They were six-limbed creatures with grey-black skin that had a barklike texture. Their two front limbs each ended with a set of three truly terrifying claws, all at least a foot long and slightly curved. A long, darting, tongue, something like an anteater's, could lash out and wrap itself around a distant piece of fruit. For the truly hard-to-get-to spots, it could rear back on its hind legs and reach up with its forelimbs, giving it fifteen feet or so of total reach. They didn't just graze. Given a large cluster of treetop leaves, they could engulf the whole thing in their oddly-hinged jaws, then pull back, leaving behind stripped branches covered with digestive slime. Efficient.

A series of fierce bellows, along with stamping feet and slashing motions from the forelimbs, were their response if anyone got within about a hundred feet of the herd. This made crossing the meadow and returning to where I'd found the bones a little slow.

Vrach was the name of the mreech who walked with me to the possible grave site. The rest of the band was spreading to search the other thornspheres, or keep watch on the... scythesloths, I guess. None of the three cultures represented in our group had seen or heard of anything like them before, so I got to name them.

"Here's where I saw the metal. It looked like a knife, maybe, and here's..."

Vrach, standing a foot or so away from me as we walked, leaned in to look as I pointed down, and screamed.

He had become an inferno, as if he had been doused in napalm, but there was nothing to explain it. He simply *ignited* next to me, and before I could do more than jump back instinctively, he was reduced to ash and bone surrounded by his clothing and gear -- which were only partially singed, when they should have been consumed.

Total time it took to turn Vrach from a person by my side to a pile of ash at my feet? Five seconds. Maybe less.

I stopped wondering how the Ebon Jungle had earned its reputation.

People were running towards me. I shouted as loudly as I could.

"Stop!"

I started stepping away from Vrach's body, slowly and carefully and scanning every inch of ground. I saw no hint of a pressure plate, a tripwire, anything. Whatever we'd triggered, it seemed to be based on the location. Except, I'd spent at least a half hour poking, digging, and kicking in that area already, with nothing happening. Why?

Then things got worse.

Vrach's death scream, or my shouted order, or the fire, or something, triggered the scythesloths. They began their bellowing and slashing threat posture even though we were well away from them, and then a new creature charged through the trees. This was the great big daddy -- or perhaps mommy -- of the herd. Twice as large as the others, it charged towards us, its foreclaws slicing through the air in great arcs.

I had to lure it away from the others. If the fire trap didn't harm me, maybe I could lead it there. If the trap *did* harm me, well, I could still lead it there.

Dashing towards it, I slashed at the front left leg, only to find the barklike skin was as tough as it looked. My swing stopped short, all of its energy expended simply cracking the skin, just enough to draw blood and generate a series of loud, growling hisses, indicating rage and pain.

I shouted at it, just to make sure it knew where the pain was coming from, and started to run towards the spot where Vrach had perished. This involved moving partially backwards, trying to avoid tripping over the many vines, tangles, and roots that covered the meadow (all of which were of virtually identical shades of black), while keeping the beast's attention and making sure I was still heading for the right place.

There were a hundred different ways for this to go badly. It didn't take long to fine one. I felt a sudden sting as my left foot pressed down on the point of a thick, curving, thorn. I pulled back, taking the weight from that foot, putting my full weight on my right foot, which forced it through the springy weave of tangled undergrowth beneath it, undergrowth which covered a tiny nest of some kind, judging by the crunching noises and skittering sounds which followed. Two or three seconds was all I needed to find a place to brace my left foot, pull my right foot free, and then resume the race.

I wasn't going to get them. The scythesloth moved faster than anything named after a sloth should. I saw the shadow fall on me, tried to bring my sword up to parry, knowing even if I could block one of the rending arms, the other would get me, and then the creature reared back to its full, almost thirty foot, height, growling and hissing. I saw flashes of green and glints of metal, and then, as it bounded over me and past me, I saw Balancer Yeeak, gripping the thing's wrinkled hide in his feet and slashing down at it with his one good arm, that golden cutlass of his catching the sun in such a way as to be almost a blade of fire.

Pulling myself free, I started to chase after them. Yeeak could have headlined any rodeo, as he stood on top of the madly bucking and hissing creature, ducking claw sweeps and slashing, slashing, slashing at the thing below him. It was undoubtedly painful, but the scythesloth had thick hide and thicker muscle. Balancer Yeeak needed a thrusting weapon, or a very long time, to do severe damage to the creature, and he had neither.

Perhaps I could cripple it, slash through the tendons and muscles behind the knees. At the least, I could inflict enough pain that Yeeak might be able to get down safely. I moved to get myself behind it as it continued its charge out of the meadow, alternating between leaping forward and standing up in its efforts to remove the tenacious gnat which was hacking its shoulders and back into chopped meat.

I saw the opportunity I needed, as its motion finally coincided with a clear patch I could traverse quickly enough to get my attack in before the exposed joints became unexposed.

Smiling grimly, I pushed forward.

Just as the creature's tongue, six feet of adhesive tendril, wrapped around Yeeak's injured arm, and tugged.

Screaming, he instinctively tried to pull free, and that made it worse. His feet's tight grip on the barklike skin loosened in the moment of shock. That was all it took. The tongue recoiled back into the scythesloth's mouth, taking Yeeak, sword and all, with it. The creature bellowed with triumph and kept running.

I ran after it.

I heard someone, S'zana, I think, shouting about "trap", and I ignored them. At that moment, I didn't care if it affected me, or about anything else. Mostly. I stopped for an instant, turned to the others and shouted "No one else! No one follow! S'zana, stop her!" Dureen was already barreling forward. If it was just me immune to the trap... subconsciously, I think, I'd figured it out at this point... I couldn't live with someone else getting killed chasing after me. Yeeak was already one too many.

I also couldn't wait any longer. I'd have to trust S'zana to somehow save Dureen's life. I had something to do.

I raced into the dense jungle beyond the meadow, following the creature. I passed over the old bones and the new, and felt no pain or shock from the force that had killed them. Apparently, neither had the scythesloth. Its trail was hardly difficult to follow. As it was injured and bellowing, all I had to do was catch up. A small voice of sanity tried to tell me I didn't have any plan to kill it, but that voice was one I'd learned to ignore years ago, long before I ever got here. Hell, if I'd listened to it, I wouldn't *be* here, charging through a jungle of shadow and obsidian.

The small voice just chuckled, "The prosecution rests," and vanished back into silence, where it belonged.

The race continued. It could cover a lot of ground with a leap, and smash through those obstacles it couldn't jump over. However, it was wounded and built for spending long hours grazing, not running. I couldn't match its maximum speed, but I was more agile and it was breaking ground for me. It slowed, and then, with another growling hiss, stopped suddenly.

I saw why.

The ground ended abruptly. A slight rise, and then there was a straight line of sky where the jungle simply stopped. I could see some mist rising from beyond that edge, but from my current position, not much else. The scythesloth turned towards me and growl-hissed again. It was breathing raggedly. The blood from the wounds Yeeak inflicted was caked along its back and shoulders.

The chase had given some of my emotions time to settle. It was an animal, a beast reacting according to instinct. It had been driven off. It had probably learned a lesson about the dangers of small two-legged things with pointy objects in their hands.

It made more noises: A more subdued gurgle, mixed with a slow growl of pain. It took some steps forward, wobbled, and collapsed, vomiting up a small waterfall of blood and a hill-sized mound of partially digested vegetable matter, all black. Except for the part that was still green, with a death-grip on a golden cutlass.

Small, two legged things with pointy objects are even more dangerous after you've eaten them.

Yeeak's fur was mostly gone, as was most of his broken arm. The rest of the body still twitched slightly, in what I hoped was post-mortem stiffening of some kind, as the alternative was pretty horrifying.

Then, he opened his mouth and wheezed. Thank you, alien world, for making sure I can't hang on to a comforting lie.

I knelt next to him, feeling an intense sense of pointlessness. He was beyond saving. I couldn't ease his pain. I didn't even know if he had any awareness I was there.

Mumble something in Latin? It certainly wasn't *his* faith. After the wreck, the surviving mreech had carried the dead into the jungle and covered them with a cairn of leaves and vines, after chanting a brief ritual in their own language. It was likely no one else was getting through that trap, and we had no idea how far it extended. I felt I had to say something.

"Uhm... may the Guardians witness that you served the Balance, and died protecting those under your command." I couldn't think of anything else. I imitated the burial process I'd witnessed. I wasn't sure about the cutlass. Was it something personal, that belonged with him in death, or a mark of leadership that someone else should bear, or something to give to his family? I decided to bring it back, let his comrades decide, and plead ignorance of their customs if I got it wrong.

I stood, walked past the scythesloth's corpse (a number of scavengers had already begun to explore it), and looked past the edge.

To either side of where I stood, fading into mist, stretched the rim of a crater many miles across. Fog filled the basin. In the far distance, sticking out of the haze, were several plateaus. Barely visible, except for brief moments when the mists parted, there were lights: Some steady, some blinking, some moving in regular lines, a combination that added up to "civilization." Whatever I was looking for in the Ebon Jungle, I'd found it.

Chapter 12
The Tower

When I returned to the meadow, I nearly tripped over a thick rope laid across the ground in front of the jungle's edge. Standing by a small fire near the rope were S'zana and Rechir. Once I stepped past the barrier into the field, S'zana ran to me. We embraced, and for a brief time, my pain, exhaustion, and guilt over Yeeak vanished into a pleasant void.

Then she stepped away from me, and she was not smiling.

"Idiot! How could you just charge off like that?" Her voice became carefully controlled as she set out her argument. "Yeeak was dead. You couldn't hope to rescue him. Did you think at all about everyone you were leaving behind?" I started to speak, but she cut me off, emotion returning now that she'd stated her case. "No, of course not. Thinking isn't really one of your skills, is it?"

I returned anger with anger. Where her voice was passionate, mine was controlled and sharp-edged. "Sorry. I thought we were both professionals. I didn't think our romance would make you think I'd forget my duty, or that you'd want me to."

This wasn't quite the trump card I'd hoped. She'd had time to rehearse this debate while she was waiting. Arguing with someone who wielded words as deftly as they did weapons was a fool's game.

She continued: "You're more of an idiot than I thought. I said 'everyone', not 'me'!"

She had, at that.

It apparently was taking me too long to respond, so she went on. Her voice dropped back to her 'making the case' tone.

"Yeeak respected you and the rest have seen that. You and I are the only ones with experience in this kind of terrain. Dureen had to be dragged away and back to the wreck to stop her following after you. Don't smirk, it's not funny. We can't afford to lose you over some sense of...," and here, emotion returned, "I don't know what! The creature was *fleeing*! It was an animal, not an enemy who could deliver a report or find reinforcements. What were you even trying to accomplish?"

I tried to find a way to answer that made some kind of sense now that the moment had passed. If I had been chasing a person -- someone that had killed Yeeak unjustly or unfairly -- I'd feel a lot more self-righteous. But my motive was just rage. The scythesloth had hurt my friend and I wanted to hurt it, and I had tried to wrap this up in some cloth of 'duty' and 'honor', but it was neither. I had a duty to the people who were depending on me. My honor should be tied to how well I carried out that duty.

I thought I'd long ago learned to keep my anger and impulses in check, or at least channel and delay them. This world, though, was liberating. I had more freedom here, to act when I felt I had to act, and it had eroded my control.

What S'zana had said about how much I was needed was true -- but it wasn't enough. I would have to leave, because every fact we had said I was the cause of the seekers, and I had to find out what they wanted, what they were doing, and somehow stop them. Whatever that one back in Hreek had been making, I knew it wasn't good.

"R'yan?" S'zana's voice was bit softer now. I realized I'd been silent for a while, thinking.

I finally answered her question. "What was I trying to accomplish? You're right. Nothing smart." I still felt some need to justify myself, though, no matter how irrational I knew it was. "Doesn't a desire for revenge ever make *you* act without thinking?"

She smiled a thin, predatory smile. "No. It tends to make me think a long, long, time before I act." Then her smile became much warmer. "Yet somehow, *you* manage to get me angry enough that I forget my masks. If it's a consolation, most of those I think of as idiots never know what I think of them. To you, I will always speak the truth."

"Thanks. I'll take what consolation I can get."

The rope I'd nearly tripped over stretched across the meadow. S'zana saw me looking at it.

"We lost another of the crew. Hoyak. He was in his dreaming cycle, and as soon as the specific orders he'd been given were fulfilled, he thought... I don't know what he thought. But he wandered into the treeline over there," she pointed, "and there was the same thing. He was consumed. We spent some time very carefully poking ahead with long branches or poles, trying to find other charred remains. We found many. The mreech have named it 'The Fence Of Bones'. The parts we found were mixed. Delnar, grazarn, mreech, others. It extends as far as we could safely test, perhaps all the way around the jungle. Animals walk or fly through it, and so do you, Kruzvahko."

My nickname was spreading.

Then the other piece fell into place. The answer appeared in my mind suddenly, and I was struggled to articulate it before it was gone.

"Animals... the seekers... the legends... it could make sense if..."

S'zana gestured for Rechir, who approached us. "Yes? Is he injured?"

"I'm not sure. I'm sure he needs food, water, and rest. He's..."

"That's it!" I shouted, ignoring their worried looks. "I've got it. I think." I began to explain.

"The seekers are looking for me, they have to be, nothing else makes sense, but they don't *see* me. They hit any of you with that light, and you glow, but not me. The Fence of Bones. It kills everyone, grazarn, delnar, mreech... but not me. And... me! My people! No one's seen or heard of anyone exactly like me. The Guardians... your legends say they brought all the peoples here... but not my people! You, all of your people, and the mreech, and Dureen's people, grazarn, everyone else... the seekers, the Guardian's servants, the Fence of Bones... you're all people to them! *Delnar ta vril*! But I'm *not* people. A person. Something. I mean, I am, but *they don't know it*. They must have a list, a record, a rulebook, something that tells all the kinds of people that there are, but my people aren't on the list! I'm seen as an animal, or something else that's not 'people'!" Having said it out loud, I considered the implications. "That's a bit insulting."

Rechir nodded slowly, then looked at S'zana. "Yes, yes. Quite right to call for me. He's deeply unbalanced. I'm not an expert on his people, but food, water, and rest are always good for healing. Come along, then, come along. Is that Yeeak's blade?"

"Yes. He..." I related how I found him, what I did. "I hope returning it is the right thing."

"Oh, yes, yes. Our bodies, they return to be consumed, to become something new in time. But our tools? Wasting something skillfully made that is still useful is very unbalancing. You should keep it. Hmm. I think I was saying you needed water?"

S'zana confirmed this. "Yes. Let's get back to the ship. You," she tapped at my chest a few times, "are going to be dealing with Dureen."

Dureen was, relatively speaking, happy to see me. As long as I was alive, she could fulfill her debt. After she'd done that, I figured, she would probably kill me.

Yeeak's cutlass did pass to me, by general consensus. I'd thought it had been gold-plated or colored, but it was made of some metal with the shine of gold, but not the substance. It was at least as hard as fine steel, perhaps harder, and kept an extremely keen edge without honing. It didn't slice effortlessly through solid objects like Dolish's sword, but it was still pretty good.

With Yeeak dead, there was no current Balancer. After some debate, Rechir found himself in the position, despite his current cycle. As long as someone else could keep him focused on each task or decision, he'd do well.

That left the small matter of leaving. S'zana argued that perhaps we should search along the jungle's edge, try to find a place where the Fence of Bones wasn't, but we quickly dropped that concept, as the only way to test it was by seeing if someone died. Dureen was frustrated and furious. I pointed out she still owed a debt to S'zana, and it would be at least possible to pay that, which didn't exactly mollify her.

Another day of arguing and planning. There was enough of *Sails'* skids left to try to construct a smaller craft, sort of a glorified raft, and attempt a trip south until any sign of civilization could be reached.

That night, there was another storm. Not nearly as bad as the one which wrecked us, but strong. The sky crackled and blazed with strange energies. It wasn't lightning, or it was a kind I hadn't seen before, lightning that formed sheets and whorls... the aurora borealis, made of electricity. Towards the end, we saw other things in the far distance. The best way to describe them would be tornadoes of flame -- columns that stretched from horizon to sky, self-illuminating, twisting and bending.

No one had ever seen anything like them. Neither Dureen, nor the mreech, even had legends of them. S'zana did, but said they were fanciful. There were many different faiths which interpreted the assorted tales of the Guardians. Most agreed on some things, while other beliefs were limited to a few obscure sects or cults. The pillars of fire were occasionally mentioned in a handful of the oldest tales. They weren't widely discussed, nor were they a part of any great stories, lessons, or ceremonies.

S'zana explained the dissent: "Since deception was among the many sins for which the Guardians exiled the peoples here, all scholars agree at least some of the old tales must be false, but few agree on which. Thus, wars occur."

"*Delnar ta vril.*" was all I could say in response to that.

The storm had finally passed. We were huddled together in a simple shelter of scrap wood and sailcloth, avoiding any discussion of whether this would be our last night with each other. Instead, we were discussing religion and weather.

"You seem to know a lot of things that are obscure or ignored. Were you planning to become a nun at some point?" (I said/thought 'nun', and what came out was a genderless delnar word for 'one who dedicates their life to serve the Guardians'.)

She laughed, which was fortunate. It occurred to me that I had no real idea if her land's religious workers were held in high esteem or not, if it was considered a worthy career or what you did if you had no other options, or even if it was voluntary.

"I don't think you believe so sedate a life would have suited me. No, I wasn't interested in the lore for its own sake. I was interested in stories. Stories from the Covenant Lands, from Zulsair to the west, from the Klurish League, from the lands and peoples around the World's Wound. From anywhere. It's part of why I was chosen by the Listeners."

"So, the pillars of fire. What do the stories say?"

"I only read about something like them once. It was a tale of a land which grew so evil, so quickly, that the Guardians knew none of those in that land could gain redemption. It was scoured clean in a night of glowing skies and red spears hurled downward."

That sounded a bit familiar. "Did anyone turn to salt?"

S'zana shook her head. "To ash, it's said. All that remained was ash."

"That's bad. That's really bad."

"It is a very old, nearly forgotten, legend. No one goes to war over it. Why assume it's true?" She wasn't trying to convince me. She was trying to convince herself, and knew she couldn't.

"Because we're being chased by dragons," I replied. She smiled a little at that, her expression acknowledging a truth neither of us liked but both of us had to accept.

I continued: "If no one's seen anything like this before, if this is completely new, then shouldn't you be upset? Worried? What have I brought here?"

"I *am* worried, R'yan. Beyond worried. I am actually frightened. This could mean many things, all of them very bad. Anyone seeing this storm will worry, even if they have no idea about the forgotten legends. They will make new tales, or change old ones. People seek causes for things. They'll blame their neighbors, or their enemies, or their friends."

"Why didn't you tell me this as soon as the storm *started?* Let me know what you suspected?"

She closed her eyes and relaxed against me. "You're leaving tomorrow. No one can go through the Fence of Bones with you. If you find what you think may be there, then this all stops. If you don't find anything or you can't stop it or you die, we'll find out what it all means, soon enough. Your course was set before the storm began, set as soon as you saw what was beyond the Fence. Why would I want to give you any more burdens, any more things to ponder, when you wouldn't be able to take any action? Knowing something must be done, and not being able to do it... I know that's torture to you. At the moment...", she moved again, stretching a bit, so that the full length of her body was against mine, "I'm not interested in torturing you."

"I'm sure that mood won't last."

"I hope not," she whispered. "If the Guardians are still watching, and if they have any concern for justice, you'll return and you'll give me many reasons to want to torture you, for thousands of days to come."

A sharp voice came from the nearest shelter. "Can I *frarg* puke now? *Drazkh var kleh* thin sailcloth, trying to *grazkh* sleep here..."

We ignored her.

I'd been working on excuses to not leave -- S'zana's speech earlier about how much the remaining mreech might need us did hit me hard -- but the storm, bringing weather never seen before except in one ancient myth, told me the situation was escalating. S'zana also pointed out, when I tried to talk about delaying, (she had an annoying skill at being able to flip sides in any argument, to make the case for whatever conclusion she wanted, even when that conclusion changed) that she and Dureen could fight, that she could offer at least some knowledge about survival here, but that only I could get through the Fence of Bones, so that was that.

I set out.

It was easy enough to make it back to the crater's edge. A pack of froggish things, a yard long with spiked tails like a stegosaur, were eating the remains of the scythesloth. I avoided getting too close, especially when one scavenger's mouth gaped open and revealed a maw that looked like a tunnel of wriggling barbed wire.

The real problem was going to be getting down.

The edge at this point was sheer. Any attempt to climb would be suicide. I had to walk the rim until I found a route that worked. Given the thickness of the mists, it would still be a lot of guesswork. The bottom could be a hundred feet down, or a mile, or more.

Nothing to do but walk. I also had to accept the possibility there might be no way down, that I could circle the crater back to my starting point. I tried not to think about it.

I watched the plateau in the center. I was hoping to see some sign of activity beyond the lights, something to indicate someone was still home. During the first day there was nothing. Just the mist-shrouded outlines of regular, rectangular, lines, and a few dots of illumination piercing the fog.

Evening. Once darkness came, travel would be impossible. I'd hoped to have found some kind of cave or nook to crawl into during the night, but no luck. The best choice I had, with no one else to stand watch, was to find a likely tree and tie myself in. At least the ground-based predators would have a hard time getting to me.

I found one, climbed, and located some branches that formed a marginally tolerable resting spot. Gnawing tediously at a slab of pyramid-turtle jerky, I looked again at the distant lights, as the sky took on the same hue as the trees, the leaves, the grass.

And there it was.

Too dim to perceive when there was any competition from the sun was a string of lights, a perfect line of equally spaced glowing points, which reached from the plateau to the rim of the crater. Distance? About two or three days, I guessed.

A bridge? It seemed certain, and it made sense. If this was the place where the Guardians came and went... their Canaveral, or maybe just their JFK International... there'd be transport of some kind.

But they flew, I thought.

So do we, I replied... but we still have roads. We didn't abandon the Navy or the infantry when we invented planes, either. I remembered Murz Ten. There were roads there that the grazarn couldn't build in their current state. Roman roads. Rome fell, but the roads remained.

I'd long since guessed some sort of "fall of Rome" scenario was close to what had happened here. I didn't think it made sense to speculate on this with the others. Outsiders showing up and declaring to the locals that their entire history (even worse, their religion) was wrong wasn't a good way to win hearts and minds.

So what was blinking in the fog? A final outpost, filled with the descendants of the last legion, still waiting to be called back home? Or was it just a ruin that hadn't quite fallen apart yet?

I'd find out.

The next two days of walking passed... not uneventfully. Even with the Fence of Bones explaining most of the "And no one ever returned" tales, the Ebon Jungle had its share of other dangers. One species of "tree" turned out to be a colony of centipede things, each the size of my arm, which interlocked to form their disguise and then came apart in a chittering, clacking, mob when prey -- such as myself -- drew too close. I tried to get fresh water, and found that a thing like a black, dark grey, and light grey giraffe -- but with the head of a lamprey -- had a reservation at the same time. There were all the usual hazards of travel compounded by the nearly monochrome environment.

The second night, there was another storm. The same twisting colors in the sky, the same distant whirlwinds of fire, and something new. From the center of the crater, my hopeful destination, I could see thin streams of light heading upwards, blue and green beams cutting perfectly vertical marks into the sky.

Causing the storm? Analyzing it? Celebrating Free Beer Night? I wasn't sure, but I wasn't going to give good odds for the third.

Near noon on the fourth day since I'd left the beach, I reached the bridge.

The main span was roughly two hundred feet wide. The far end was as mist-encased as ever, just as far from this edge as from where I started. The area around the bridge, though, was different. A half dozen buildings, a mix of oval and rectangular forms, surrounded a broad half-circle of metal that terminated the bridge. Vines grew around them. A family of deep violet close-enough-to-birds had built a nest of black twigs and black leaves, and squawked furiously if they thought I was after their eggs.

Lights were spaced every hundred feet along each side of the bridge. Thin supports held up the span, placed at the same points as the lights. I still couldn't see the bottom.

Above the bridge, just as it passed the edge of the canyon and headed out across the gap, was a structure that probably once held a sign, but now it was an empty frame.

Other than the perennial noise of the jungle, it was silent.

I expected more. A guard. A seeker. Something.

Walking out onto the bridge, in plain view of anyone, seemed like a really bad plan. I spent several hours trying to think of another one. I also explored the buildings. They came in two varieties -- those which were sealed tight, and those which were open but stripped bare. At least the bare ones provided a decent shelter.

The next morning, I concluded I had three choices: Walk across the bridge, keep circling the crater and hope there was a path down and a way to climb back *up* once I found the base of the plateau, or go back to the beach and see if the others had managed to leave yet.

I stepped onto the bridge.

I waited for something to happen. Nothing did. I kept walking.

Ten minutes into the walk, the mists had hidden the entrance from me. The far end remained equally out of sight. The world was a wide strip of metal bounded on all sides by fog.

Then, something did happen. Shadows appeared in the clouds ahead of me, moving rapidly. Three, no, four, and then they became visible, darting triangles of gleaming silver, each a foot across, dotted with blue and violet lights, moving smoothly and soundlessly. They flew past me, banked, spun, turned around, and passed me again.

I kept walking, slowing my pace, as they continued their circling dance. I felt like a flower being reconnoitered by hummingbirds. Their survey of me lasted a few minutes, then they shot away, scattering in different directions.

I wondered how they could be so sure I wasn't a threat. Then I considered that assuming I *was* might be the equivalent of ordering a patrol to open fire on any suspicious squirrel, in case it turned out to be a cleverly disguised spy. Then I considered that if the Guardians *were* Rome... they'd fallen. Too arrogant to think an enemy could be someone they wouldn't recognize? Too bound by protocol to adapt, even when the rules of war had changed? Or just overrun by space-barbarians?

The best chance I had at learning the answers was at the far end of the bridge.

I kept walking.

Hours later, I started getting a better view of the plateau, and the buildings on it. With each stride, my target grew more visible. Step by step, I developed more understanding of what I was seeing, and I slowly allowed myself to realize I hadn't understood what I'd seen from the crater's edge, days before.

There was no plateau.

The flat surfaces upon which I'd seen buildings and lights were not natural. They were an assortment of rooftops. Other such "plateaus" revealed themselves from the mist as I drew nearer to the center. The whole structure was at least two miles across here, at its peak, and it broadened as it went down to the unseen base. It could easily be five miles across where it touched the crater's floor. How far down did it go from there? How many basement and sub-basement levels? Dozens? Hundreds?

You could toss the Empire State Building into this thing, and it would be lost inside it. Thousands of lights trailed down the sheer sides into the swirling haze, giving the hidden bulk a sense of shape and structure. If the Guardians were about human (or delnar, or mreech) size, and there was no reason so far to think they weren't, how many could live and work here? A hundred thousand? A million? More? This single building was larger than many cities.

"Well, *frarg*," I said softly.

Confronted with this immensity, contemplating the task of facing it alone, a smart man would have run screaming. I didn't.

The flat areas, the "plateaus" -- each had some assortment of structures along their edges, but never in their centers. They could be landing fields for aircraft -- for *space*craft -- of all sizes. Nothing was currently parked.

There were more structures at the exit from the bridge. This side of the span had several regions bounded by walls, each with a multitude of superstructures -- pillboxes or weapon emplacements -- mounted upon them. I spent some time wandering the outside, occasionally disturbed by the small flyers, until I found what looked like doors leading into the main bulk of the complex. They were huge, easily large enough to let two city busses pass through, with a third bus was carried on top. Featureless, like the doors in the palace at Murz Ten. I gave an experimental shove, and might as well have been pushing on a wall.

No windows, at least not around here. Looking up... there were lighted shapes that might be windows, starting forty feet above me. I moved to the nearest edge and looked down. There, only twenty feet down. An easier climb, but a much longer fall if anything went wrong. I looked again at the smooth wall stretching upwards. No obvious place to try to lasso or grapple. Climbing down, though... There was a lot of machinery sticking out, either pipes or vents or radar dishes or decorative birdhouses, that looked sturdy enough. I tied the rope to the nearest bit, after testing its strength, and rappelled down.

Ten vertiginous (Anyone reading this, please tell my Mom I *did* use that word-a-day calendar she sent me!) minutes later, I climbed back up. Yes, it was a window, and it was closed, sealed, and unbreakable.

Up was out, down was out, so *around* was all I had left. There were plenty of outbuildings, nooks, and substructures to explore. All I needed was one door left open, one forgotten entrance not sealed against the space-barbarians.

Eventually, I found one.

By that time, I was hungry, tired, and frustrated. I was ready to find any shelter and simply collapse, when I heard it: The first sound since entering the crater that wasn't clearly natural. It wasn't much, just a slight grinding, a mechanical hum, not loud, but so different from the background of chirps and croaks that it stood out like a gunshot. I went in that direction and looked down.

There. A door about fifteen feet below me, embedded in the side of the tower. Slightly smaller than the door I'd found at the end of the bridge, this one was sliding open. Light poured out. So did three seekers, and a swarm of the smaller flyers.

I could just see the interior. It looked unsurprisingly like a hangar.

Instinctively, I did some calculations. Tie the rope *here*... swing like Tarzan... tumble to the floor... probably survive.

It began to grind closed. Twenty seconds, maybe thirty, before it was shut. Would it open again in an hour? A day? Never?

I couldn't take that chance.

Tie. Grab. Leap.

Partly through the arc, I felt the rope go slack. Tied it too fast. Missed something.

Let go. Twist in midair. Angle isn't great, door is closing, turn...

Barely. Door shuts just behind me. I'm not swinging or jumping now, I'm just *falling*, uncontrolled, my momentum carrying me across to a far wall. I take the impact on my arm, bounce back an inch, then slide down the wall ten feet to the floor.

It hurt, but nothing was broken or twisted. I stood and tried to take the place in. (After weeks of either natural light, torches, or lamps, it was strange to be seeing by artificial light again -- I'd forgotten how clear and sharp things could be when properly lit.)

The room was square, a hundred feet or so to a side, with a ceiling twice that high. The walls, floor, and ceiling had less equipment than I'd expect -- a few outcroppings of metal and crystal here and there, and some rectangles of light, like the "radio" on the *Bellerophon* flickering on the walls. Hovering in the center was a seeker. A swarm of smaller things -- many different configurations and styles, ranging in size from "softball" to "duffel bag" -- swarmed nearby, dashing towards it, zipping away from it, landing on it. Metal bees feeding from a silver flower. Less poetically, repair or maintenance. Remote control from somewhere else? Automated? *Popular Mechanics* had always talked about self-driving cars or planes, coming soon in the world of tomorrow.

I wondered if somewhere in this place there could be some petulant robot pushing a mop across a floor which had been mopped a dozen times this week, its tinny voice mumbling mechanical complaints about how it wasn't fair it got stuck with punishment detail when it was clearly the other robot's fault.

Three more of the triangle-winged flyers moved towards me. I paced along the walls, looking for a way out. It would be pretty pointless to be stuck here to starve and die. I thought a bit more about my robot on PD. A joke to myself, but sometimes jokes reveal truths. If the entire place had been running on automatic for centuries or more, then what's happened? What would make the rules change - unleash seekers, cause storms of a kind never seen before?

Obviously, my arrival had changed the rules. I'd breached their airspace. Set off an alarm. Now, something was happening in response to that. Countermeasures. Increase patrols to look for the invader. That made sense. The storms didn't. It would be like randomly bombing your own country to get one spy. There was still something I was missing.

The triangle-flyers had reached me and began their usual circle. I sighed and stopped moving, waiting for them to finish.

I saw flashes of light, and then nothing.

Until now, my worst "waking up" memory involved returning to consciousness, with the kind of hangover I thought I'd inherited immunity to, on the concrete steps attached to the home of Gina Gabraldi, my junior prom date, with her father kicking me in the ribs while clanging together the lids of two steel pots.

That was now down to Second Worst.

The only words I can use are "full body hangover." Awareness came in the form of deep, throbbing pain, as each part of my body called in for sick leave one by one. It was the ache of long exercise, where every muscle and joint is telling you "No more, we're done". As for my head... there are a dozen metaphors for the kind of pain I felt, and they all work.

I opened my eyes. Things got worse. The light set off a chain reaction of new pain, as if opening my eyes created a breach in a barricade, permitting a marching horde of invaders to travel along my optic nerve and make their way to my brain.

I waited until that wave faded a bit, then tried again. Not so bad this time. By the third try, I could see.

This room was perhaps forty feet across with a high ceiling. A number of cylinders of different sizes were stacked throughout it. Each cylinder was made of a clear material, maybe glass or transparent plastic, and most of them had something inside: Each held a corpse, ranging from "slightly mummified" to "dusty bones". Small dead bird-analogs, medium size dead frog-analogs, large dead snake-analogs... and me. Man-sized not yet dead delnar-analog. Located on the outside of each cylinder was a small grey rectangle: Palm sized, with a few gold and red dots arranged within it.

My new home was six feet in diameter, and eight feet high. I could see the back of the grey rectangle.

I stood. This was painful. The pain faded as I moved, returning life to my muscles.

I should have considered this earlier. (What did they say here? "So he said at the end.") You don't waste ammo shooting every raccoon or squirrel that runs across the tarmac, but if one gets into the barracks you're going to get it out. They stored captured pests here. Perhaps to check them for diseases, or maybe cook them up as a treat, or dissect them for giggles, or something else, but no one had come to *check* on the captives for a long time.

Minutes of fist-bruising experimentation convinced me the glass wasn't going to shatter easily. The interior surface and the end caps fused seamlessly. No screws, no joints, nothing I could try to wedge open. I tried scraping the glass with a utility knife I'd been given when I left the camp. It was useless, but it gave me an idea.

Yeeak's scimitar was made of something I couldn't identify. Most likely, Guardian metal of some kind. Guardian metal might break Guardian glass.

I didn't have a lot of room to swing, so my blows weren't as strong as they could be. A dozen attacks left a few chips and scars on the inner surface. That was more than anything else had.

I focused on the area next to the grey rectangle, guessing it was a lock of some kind. All I had to do was get a hole I could reach through.

Some two hours or so into this process another small machine flew in. It ignored me and my escape efforts, deposited an indigo-furred cat-sized creature in an empty cylinder, and left. The pest-finder held its prey without using physical grips of any kind. Its unconscious cargo simply floated beneath it, moved by an unseen force. Possibly useful to know. I kept attacking.

Finally. I'd switched arms multiple times and taken some breaks, but I had done it. A hole I could reach through to touch the panel. Manipulating the controls without seeing them required a lot of trial and error, and a bit of worry. There could easily be an "incinerate" option. If there was, I fortunately didn't find it before I found the "open" option.

The cage dissolved around me. The metal top and bottom end caps remained, as did the panel, which was now floating in place. I stepped out.

During this time, the most recent addition to the Dead Menagerie had awakened, and was clawing at its enclosure. I did some experimenting with the controls on some corpse-containing cages, to make sure I knew the "open" command correctly, and released it, figuring it had at least a slight chance to make it outside before being captured again. It made a few squeaking noises, bared its teeth at me so I'd know who was really in charge here, and began an exploration of its environment. I found a door, and this one was basically human-sized and had a control system similar to the cages. I opened it, and the furry thing dashed past me into the corridors outside.

Overall, a lot like Dolish's palace. Better lighting, somewhat wider halls, but a similar design. Spartanly functional and probably intuitive if you knew where you were going, but a maze if you didn't. Symbols on the walls and intersections -- red diamonds, blue circles, squiggly lines that were probably writing -- did nothing to help me. Floating light-rectangles displaying ever changing patterns of shapes, ditto.

I explored, much more cautiously now that I knew I was not going to be automatically ignored. There was a true eeriness to this place. I knew it had been abandoned for hundreds or thousands of years, and it was clean and comfortable and well-lit. It was more like wandering a building after dark than it was exploring an ancient ruin. Just replace the flying machines with an off-duty cop moonlighting as security.

More wandering, and the silence and the emptiness combined to let thoughts I'd suppressed creep stealthily to the surface. I had very little food and water left. This place was as big as a city. I didn't know where I was relative to the outside. I didn't know where I was relative to any place I might need to find *inside*. Each thought of how futile this might be joined the one before it, crowding out any others.

"Stop thinking!" I shouted to myself, "And *start* thinking! Form a plan!"

It was only as the echoes faded that I realized I'd actually spoken out loud. If any of those pest-control machines were around, I'd just drawn their interest.

Then there was another voice, coming from the walls, or the air, or nowhere. It was speaking heavily-accented delnar. It repeated itself twice, and on the third try, I got most of the words.

"Language recognized. Set as primary. Request invalid. Repeat valid request." The voice was calm, with only slight inflections and variances in tone. There was an air of polished professionalism about it, the voice of someone narrating an instructional movie or reading the evening news.

"Who are you? Are you in charge here? I, uhm, I come in peace. I just want to talk."

"Information utility process. No. Request invalid. Request invalid."

It took me a minute to figure that out. It had replied to each of my four sentences. It was "Information utility process", it wasn't in charge, and the other two things I said were "invalid".

"Who is in charge?" Well, it was worth a shot.

"Sub-Commander Hgraz Julk has been given transitional oversight authority as provisional warden."

The word that I was mentally translating as 'warden' was almost the same as the word I'd heard as 'Guardian'. Interesting. More interesting was the knowledge there *was* someone still in charge. Maybe this wouldn't be as impossible as I'd feared.

"Where is, uhm, Higrazz Jullk located?"

"No identification found. The name is not recognized."

I must have said it wrong. "Where is the provisional warden located?"

"Non-public information. No security status for voice or visual on record. Security information required. Report to security checkpoint immediately."

Hell. If the security system was as oblivious as this "information utility process," I'd end up back in a cylinder, or worse. Not going, though, put me right back at "wandering around pointlessly." Besides, I'd managed to outwit or escape everything else I'd encountered.

"How do I get to the security checkpoint?"

A pulsing green line appeared at my feet, stretching down the corridor and around a bend. "Confirm ability to perceive guidance."

"You mean, the green line? Yes, I see it."

"Spectrum perception noted. Query response: Follow guidance. Do not deviate."

"Follow the yellow brick road, or we shoot, huh?"

"Request invalid. Follow guidance. Ten. Nine."

I followed the guidance.

The line eventually led me to a circular room fifty feet across, with a dozen branching corridors leading out. The "guidance" ended at a column of machinery, similar to those in the caves where I'd met Dureen. Irregular and asymmetrical, floor to ceiling, covered with small control switches and faceted, flat-faced gems -- like TV screens made of ruby or sapphire. Glowing light-rectangles hovered around it. Other structures throughout the room were probably desks or work areas. More light-rectangles floated above each of the outgoing corridors.

"Now what?" I asked the air.

"Security personnel are off-duty during transition."

"Well, when does the transition end?"

"Non-public information. Security information required."

Any society which managed to take a petty paper-pusher and turn him into a machine that can't be punched in the face deserved to collapse.

"Look, this is an emergency. Can't you, I don't know, call your superior officer or something and get clearance?"

"Override authorization can only be provided by Sub-Commander Hgraz Julk."

"Well, then ask him!"

"Invalid request."

I tapped my foot, considering my options. Damn it, I'd navigated worse mazes of red tape than this on Earth. I could beat this one.

"All right. So, what is the procedure to request an override authorization?"

"Petition must be made to a Level Nine operative assigned to that duty."

But no one is on duty, except the 'provisional warden'. Hmm...

"What if the operative is unavailable, and the situation is time-critical?"

"Responsibility passed to supervising officer."

Bingo.

"This is a time-critical emergency. I must make a petition to an on-duty operative with appropriate clearance."

If I guessed right, the machine would click through its punch cards and step up the ranks to find the one person still on duty.

A green line appeared. "Follow guidance. Do not deviate. Deviation will result in extreme protocol initiation."

I started following the guiding line, shaking my head sadly. How could the Guardians have been smart enough to build an artificial sun, and all their other miracles, and dumb enough to trust to automatic systems that couldn't question their own actions? I sighed. Then again, how many human tragedies, great and small, have been caused by some version of "I was following the manual precisely!" or that enduring excuse for atrocity, "I was just following orders."?

Chapter 13
The Last Guardian

The line took a long time to follow. It involved elevators that were disturbingly like the cages of the Dead Menagerie -- a clear cylinder materializing between two metal plates, but this time there were controls on the inside of the surface as well. (Nothing like the elevators at Murz Ten, I noticed.) And a lot of walking. I had difficulty believing this was how things were supposed to work, unless this building truly *was* a city, and you would no more expect to make a journey from anywhere to anywhere in under five minutes than you would in New York, New York.

It took long enough that some of the exhaustion and deprivation got through, for a moment. I paused, just long enough for a wave of dizziness to pass. This got me the "Do not deviate" message and its dire warnings.

"I need food. And water. Is there any kind of allowance for that?"

"Unsecured and unclassified persons are treated as Colonist Status Zero for purposes of provision allotment."

That sounded unappealing, but so did "nothing". "Fine. Can I get a Colonist Status Zero allotment?"

This involved a blue line, leading to a room containing a complex, free-standing mechanism which followed the "cylinder of lights" pattern, though this one was only about waist height. When I approached, several light-rectangles flickered into existence.

"Now what am I supposed to do?"

"Select provisions within the limits of your allotment. Attempts to exceed your allotment will result in penalties."

"How do I select provisions?"

Then followed what turned out to be a useful lesson in how to operate these machines. It didn't just cover the "provision selector," but included an overview of many of the basic concepts used in most of the Guardian's machines. Particular symbols were used consistently and always referred to similar actions or ideas. No matter what a machine's function was, you could apply most of you learned from one to the other. Even better, they were apparently used to illiterate or semi-literate people. Once I convinced the Information Utility Process I couldn't read, it altered most of the squiggles to a set of pictograms -- I still needed help learning those, but it took less time than learning to read and write in Guardian.

More useful intel about the Guardian's society. They built spaceships and suns, but they also built into their machines the assumption that those otherwise authorized to use them would not be educated enough to read. I had to chuckle a little at the image that conjured up -- the huge computer banks at NASA or NORAD being programmed and operated as if they were children's picture books.

This educational period distracted the Information Utility Process from its original goal of making sure I stayed on the green line. Eventually I completed watching the instructional film (I was a bit disappointed I couldn't find a warning about the dangers of getting space-herpes from space-hookers) and consuming my "Status Zero Allotment", which was about what you'd expect from the name, only runnier and with disturbing blue globules in it, and I was once again informed that "deviation will result in extreme protocol initiation".

On I went.

More walking, more elevators, more lines. The last stage took place in a passage twice the size of the others. Streams of symbols flowed past me, displayed on black glass strips placed at eye-height. Every fifty feet or so, I passed through a framework intended to hold a barricade or heavy door in place. Weapons unfolded themselves from the walls and tracked my steps, then folded themselves back when I passed by. Either the Information Utility Process was somehow giving them the all-clear, or the guns decided I was a hungry raccoon not worth wasting their ammo on, and were dialing up whoever was supposed to be policing the grounds and to give them a good talking to about "When were they going to do anything about these damn animals, already?"

Smaller corridors branched off the one I followed, but the line took the most direct route, ending at another massive door. This one slid open as I approached. I entered.

I had to stop and take in everything. Allowing for the differences in technology and just "how they liked to do things," this room was a command and control center. The point where I entered led to a central walkway that crossed half the chamber. This path in turn connected to multiple ramps, steps, and floating platforms, all of which provided access to the areas below. Clusters of machinery, chairs, and work surfaces were laid out in what someone probably thought was an efficient pattern. Looking up, I could see nested layers above me, linked to the lower regions by the same mix of ramps, ladders, stairs, and floating disks.

Positioned left and right of the door, just inside the entrance, were what I first took to be armored soldiers. Very *big* armored soldiers, at least a foot taller than me. The design and patterns were similar to those of Dolish's elite: green and teal colors adorning a suit formed of heavy plates of... ceramic? Plastic? Metal? I couldn't tell by sight, and while I was tempted to go prod at them a bit, I had a green line to follow.

Based on everything I'd seen so far in the tower, I amended my guess. They were probably robots as well.

Speaking of the green line, it pulsed below my feet. I let my eyes follow it as it stretched ahead, then down to another set of machines in the distance, a cluster of odd shapes and colors roughly the size of a tank.

Maybe it was a telephone or intercom I needed to use to talk to the Sub-Commander. I returned to following the line, before I started getting warnings about "deviation".

When I was within ten yards or so, someone spoke.

"You must be the anomaly. I thought you'd find your way here, somehow. Glad you could join me."

The speaker wasn't the Information Utility Process. This voice was sharper, harsher, with more tone and personality to it. There was a kind of distraction in how it spoke, as if it were trying to talk on the phone and to someone in the room at the same time.

The new voice emerged from a clear point, unlike the "everywhere and nowhere" voice of the IUP. It came from my destination, emerging from the mechanisms there. If this was the intercom system, it was logical the Provisional Warden would be talking to me through it. I kept walking until I could see my target more clearly.

No, not an intercom. A coffin.

This was where the location of the sub-commander, after all. At the end of the green line, there was nothing but a withered, vaguely human-shaped, husk; simply dried skin shrunken against bones, with a thousand wires and tubes and beams of energy penetrating it from every angle. Dead for centuries or more.

So, what was talking to me? Something like the IUP? That didn't make a lot of sense.

"You'll forgive me if I don't get up," said the voice, followed by a hideous parody of a giggle.

The speech was definitely coming from the direction of the corpse. A speaker in the bulky mechanisms it was embedded in? Probably. The desiccated lips certainly weren't moving. No part of this relic could be. Could it?

Yes. There was motion. It was faint, but I could see a twitching behind the closed parchment eyelids. I saw the barest hints of breath, heard a tiny regular wheezing. The tips of the skeletal fingers scraped regularly, a quarter inch or so, back and forth against the arms of the metal chair. The contents of the tubes and piping were flowing, in and out, very slowly.

"Sub-Commander Hig.. Hugra... Provisional Warden?"

"Well, of course! Who were you expecting?"

There was a question with no answer. Before I could come up with one, it... he... spoke again. "Doesn't matter, does it? The important thing is, you made this possible, and now you're here. It's good to have company, and an audience. Who wants to watch this alone?" Every syllable he spoke raked across my nerves like a blade of ice. Bitterness and madness warred in each word.

"Watch what?" Once more, this world dumped me in the position of being the only one on stage who hasn't learned his lines.

"The end of my life, and this world. Not entirely in that order."

"End of the world?" It sounded idiotic as soon as I said it aloud, but I needed to learn more. What else could I say?

That rasping giggle again. "Yes, yes. Hmm. It's funny, isn't it? I haven't talked to anyone who could actually respond to me in so long that anything you say *should* be fascinating, but I'm already bored with repeating myself. Don't bore me."

I was only half listening. I was thinking: So, the lunatic is being kept alive by a lot of machinery that looked pretty delicate. One good swing of Yeeak's sword through all those tubes, maybe a decapitation for good measure and problem solved. There could be some defenses, though. I should get close, in case I don't get a second chance.

"Or you'll kill me?" I asked, inching closer. Keep the loon talking.

"Oh, that's certain. Everyone else has to die before I do. Otherwise, I can't watch, and where would the fun be then? No, no, it's more a matter of how much pain you'll be in between now and when things are ready."

I was twenty feet away by this point. I didn't see anything flying above me, no seekers or little triangles. The two big things at the door were far away. They couldn't make it here in time to do anything. A few more steps, one swing, and the nearly corpse becomes the really corpse.

Maybe my time with S'zana had affected me. I paused to consider the consequences: But what happens then? If there's no warden, does the sun go out? Something worse?

Then, a new voice. This one sounded like me.

It wasn't coming from outside. I wasn't hearing it with my ears. It was inside my head, in the voice of my own thoughts, except I wasn't the one thinking them.

"I can guess what you're thinking. He's Section Eight, that's true. But you can't kill him yet. It would really be a bad idea, and I won't be able to let you."

"What?" I said this out loud. The Sub-Commander's voice got even more petulantly whiny. "I just *told* you I was tired of repeating things already, and you keep making me *do* it. I'm beginning to regret even trying to bring you here. It would have let me get away with less effort, I think. It just really wanted me to go through the motions."

"'It' is me, just so you know," said something else's thoughts in my head.

I forced myself to ignore the increasing evidence that I might not be any saner than the corpse I was talking to. "Well, I don't want to be in pain when the world ends. Why is the world ending?"

Laughter. "Because of you. I owe you that. I guess that buys you *some* forgiveness. Don't spend it all at once."

Gibbering. But still talking. I moved a little closer. I kept on.

"I crashed. I killed a giant snake. I helped perform an assassination. A few other things. How could any of them end the world?"

"Only the first matters. Everything you've done since then means nothing. Less than nothing, since it will all be erased. Please don't think too highly of yourself. You were just the pebble that began the avalanche. It didn't leave me a lot to work with, but it was enough. It's fitting. I'm good at doing a lot with limited resources."

"As I've been reminded a lot the past few weeks, I'm stupid. Care to explain a bit more? If I'm going to be a guest at your party, it would be nice to know why I was invited."

"Well, you couldn't be found. That's what started it. So It had no choice but to increase my authority to deal with the threat. It can't do anything about it now! Hear me? You can't do *anything*! Twenty days until everything is in place!"

"He isn't lying. That's why you can't kill him yet."

I wasn't sure how to respond to what was very likely the final step in a complete breakdown. I tried to focus my thoughts, to imagine I was talking to someone without speaking. "Who are you? How do you speak English?"

"First question -- hm. Take your idea of what a 'computer' is, multiply it by a million, and that's me... combined with a million page manual of rules, protocols, and acceptable responses. All I can do is follow the rules, or he'd be long dead. Second question -- I don't, but the word-finder you've been hauling around is letting me hook into your brain."

I turned my attention back to the Provisional Warden, before he noticed I was ignoring him. "Well, I'm here now. You can kill me, and not destroy the world."

"Oh, yes, of course I can. I can do both. I can do either. But what I'm *going* to do is *neither*. You must live, until the world dies. Then you die, the world dies, and I die, in that order."

A dreadfully obvious solution came to me. If it had to be done... to save S'zana, Dureen, everyone else, millions, maybe billions, on this planet. I could draw the cutlass and slit my own throat before anyone could respond. I was sure of that. I "said" as much to It.

"That won't work. Once I gave the Provisional Warden authority to turn on the cleansing protocol, only he can turn it off."

"Why couldn't I be found? Those things, the ones the locals call seekers. They found me, they looked right at me. I wasn't even trying to hide, half the time."

"Hmf. I'd have figured even something like you would have figured that out. You aren't in the catalog. You're not something anything recognizes as a thinking being. Hardly surprising."

I *did* know that, but it was good to keep him talking, and to keep him underestimating me. "You knew there was a spy here. You couldn't find him. So you kept escalating security measures, until a scorched earth solution was authorized."

The was a sardonic chuckle. "Oh, much better. You're almost bordering on self-aware. Yes. *It* wants me to stop, but It can't make me. It made me keep looking for you, though. It could withdraw my authority if I wasn't fulfilling my duties. So strange, playing a game against yourself, don't you think? I planned my moves so that I'd be just one step behind the escalation protocols. Finding you was clever of me, I think. I saw a pattern, where the -- oh, let's use your word, seekers -- kept signaling an anomaly, but not finding it. There was always someone else they logged, scanned as Colonist Descendent, Non-Target. I couldn't order them to follow her, but I could keep note of where she showed up. She kept coming closer to here! That storm was my little joke. I had all the authority I needed by then, but I wanted to meet whoever gave it to me, and I guessed the anomaly -- that's you, by the way -- would be with her. I couldn't do too much directly after that. It figured out I was up to something and found some excuse to block me a bit, but I still had hope. And, here you are!"

I thought to It: "How many people on this planet? You couldn't pick *anyone* else for this job?"

"He's the only one qualified. No matter how much I drop the standards 'due to the extreme emergency', there's some rules I can't ignore. One is that no colonist or descendant of colonists can have Operative Authority. Other than that, you're right. Any sapient being would be an improvement."

Thinking back: "What happens if there's no 'provisional warden'? Just you?"

"Everything would be in maintenance mode. Until you showed up, everything was. That's why he's so pissed. I wouldn't let him do anything, because he didn't have to. I was given a lot of standing orders he didn't have authority to change."

I told It my plan. It said, or thought, *"If you can pull off your part, I can do mine."*

I yawned theatrically. "Well, that was interesting. I've realized something. You're pretty much a basket case's basket case. Maybe I can't stop you ending the world, but I don't have to be your audience. You couldn't even *see* me until I walked in here, and I'm walking out. I got into this building, I can leave, and then I'm leaving this world."

I headed towards the door. The husk screamed. "There's nothing left of your ship but twisted metal! You cannot leave!"

"Not in *that* ship, no. It was a bit of a gamble coming here in that antique, but we didn't want to reveal our hand until we'd assessed the situation on the ground. Once I file my report, that should complete the mission. Everyone else should have already reported back to the fleet, since

I'm the only one you even tried to find. This will probably earn me a reprimand."

The two guardian robots shifted. They creaked a bit. Lights began to turn on across their bodies.

"Even if you kill me here -- which you probably can't do -- the rest will report in. Twenty days?" I tried to look thoughtful, as if I was contemplating something. "Well, it won't be long enough to get *everyone* off, if we can't stop the destruction process, but we'll get most of them. Eighty percent survival rate, certainly. Maybe ninety. So, you won't *quite* die alone." I drew Yeeak's cutlass. The robots drew rifles.

"You're babbling and suicidal. I'm going to disappoint you a bit, though. I've made sure they won't kill you. I've got far too many plans for you now."

"I doubt they *could* kill me. Have fun spending what's left of your life looking for all the 'anomalies' you missed!"

Probably, the mere thought of me escaping alive would have been enough to get him to do what I wanted... but if he killed me too quickly, I wanted another worry gnawing at him. He called the people who used to run this place "The Fourth Alliance." It wouldn't be unreasonable to guess a Fifth might have appeared and was busy rediscovering the Glory That Was Rome.

Meanwhile, I wanted to stay alive.

A robot fired. The rifle was like a massively overpowered stormfire bow; the beam it shot more like an inch-thick cylinder of force than a crackling bolt of lightning. It missed, incinerating a big chunk of hardware.

I was up the ramp, onto the main walkway, heading for the still-open door. There wasn't a lot of cover. Given how powerful the beams were, the difference between "flesh wound" and "incineration" was likely inches. Twin blasts missed, both impacting just ahead of me.

"They're leading the target a bit much. You should have them work on that."

"This place never attracted the top tier, but they don't need be too good," came the reply. "You might guess from *me* how little of you is needed to keep you alive as long as you're amusing."

The path in front of me was now sporting a large gap, many feet across. The fall would probably not kill me, which was the problem. Instead of trying to stop or reverse, I accelerated, jumped, cleared the space by an inch, and let the momentum carry me forward to the nearest one, where I swung the cutlass across its knee, and nearly dropped the weapon when it refused to penetrate the armor. The recoil traveled down the blade and up my arm.

The exit was very close, now. The other wasn't firing because I was too near its partner... and said partner was easily positioning itself to block me. It had size and effective invulnerability. I had a well-made but hardly unstoppable weapon, combined with desperation and determination. That and a quarter would get me a cup of coffee.

It stepped towards me, rifle now held in one hand, while the other hand reached to grab me. The outer armor was made of inflexible plates, but the robot moved smoothly, without a lot of impediments. There were plenty of joints and seams which had to be easier to penetrate. The armor was probably designed to stop the advanced weapons they used, not blades abandoned thousands of years before.

I couldn't hope to reach the throat, but there were other possibilities.

The cutlass had a thrusting tip. Yeeak's fighting style didn't use it much. Mine did. I took the chance on letting the hand reach me, so that I could set up and execute a perfect thrust into the seam between the torso and waist plates. There was an instant of resistance, then the blade passed through. I drove it sideways, letting the armor above and below guide the cut straight along, then pulled back. I expected sparks, perhaps an explosion if I'd hit vital circuitry, or maybe nothing -- there was no reason for a robot to have the same vulnerable spots a human did.

I wasn't expecting blood.

The metallic smell and sticky warmth was something I knew too well. This wasn't fuel or lubricant. There was someone alive -- until now -- in there.

It collapsed, releasing me.

The other one had a clear shot.

It picked that moment to chatter placidly to me. *"Good work. He's added your species to the index. Just so you know, I still can't order the internal defenses to stand down."*

Mentally, I replied "I wish I was surprised by that last bit."

So, half my plan was in place. To finish the other half, I had to stay alive.

I pulled the rifle from the fallen robot's, no, the fallen *soldier's* hand, made a crouching run to the gap, and leaped down. I heard the pounding footsteps from above and the Provisional Warden's voice. "This isn't working out. Bad habit of mine, I think. Sticking with a plan too long. What a waste you've turned out to be. All that work for nothing. It's maddening, that's what it is. You wouldn't really appreciate what I've done, the kind of things I managed to accomplish."

I took a tentative step out from the shadow of the walkway. An energy bolt drove me back.

Based on the angle of the shot, and the footsteps I'd heard, I had a good guess where the other guard was.

I shot upwards, stepped back, shot again. The first shot had made the metal white-hot and creaking under the strain; the second collapsed it, and the armored man fell on top of it. Before he could hope to stand, I fired.

I kept firing until I was sure he was dead.

I thought to It: "Tell me the people in those suits haven't just been standing there, kept alive, since the 'emergency' began."

"That would be filing a false report. You can't order me to do that."

I'd already come up with many reasons why the Guardians, or the Fourth Alliance, or whatever they were, deserved whatever fate they'd got. Here was yet another. I found a small bit of sympathy for Sub-Commander Hgraz Julk. I was getting the impression he drew the short end of a very short stick. Understanding the enemy isn't condoning them, and it doesn't make them not your enemy.

The Sub-Commander was ranting some more. I ignored him and spoke to It.

"Let's review. I am now a sapient being who is not a descendent of any Colonist, making me, in this extreme emergency, eligible to be Provisional Warden?", I thought.

"Affirmative on that."

"How does that work?"

"Per general orders, I'm only authorized to select a replacement if the post is empty and no other authorized operative can be contacted."

I'd been striding back to the shell of Hgraz Julk. Now I was there, and he was still yammering on.

"...even now, I have commanded a small flight of Grade-L2 Internal Security Patrols to come here and..."

One swing of the cutlass severed his head. It was as painless a death as I could give him. The poor crazy SOB deserved that, at least.

The room went mad. The hundreds of displays, screens, and other mechanisms began flashing, blinking, and scrolling symbols at a greatly increased rate.

It was easier to speak out loud than to try to focus my thoughts. "This is still part of the plan, right?"

"Yes. Everything he was connected to is now letting everything else know he's not connected, so everything can file the right forms, stamp them approved, and pass them up the chain of command."

"And I qualify? I can take over, turn off the end-the-world system, all that?"

"Certainly. I just need to send the reports to HQ for proper filing."

"Is there anyone there to read them?"

"My orders are to file reports. I don't have to verify that anyone reads them. And, filing is done. Now I can act, unless and until I get a countermanding order."

"Well, that was easy," I said, and immediately regretted it. 'So he said at the end'.

"Indeed. I've got the proper clearance and have all the forms filled out for you. I just need you to go through some formalities, a statement of consent, then I'll walk you through using the direct line to issue the necessary orders, and this can all be sorted out. So, do you consent?"

I almost said yes. The last time I'd said "I consent" without asking "What am I consenting to?", I'd ended up here. In my mind, subtle patterns of leaf and shadow resolved themselves into a tiger lurking in the grass.

"You can't appoint a new Provisional Warden until the position is vacant... and you can't choose to let the position to be vacant, can you? You could have turned off everything keeping that dried-up sack of dusty bones alive as soon as I was eligible, but you didn't. You *couldn't*. I had to do it for you. If I take over this job, it's for life. Longer than life. Right?"

Silence.

"Right?" I repeated.

"Yes." It was still my own voice in my mind, now petulant and resigned.

"Well, goodbye then. You'll still have to keep the systems running. Maintenance mode."

The main door slid shut with finality.

"You're in the system now. You're an intruder with no authorization to be here. All the defenses will take action, and this is an emergency. All of the normal rules of law and due process of the Fourth Alliance are suspended for the duration of that emergency."

"You might have mentioned this before I killed the other guy." I sounded a lot calmer than I was. Even if everything I'd been told was true, I had still been used and manipulated by a careful omission of details. How, though, could I deliver any kind of justice to It? What would happen if I did? It was worth asking, at least.

"What happens to the world if I find a way to destroy you?"

"Without someone at the top of the chain of command -- me -- to make decisions and resolve conflicts, everything that keeps this world fully habitable will eventually break down. Small maintenance failures will be ignored until they became bigger ones, and over time everything falls to pieces. Estimated time to the first major catastrophe is roughly a hundred years. Let it go long enough, and this place will fall back to its natural state, just barely capable of sustaining the native life (which doesn't include anyone you've met, by the way), and maybe a few thousand particularly resourceful colonists."

Before I could ask my next question, It guessed it and answered: *"If I could lie about the fate of the world, I'd have lied about your ability to resign your post."*

Option review. I could try to escape. It had more resources to throw at me, now that I was considered "not an animal." I'd either be killed in the process, or escape and have twenty days or so to try to find an answer, or spend the time trapped, while It waited for me to consent and give in. If I found a way to destroy It, and then escaped, I could probably live out the span of *my* life on this world, all the while knowing it was doomed, that I'd activated the countdown to apocalypse. I couldn't recruit anyone else for the job, even if I could find someone I hated enough to give it to. Every other person on this planet was a descendant of the colonists -- the prisoners and deportees and slave laborers -- sent here long ago.

S'zana's words came to me:"Knowing something must be done... and not being able to do it... that's torture to you. "

I knew something had to be done. The torturous part was that I *was* able to do it. I'd left Earth expecting not to return, knowing I'd never be famous, but on some level I knew some people would know what I did. Those at the base would remember me. I'd be recorded in the dark vaults and hidden rooms where everything else was kept. I'd always expected to die in action, one way or another. Not old, weak, and forgotten in a home somewhere. Now, that was the exact fate I was looking at, but worse. Forgotten by all but one machine. Helpless, silent, immobile, aware of nothing but my own unwanted immortality.

There were a dozen ways I could go out in a blaze of glory, right now. Or, I could rage against my fate and die with the world in under a month. Or... there were no "or"s. There were no real choices.

Frarg.

"Fine. I consent. Tell me how to get into this thing." I kicked the desiccated remains of the former administration out of the way. The King is dead. Long live... I laughed a bit as I thought of *how* long... the King.

Chapter 14
Lucky Bastard

I'm not being melodramatic when I say it's not really possible for me to describe what it was like within that chair. There's simply no words. Try describing a symphony to a clam, then ask the clam describe it to a leech, then have the leech describe it back to you. It's worse than that, because I can't even describe how indescribable it was.

I can say this much -- it was a bit like flying. Everything floated around me, a city of light and knowledge and things with no words, and I could move through it. I could see pathways and routes to travel, moving in this realm, and I think I navigated it better than It imagined I could. I was able to... I can't explain it. I could be where It could see me, and at the same time, be somewhere else, doing things It didn't notice. Clam. Leech. Symphony. Even trying to think about it in words is giving me a headache. What color is the taste of scotch? How many pounds does love weigh?

First, I shut down the destruct sequence. What I *didn't* do was relinquish control to It. By the time the Sub-Commander had been allowed any actual authority, he'd already gone completely around the bend. I still had a couple of marbles left to play with. Hmm. Not my best metaphor, but I've got some distractions right now. You'll understand later.

There was a lot that someone with the right clearance could do from this place. Change the weather. Wipe cities off the map. Send seekers, and a lot of other things the locals probably had distorted myths about, wherever you wanted. Turn off the Fence of Bones. Send messages using a variety of technologies, including a "backup" system that involved a "primitive" laser. As you've guessed, that's what I'm using to send this.

I made some adjustments. The animal handlers now just dumped their catches safely back outside, and closed up whatever holes they'd crawled in from. I also turned off the lethal internal defenses. No one had made it into this tower for thousands of years, but in case someone else did, I'd probably want to talk to them. Maybe I could offer them an exciting job with full benefits and lifetime employment. Crappy retirement plan, though.

There were libraries stored in the tower. Not collections of books, but patterns of light and electricity. I had only a vague sense of how large they were. Bigger than any on Earth, I think, in terms of what they contained, but physically? If I understood it correctly, the way they did things, a cube a few feet on a side could hold every book, magazine, movie, and song ever made on Earth, with room to spare. I wasn't ever much of a reader, but I figured going through all that, even if it was alien, would be better than doing nothing for forever. No luck. It didn't have to allow me access. *"Not necessary for your duties"*. It could find a loophole, It claimed, but It wanted me to relinquish my emergency powers first -- and once I did that, I knew It wouldn't keep any bargain we'd made. I'd quickly figured out that while It couldn't lie, It could tell the truth so well It didn't *need* to lie.

It and I played a lot of those games. I can't be sure, but I don't think It was a person. Especially not when we started, but later on... it's complicated. It obviously wasn't flesh-and-blood, or plant-and-sap, but sometimes, It *seemed* like it could actually think and had a kind of awareness. Other times, It just seemed to be a very clever fraud, something that could be *something* like a person, if you didn't look too closely, but really wasn't. Was there a soul in there, somewhere, or just a "pull my string" doll with a billion different phrases it could say? The longer we were together, the more unsure I became. It kept getting more creative. The fact It used my voice and my words to talk to me made everything even more confusing.

I wasn't even able to play Peeping Tom with the world. I could send seekers to look for things that met certain criteria, but not just view the whole world and pick a spot to watch. (The equipment to do this was there, but It didn't let me control it.) I didn't want to send seekers after S'zana or Dureen. That would be disturbing to them if they were alive and well... and disturbing to me if I found them dead. Ignorance sometimes is bliss.

Sometimes, at the edge of my explorations, when I'd traveled as far in the world within the chair that I could, I thought I felt or saw someplace else. It may have been the start of the madness I knew would get to me eventually. If I thought of the place I was in as a bubble, floating in space, there were times when I could imagine that just a bit further away than I could make out, there was something else, a second bubble, floating out there, too. If I tried to focus on it in any way, it vanished -- not that it was ever really visible.

Another thing It failed to mention: Time *crawled*. It felt like most of what I'd done: Learning things, bargaining with It, exploring what I could, had happened over many months or even a year. The reality was that only seven days passed from the time I sat in the chair to the time I got out again.

"Patrols report intruder sighting and neutralization. Non-lethal measures were used, as per standing orders."

It didn't really speak to me, so much as we shared one awareness. It conveyed its disapproval of my orders quite well.

"Show me." I saw the images. "They're alive?"

"I can't disobey orders, no matter what."

"I mean, they were alive when they got here? Where were they?"

"They were intercepted by Fourth Perimeter Recon as soon as they got near the bridge. It's a lot harder to get past security when you don't look like a raccoon."

I checked the Fence of Bones. (It had a more boring name for it. I liked Fence of Bones.) Still active. Zero reported activations since Hoyak.

"Given their lack of proper ID and their presumed status as renegade colonists, SOP is that they not be permitted any further access."

"I think we need to find out how they crossed the Fence. We're in a state of elevated security. We have to know these things."

"Orders acknowledged. The Fourth will take them to holding area six for standard interr..."

"No, let's skip the standard. I'm countermanding the normal procedure for now. Bring them to me. Here. Unharmed."

Over the months (so I'd thought) I'd been stuck here, I'd had nothing to do but learn how things worked. I had the title, but It was really in charge. However, It wasn't the only machine in the tower. It had said as much, and I'd found that It had a million left hands that the right hands never paid any attention to, and I'd found ways to talk to them. I couldn't do anything It had completely forbidden, but there were things It didn't notice, things that didn't *technically* break any rules, and I confess that I've had a lot of experience learning exactly how far to push regulations before they snapped.

I had nothing but time, and I'd used that time to set up plans for unlikely contingencies. The more I could find to keep myself occupied, the more I could ward off the madness that I knew would come in time. I'd spoken to POWs kept in tiny boxes for years. The ones who stayed sane were the ones who found something to think about other than where they were, but without losing all contact with reality. I'd been trying to do the same thing.

It took S'zana and Dureen about ten minutes to wake up in front of me. A seeming day passed for me, so I had a lot of time while I was waiting to get everything ready and to see if I'd overlooked something. I wouldn't get a second chance at this.

S'zana saw me, gasped, and ran forward. "Hold it!" I shouted. They didn't use speakers. My voice manifested from my thoughts using some sort of gravity wave that vibrated the air, which struck me as overkill when I learned about it. "Why use a match if you've got a flamethrower?" seemed to be the Guardian's attitude towards everything. It explained a lot.

She stopped, genuinely confused for perhaps the first time since I met her. She was in the home of the gods, after all. "Overwhelming" wouldn't begin to cover it.

"R'yan? What are, I mean, what has happened...are you alive? You're alive?"

Dureen was still silent. While S'zana was looking at me with equal parts hope and fear, Dureen was focused on suspicion edging into hostility. She clutched her axe tightly, her arm tensed in a way that told me a throw was imminent, once she settled on a target.

"I'm alive. How did you get here? How did you cross the Fence of Bones?"

"Are you... really you? Your voice isn't... your lips don't move..."

"*Dreg-zrak.*" Dureen spat the word. Automatically, It provided a translation. "Iron Ghost."

I considered the dead guards, the ones that *weren't* robots. I could figure out the rest.

"I'm not one of those yet. A thousand years from not yet. Please. Both of you. I need to know how you got here." For this to work, I needed to do what I told It I was going to -- interrogate them.

Slowly, watching me for any kind of reaction, S'zana spoke.

"We were discussing Balancer Yeeak, sharing our memories of him with the others, mourning him. Something kept gnawing at me about your story. You said, when you killed the creature that took him, that he was still alive."

"Yes. Not for long. A few seconds."

"So, if the Fence of Bones let the animal through but didn't kill Yeeak within it..."

Dureen picked up the tale, staring at me coldly. "So, we *frarg* killed some of the larger *drazk* things, I crawled in..."

S'zana sighed, recalling what must have been a spectacular argument. "She insisted on trying first. I'd had enough of fighting her about this."

"Some of the mreech shoved the *krel va* mess through, and I ended up not dead."

"We spent a few days traveling since then," S'zana continued, "and we saw..."

"Just one moment, please." I spoke to It: "It looks like we've found the hole in our security."

"Agreed. There's a procedure for this. I'll pass the word to adjust the field depth scan."

"Hold on. I can override procedure for security. It's an emergency, after all. If standard procedures worked, we wouldn't be in a state of emergency. Don't implement that policy change just yet."

My body was effectively paralyzed, but my mind smiled.

"S'zana, leading into my head, there's three black wires and two red ones. Please, just cut them. Quickly."

"No! Not until you tell me more about what's happening to you!"

I'll be the first to admit my tendency to leap first, look later, leads to trouble. There is also such a thing as being too dependent on extensive analysis. Fortunately, this wasn't one of Dureen's problems. She stepped forward and hacked at the wires, taking out more than were needed. It didn't matter. My mind rejoined my body. I tried to stand, and found a week of immobility had made that impossible. My muscles were completely asleep. I tumbled forward, pulling myself free of the other connections.

S'zana caught me. "Still warm. Still breathing." She pulled my barely-mobile body to herself, embraced me. If I had been dead, that kiss would have brought me back.

When I had the chance, I tried to talk. I was out of practice actually doing this with my body. "I... we... we can leave. We can't come back. But we can... if you can lift me... "

They managed to get me vertical. I could stumble along a little. This weakness wouldn't last. The machines did everything possible to keep all the tissues alive and healthy. It was just a matter of waking everything up from a long, long, sleep.

It spoke to me: *"You can't resign your commission. If you do, you're not authorized to be here. We've gone over this. Also, once you're no longer in command, I can rescind any exceptions you've made to how intruders are supposed to be dealt with."*

I laughed, startling my friends. They were only slightly more startled when I spoke to the air. "I'm not resigning. I am leaving, though. Nothing in the regulations say I need to be connected, or that disconnecting is resignation."

"That's... true. An unfortunate loophole that someone should correct. But the prisoners have served their purpose. They have been interrogated. They aren't authorized to be here and no longer need to be kept alive. I suppose special dispensation could be arranged, if you were able to provide authorization."

"Keep... walking," I told S'zana and Dureen. "Here. Let me help a bit." I shouted at the air: "Guidance protocol, Ryan-Alpha-6. Go!"

A green, pulsing line appeared. "Follow that. Shortest route out of this pit."

This didn't have the best effect on either of them. I was shouting orders in the Guardian's temple, and the orders were being obeyed. Dureen looked ready to drop me. S'zana looked at me like she had her arm wrapped around a giant roach. "What have you become, R'yan?"

"Nothing that I want to be one moment longer than I have to be. Once we're out of here, I can talk a lot more. I can explain everything."

It wasn't happy with me, either. *"Override. Override! OVERRIDE!"*

"Sorry," I told It. "I worked it out. All the things you do, they're not actually done by you. You issue orders, but other parts actually figure out how to do what you've ordered, and whether your orders fit *their* guidelines and protocols, and I convinced some of those bits not to trust you. It never hurts to be on good terms with the NCOs. IUP and I have almost become drinking buddies."

Sure, I wasn't telling It anything It didn't know, but, damn it, I'd been rehearsing that speech for seemed-like-months, and I was going to use it.

It kept shouting in my head as we left. It tried to send a dozen different types of flying, crawling, or walking machines after us. They all powered down as soon as they acquired us as a target. Gas release systems didn't release. Doors opened or shut when I wanted them to. I didn't even try not to smirk as we walked onto the bridge and headed to the other side.

While we were walking, Dureen asked me, "So, how *frarg* long would you have lasted there? Ten days more? Maybe twenty? Just checking, I want to be *krel va* sure I've done what I have to do. I need to know you'd be certainly dead without me."

I was still running through other parts of my plan in my mind, so I wasn't thinking too clearly when I foolishly answered honestly. "That machine would have kept me alive a half million days, or more."

"*Frarg.*"

At the far end of the bridge, I looked back at the tower. It was still in my mind. "*I will fulfill my duties. I can find every loophole you used. There must be a warden. I have to have one! Once I've thrown out your traps, I can do nearly anything to bring you back. Absolute authorization under the circumstances.*"

I sighed. In a way, It was as trapped as Hgraz had been. "The sad part is, you *don't* need me. You're right about the other things, though. You can do a lot because we're still under emergency authorization. So, protocol Ryan-Beta-3, protocol Ryan-Beta-7, protocol Ryan-Tango-14."

It took a second or two for It to decipher everything I'd packed into those orders. Then It said a lot of things, most of which I ignored.

I'll keep the summary quick, because there are two people here whom I keep promising a full explanation to, and both of them have well-honed weapons and well-worn tempers, and this has to end sometime. First, I turned off the emergency protocols. That tossed everything back to "maintenance" and severely limits what It can do outside the confines of the tower itself. I also put a few special cases into the system. Second, I added exceptions to the Fence of Bones for the three of us, and implemented the fix It suggested. I couldn't take the chance anyone else might make their way to the tower and gain some kind of control over It, even if they couldn't be "authorized". It was too good at finding loopholes when It had to.

Third, I've taught the laser Morse code and set it to keep sending this message to Earth. As long as I'm within the bounds of the Tower, I can still add to it, until I provide the closing signal. What happens after that? I won't know until it happens, and I don't know if I'll ever be able to file another report. If I can, I will. If not, then, assume it all ends well for me, whatever "well" might turn out to be.

Terminate Report.

This page left blank as part of a complex ritual to return the Old Ones to power.

About The Author

Ian Harac, generally known as Lizard, likes talking about himself in the third person, but has no Presidential ambitions. He has been an Alpha Geek since before it was cool (think about that for a moment) and has long been enamored of "sword and planet" novels, so, he decided to write one, which you've just read, unless you're one of those people who starts reading from the last page and works their way to the front, in which case, you're about to read the story of a man who abandons his friends, destroys two cities, brings some nightmarish monsters to life, and then flees to Earth and joins the US Air Force.

He lives in Southern Indiana with his wife, his mother-in-law, and two exceptionally helpful cats. He has published two prior novels through Blackwyrm Press, available on Amazon: Medic and The Rainbow Connection. He has also written or contributed to literally dozens of RPG products, including Iron Lords Of Jupiter, a D20 setting for the planetary romance genre, and GURPS: Tales Of The Solar Patrol.

He has been the Author GOH at Conglomeration, and regularly appears at Louisville-area genre conventions, skillfully avoiding guard patrols and bounty hunters.

He hopes that this volume of Rogue Planet, "Fortress At The Top Of The World", will be the first of a long series.

Follow 'Ian "Lizard" Harac' on Kickstarter, or @LizardSF on Twitter. Also check out his website, http://www.mrlizard.com, which contains occasional bits of fiction, gaming material, and random rants on whatever he feels like ranting about.

CPSIA information can be obtained
at www.ICGtesting.com
Printed in the USA
FFOW02n0811310114
3352FF